# ROBIE MADISON

Love
Partner

ELLORA'S CAVE
ROMANTICA PUBLISHING

# *What the critics are saying...*

### ❧

## 2006 DREAM REALM AWARD WINNER

**5 Stars** "Robie Madison takes the reader on a voyage of discovery. Judan and Myrina cannot keep away from each other. When she is not in the lab trying to discover why the Outlanders are dying, she is discovering a love unlike any she ever thought possible. Can Myrina find a cure for the Outposters before they all die? Is Myrina really Judan's genetically coded mate? The answers are in LOVE PARTNER."
~ *EcataRomance Reviews*

**4 Hearts** "Madison is a gifted storyteller. She has created a world full of complex characters and amazing science. [...] *Love Partner* has added a dimension to fated mates that I had not read before. Besides the genetic compatibility there needs to be a genuine connection, and the book discusses if compatibility is enough, and is love biology or psychology. I can't wait for more from Madison she writes a terrific story sprinkled with just enough sex." ~ *Night Owl Romance Reviews*

"I couldn't put *Love Partner* down until I was done with the entire book, it was action packed and intriguing enough to grab my attention and not let it go. [...] *Love Partner* has all the ingredients for a fantastic read, and it certainly delivered that on all counts. Definitely a keeper!" ~ *Road to Romance Reviews*

An Ellora's Cave Romantica Publication

www.ellorascave.com

Love Partner

ISBN 9781419957772
ALL RIGHTS RESERVED.
Love Partner Copyright © 2006 Robie Madison
Edited by Nicholas Conrad.
Cover art by Syneca.

This book printed in the U.S.A. by Jasmine–Jade Enterprises, LLC.

Electronic book Publication July 2006
Trade paperback Publication May 2008

# Also by Robie Madison

෨

Cats and Dogs
Desperate Alliance

# About the Author

෨

A world traveler, Robie loves visiting mystical places and learning about other cultures and peoples. She's spent several years living abroad, allowing her to study human nature in a variety of settings and circumstances. These years also included a few wild exploits of her own. Multi-published, she uses her knowledge to enhance her stories. When not traveling, or planning her next trip, Robie creates characters that can do the adventuring for her.

Robie welcomes comments from readers. You can find her website and email address on her author bio page at www.ellorascave.com.

## Tell Us What You Think
We appreciate hearing reader opinions about our books. You can email us at Comments@EllorasCave.com.

# LOVE PARTNER

# Prologue

*1100<sup>th</sup> Year of the Great Sand Lizard, Dakokata*

Slabs of shale-like rock stretched across the wasteland, their smoothness marred by row upon row of steep-sided cones. Despite their deceptively benign appearance, Judan Ringa was not taken in. He started counting and reached eight before the first eruption burst on the horizon sending a searing hot geyser of water and gas straight into the air. He refocused on the next string of cones and started counting again. Predictably, the eruptions spouted with increasing speed. The force of the geysers eroded the steep sides of the cones, sending a thick, liquid mass oozing across the uneven landscape in a series of steamy rivulets.

Judan shifted his gaze downward to the young boy who stood motionless in front of him. Normally he'd be honored that in all things Zane sought to emulate him, but not here at this exhibit.

The first time his own father had brought him to the OtherWorlds he'd been older than Zane, at least seven. Even so he'd quaked in his boots when the holographic geysers had erupted so close he'd thought he felt the spray and the heat burning his skin. And, when the last geyser had erupted at his feet threatening to carry him away, only the steadying pressure of his father's hands on his shoulders had prevented him from turning tail and running.

Judan flexed his hand towards the boy, but left it hanging uselessly at his side. Past experience had taught him the boy resented being thought so weak. At three and a half, Zane imagined himself to be as fearless as Judan, a man of thirty-three. But, whereas the OtherWorlds had captured and channeled Judan's need to learn and to challenge himself, he knew quite clearly that for Zane the OtherWorlds represented one more way to harden himself against the pain of loss.

He couldn't blame the boy for his angry sullenness. Or worse, his desperate attempts to suppress all his emotions and feel nothing. Unlike the simulated wasteland before them that could be repaired in an instant for the next visitor, Zane's life was permanently scarred by the death of his parents.

Yet, what Judan the man understood was that it was not his training that made him appear fearless, nor had it gained him the position of *Ktua* at an unusually young age, since most of the other members of the *Ktua* were in their fifties or older. It was the fact that he'd never forgotten that seven-year-old boy with the quaking boots. But Judan worried he would never be able to tell the story of that boy so Zane would understand.

Memories of his own father flooded his mind as the last geyser burst at their feet and he allowed the sorrow to play across his face. Zane's eyes grew round with surprise when he turned to look up at him.

"What happened, Judan, you look sad?"

"I was remembering your *Datuk*. We used to come here a lot." *Until I became too busy.* "I miss that time."

Judan watched Zane's face carefully as he spoke, but it seemed the boy absorbed the information without a flicker of emotion.

"Come. Do you want to try another exhibit before we go back to see what your *Nenek* has prepared for our meal?"

Zane looked down at his feet and shook his head as he scuffed the toe of one shoe across the floor. Judan breathed a private sigh of relief. The boy did feel the loss of the man he'd called grandfather and that gave Judan hope.

When Judan's cousin and her husband had been killed they'd left ten-month-old Zane behind. Since, under the law, single people were disqualified from adopting, Judan's parents were the only couple left in the family who could take the child in. They'd done their best, but already Judan's father had been dying. What should have been a time to prepare for the end of the *Rakanasmara* between them was now turned to the task of raising a foster son. Despite his ambitions as a rising *Ktua*, Judan had also accepted a responsibility for the child.

"*Nenek* asked you to take me out today, didn't she?"

"Don't you and I always go out before I leave on a mission? Why should today be any different?" Mentally, Judan prepared himself for the battle he felt might be coming with the boy.

"*Nenek* says I'm too much of a challenge," Zane muttered.

Judan stared down at the boy. Hard.

"I heard her say so," came the defiant little voice.

"We are all having a hard time adjusting to your *Datuk's* death, especially your *Nenek*. Right now life is too much of a challenge, which is why she needs you."

Zane sighed loudly. "I still would like to go with you."

"I know." Judan wondered how he'd gotten off so lightly. "I appreciate you staying with your *Nenek*."

"Will you be visiting Lorre?" Zane asked eagerly.

"Probably. What would you have me tell him this time?" Judan teased, pleased by the change in topic. Although ten years younger than Judan, Lorre was his favorite brother and also Zane's favorite foster brother.

"Tell him I want to be a great Outposter too."

Judan laughed. "Being an Outposter is a dangerous life and your *Nenek* has a tender heart. She'd worry with a third son in danger."

"You were an Outposter, Judan, before becoming a *Ktua*. Besides, I am not really *Nenek's* son."

And that, Judan thought, was that. With nothing more to say, they walked along in silence for a short while.

"What if she doesn't want me?" Zane asked, sending Judan's heart plummeting.

"She?" He hoped the boy wasn't thinking what he thought he was thinking. He was.

"Your partner. Like Dare's partner didn't want me."

After his father's death, Judan's mother had considered sending Zane to her nephew Dare, who was now partnered and had a son of his own. But soon after Dare had secured a job on a satellite research station and the plan had fallen through. Believing himself unwanted by both Judan's mother and Dare, Zane had obviously invented this newest torture for himself. He'd begun to obsess about Judan's potential partner.

"You know I wouldn't choose anyone who didn't also want you. We come as a package." Judan's words rang hollow in his ears, although he spoke from his heart. It was also the closest he'd ever come to directly acknowledging what they both wanted but could not have—to be a father and a son to each other.

A small hand crept into his and he gave it a quick squeeze as he looked down. This time Zane's face did not hide the fear beneath the bravado.

It was a stupid thing to have said to the boy. The *Rakanasmara* came, or it did not come. The *Rakanasmara* did the choosing. It could not be influenced.

But without *Rakanasmara*, he would not be able to have Zane as his son.

# Chapter One
*Technikon Laboratories Consortium (TLC), Three Months Later*

෨

Five levels beneath the planet's surface the train whined as it banked into the curve. The sudden movement jostled Dr. Myrina deCarte awake. She blinked against the bright lights that illuminated the car and kept the darkness of the subterranean tunnel at bay, then winced as the train screeched to a halt at the next station. *Blast.* She really could have used the thirteen more minutes of sleep before the train reached her stop. Sometimes life just sucked. She never slept well when she had to go off-world, even if it was only as far as one of the satellite meeting stations orbiting TLC.

This time she'd spent two sleepless nights at a satellite station, meeting with the Hulite representatives and giving them the bad news. According to her tests three of the five mining bases they'd recently scouted were unsuitable. It seemed the planetoids' atmospheres contained an unusual property that would leech high concentrations of electrolytes from the bodies of the Hulite miners. As a result, the workers were in danger of experiencing severe hypokalemic reactions due to rapid depletions of potassium from their systems. With the speed of the leeching, supplements weren't going to help the problem. Hardly worth the cost of the mineral they wanted to extract from the otherwise barren hunks of rock.

Stifling a yawn, Myrina scrubbed her hands through her short, light brown curls, massaging her scalp in the process. She needed sleep in the worst way. Deep REM, dream-inducing, blissfully uninterrupted sleep. And she planned to get it just as soon as she checked in with her assistant, Kikki San.

The doors of the train slid open and Myrina stumbled to her feet and out onto the platform. The paintball designs on the transit station's walls always reminded her of a basic biology class. Around her everyone walked purposefully toward one of the three exit tunnels. And she would too, as soon as she remembered which tunnel led to her lab.

"Dr. Myrina deCarte?"

Myrina stifled a groan at the sound of her name. *No, no, no. This can't be happening! Not now.* Yet sure enough, when she turned around there stood an earnest, clean-cut messenger sporting a vid screen on his T-shirt. *Damn.*

She wasn't up to smiling at him, but nodded politely enough to indicate she would hear the message. It wasn't the kid's fault that she'd endured two sleepless nights and a four hour train ride from the southern docking port. On cue, the face of Fenton deMorriss, TLC's Foreign Affairs Director, filled the vid screen. *Double damn.*

"I'm sorry to interrupt your plans, Myrina, but I need to see you immediately regarding the Dakokatan crisis. Please come directly to my office before heading to your quarters."

In her opinion, deMorriss was a pompous stuffed shirt, even if he issued orders with a polite please and thank you. His precise manner was the perfect foil between the brilliant but often taciturn scientists who worked for TLC and their frequently demanding foreign clients. Well, right now she was feeling pretty antisocial, so she didn't give two hoots what kind of crisis the Dakokatans were in. She was not going to submit to deMorriss' demands until she'd slept. At least that was what she told herself as she waved the messenger away and headed for the little-used elevator. Unfortunately her protests were all talk. Turning down a request from deMorriss was exceedingly unhealthy to a scientist's future at TLC since he brought in the clients and the money.

Ascending five floors, Myrina exited onto the ground floor of a garden rotunda. She squinted and automatically shielded her eyes against the brilliant sunlight streaming in from the glass dome four floors above. Silently, she cursed the fact that her sunglasses were back in her apartment. She stood for a moment assimilating the heavy, perfumed scents that penetrated her nostrils, an abrupt change from the slightly stale air that had circulated in the satellite station. Temptation beckoned, urging her to wander aimlessly along the narrow pathways and lose herself in the color and the noisy chatter of the birds that flitted high above her.

Instead she turned right and walked to the bank of escalators that would take her two flights up to the Directorial offices. En route she dredged up the few facts she remembered about the newest members of the Confederacy. Dakokatans were green-skinned humanoids who lived on the periphery of the Confederacy's boundaries, which probably explained why she'd never met one.

Pausing to press the blue button that would open the doors to deMorriss' office, Myrina walked in unannounced. "This better be goo—"

She came to an abrupt halt when her scalp began to prickle as if she'd touched a live wire. Her hair tingled and for about two seconds she swore the current shot straight to her roots. Briefly she wondered if deMorriss had somehow statically charged his intricately woven Yettati carpet to jolt her awake. He knew darn well she'd be tired and therefore cranky after her meeting with the Hulites. But since he himself stood on the carpet looking unaffected, she supposed not.

Almost afraid to check, she tentatively brushed her hand through her hair. Sure enough, something odd was going on. The usually curly locks seemed a little straighter and crackled under her touch.

"Myrina, please, come in," Fenton deMorriss said with a brisk wave of his hand.

Speculation put deMorriss' age anywhere between forty and fifty. Almost nothing was known about what the tall, barrel-chested man had done before joining TLC, except that he spent his vacations training with one of the Confederacy's elite tactical squads. At the moment, his pale blue eyes, set off by the Tigalian blue silk of his tailored suit, gleamed rather sharply. Not a good sign.

A second wave of electrical impulses washed over her skin, covering her in goose bumps. Despite the insulated material of her jumpsuit, she shivered as if she'd been hit by a blast of cold air.

*Damn, this is getting weird. What's wrong with me?*

She plastered a smile on her face and fought the urge to rub her hands along her arms to ease the strange, tingly feeling in them. Now was not the time to display weakness. She forced herself to stand a little straighter.

"I'd like to introduce Ambassador Judan Ringa," deMorriss said. "The Dakokatan Warlord arrived yesterday."

*Damn.* She'd been so focused on maintaining her equilibrium she'd been completely oblivious to the Dakokatan's presence in the room.

"Ambassador," Fenton continued. "May I present Doctor Myrina deCarte, TLC's top genetic environmentalist who specializes in colonization dissonance."

Nope, definitely not a good sign. Fenton was resorting to his most nauseatingly congenial greeting. And as introductions went, this one stank. She was TLC's *only* genetic environmentalist who specialized in colonization dissonance.

*Don't go soft. Fenton isn't being congenial.*

She'd learned long ago deMorriss was a consummate politician who never said anything without a purpose. Unfortunately he also enjoyed leaving people clueless until he chose to enlighten them.

She turned to face the Warlord, only to choke on her next breath at the sight of her first Dakokatan. The man standing before her was well over six feet tall, with eyes that flashed like twin emeralds. A sharp contrast to the slightly washed-out tinge of green on his face, which was the only exposed skin she could see because his hands were hidden behind his back. Dressed all in black—boots, leggings, shirt and a huge cape studded with black quills that clicked when he bowed slightly in her direction—he looked more than a little dangerous. The folds of his shirt emphasized his wide shoulders and his long, lean torso, two features she particularly liked in her men. His leggings hugged his muscular thighs like a second skin, accentuating the prominent bulge at his crotch. Definitely a dangerously attractive presence, one that screamed *bed, naked, now.*

*Whoa, now where did that idea come from?* Probably from the same source as the pesky possessive pronoun "her". He most definitely was *not* hers and she must be delirious from sleep deprivation to have entertained the thought. At least that was the plausible explanation she gave herself, though it didn't quite explain the sudden ache in her breasts. Underneath the sturdy jumpsuit material her nipples beaded into hard, sensitive points. She hadn't experienced this kind of instantaneous lust for a man in a long, long time—if ever.

"Dr. deCarte," the Warlord said. He straightened and his movement focused her attention on his head and the incongruous, straw-like thatch of hair. It looked like a bad wig.

Fascinated, she skimmed over the man's rough facial features, doing her best to ignore his forceful stare. The instant attraction was there all right, at least on her side. In her hallucinogenic state, she even imagined she caught a faint but tantalizing whiff of sandalwood surrounding him. The scent zinged a wave of heat straight to her womb. As for the Warlord, he looked as if he'd never seen a human woman before, which just wasn't possible if he'd spent the past day at TLC. Never one to particularly care about how she looked, she was suddenly self-conscious over her rumpled appearance.

"Warlord." She returned the formal greeting and then ordered herself to walk to the nearest chair before she collapsed in a heap on the floor. A strange kinesthetic reaction mixed with exhaustion and lust wasn't the most steadying combination in the universe, especially if she was supposed to be alert and intelligent about some as yet unspecified crisis.

"What seems to be the problem?" she asked Fenton, obstinately trying to ignore the Dakokatan and her lustful thoughts towards him. Out of the corner of her eye she caught the restless stir of the Warlord's cape. He wanted her to look at him. She refused, aware there wasn't a rational explanation for her stubbornness.

Fenton smiled and affably waved the Warlord into the closest available seat before he himself perched on the arm of an overstuffed chair. Myrina bit back a grin. deMorris was only six feet tall, but he obviously wanted to keep his position of power in front of the Dakokatan.

"The Ambassador is faced with a small problem, Myrina," deMorriss said.

*Small? I'll just bet.*

The Warlord gestured impatiently. "I hardly call seventy-seven Outposters stranded on a planet a small problem, Mr. deMorriss." The comment that should have been full of emotion was delivered in an unnatural monotone.

Myrina felt slightly dizzy and her scalp continued to tingle, begging for a massage. Annoyed at her body's reaction, she now wondered if the Dakokatan had something to do with it. Of course, at the moment, she had no way of confirming her theory except he kept staring at her as if he expected to see something. The question was, what?

"Let me guess," she said. "You achieved a ninety percent or better compatibility rating and decided what the hell, let's colonize."

The Dakokatan's rugged features hardened. "After the initial investigation, the Outposters were sent to Hitani to conduct ground tests. We had no intention of colonizing the planet until the primary data was verified."

Myrina caught Fenton's scowl and backed off on her next logical comment. Every colonization test ever devised tended to look at the points of compatibility between the home and new worlds and blithely ignore the potential problems. There were always factors that were considered irrelevant to the selection process. Many times, as in the case of the Hulites, only extreme consequences and potential lawsuits prevented those fueled by economic greed from raping the land. In other cases a cultural bias overlooked some aspect of the new ecosystem that later played havoc on settlers' lives.

"Why can't they be evacuated?" she asked, despite the fact she could guess the answer.

The Warlord's hands gripped the arms of the chair and turned a luminescent white. "The Outposter who boarded the reconnaissance ship with the medical logs died within an hour of leaving the planet."

Again she was struck by the lack of inflection in his tone, as if he were purposely trying to suppress his emotions. She bit back a shiver of fear. Humanoids, no matter what kind, seemed hell-bent on making their mark on every inhabitable planet they could find, with little thought to the stress on the new environment or themselves. As it was, she could probably find the glitch in her sleep, but decided not to press her luck. There was still the matter of Fenton's odd introduction to be explained.

"I take it the Outposters on Hitani are sick," she said. Why else would they be examining medical logs?

The Dakokatan gave her a curt nod.

"Fine." She gripped the edge of her seat for support, still unable to bring herself to look the Warlord in the eye. The intensity of the odd reaction was fading, but she still didn't trust herself to stand. "Send the medical data-chip to my lab along with the body of the dead Outposter. I'll let you know what I find."

The quills on his cape clacked in protest as the Dakokatan stood. *"Tak tahu adat mati."* He whispered the words rather fiercely before turning to face Fenton who had shoved himself into a standing position. Myrina wondered if she'd just been introduced to the seamier side of the Dakokatan language.

"Mr. deMorriss, straighten this woman out and get her on my ship by tomorrow morning." Not waiting for a reply, he stalked out, his black cape billowing behind him like the wings of a great bird.

Myrina promptly collapsed against the back of her seat and closed her eyes. The tension ebbed out of her. *So I was blunt. So sue me.* Unfortunately it was within the bounds of possibility the Dakokatan Warlord wanted to do just that. She cracked an eye open and caught Fenton glaring at her. *Oh boy, here it comes.*

"Myrina," Fenton said, repositioning himself on the edge of his desk with an exasperated, paternalistic sigh. "You need to work on your manners. The Confederacy has been courting the Dakokatans for some time. Despite their isolationist policy, they're explorers and would make an excellent ally in the virtually uncharted southeast sector.

"The Confederacy didn't have much luck opening negotiations until Ringa was appointed a Warlord about four years ago. Since Ringa is the most likely candidate as the next Council Commander, the Confederacy intends to fully support his request for help in this crisis."

"Come on, Fenton. Since when do you kowtow to the bigwigs? You know as well as I do that no matter how sophisticated the criteria for selecting a habitable planet, there's always something that's not accounted for. Some environmental factor that's seen as perfectly harmless until someone gets killed."

Fenton shrugged a little too carelessly. "You can assess the situation yourself more thoroughly when you reach Hitani."

Myrina surged to her feet, a ripple of alarm streaking down her spine as Fenton's words sank in. She hadn't paid much attention when the Warlord had mentioned his ship and her in the same breath. She did now for one simple reason. It distinctly sounded as if Fenton had said she was going out into the field. And he knew full well that was impossible.

"Are you actually suggesting I take a cruise with that guy?" she asked, hoping against hope she'd heard wrong. "My equipment is here. My data banks are here. My own staff is well-trained and used to my methods."

As if he wasn't stabbing her in the back, deMorriss laid her assignment on the line. "Myrina, I'm not suggesting anything. I'm telling you. I've juggled assignments over the years, but not this time. With one Outposter already dead the status code is now at red alert. You know as well as I do that means a field assignment because conditions on the planet have become so unstable. You *are* the only one qualified to handle this problem and it can't be done in the lab.

"You'll be accompanying the Ambassador on the Dakokatan Speedlite back to Hitani. You'll have your own quarters, lab, Dakokatan staff. Whatever you need. Given his apparent urgency, I have no idea why Ringa is giving you until tomorrow morning, but if I were you, I'd be thankful." The humorless smile he gave her didn't quite reach his eyes. "Look on it as an adventure."

She hated him for making her beg. "I can't, Fenton. You know I can't go on that ship."

He circled around his desk, cutting off his support and any hope she had of talking her way out of the job. "Myrina, I know you must be tired after spending two days on the satellite, so sleep for a while if you must, but don't make the mistake of taking this assignment lightly. Your career is on the line with this one and you've already managed to piss the

Ambassador off. If the job is so easy, find out what's wrong, impress the man and come home."

A few choice words lodged in her throat while her hands itched to take a couple of swings and deck the man. He was trying to scare the shit out of her and doing a damn good job of it, but she had no intention of giving him the satisfaction of seeing how frightened she was.

Fists clenched, her stomach roiling, she stormed out of Fenton's office. The man had just broken an eight year agreement never to send her on a field assignment. Not that it would do any good to remind him of that. She had nothing in writing, only his word, and she'd just discovered how reliable that was.

She made her way to her quarters where she stripped off her standard-issue TLC jumpsuit, washed up, set her alarm and collapsed into bed. Exhaustion tugged at her bones but her brain wouldn't follow suit. Defeated, she sat huddled in the middle of the bed, her arms wrapped around her legs to stop the shakes.

From her vantage point, she gazed around her room. This apartment in the TLC complex was the only home she'd ever had as her own and she was terrified that after tomorrow morning she'd never see it again.

* * * * *

Powerless to stop the heated energy from surging through his body and priming his cock to a painful erection, Judan Ringa stalked down the hall and boarded the first moving staircase he came to. Even then his body, like his mind, was too restless to stand still for the ride. The woman had done this to him and he was sure the Foreign Affairs Director had noticed his reaction. He took the stairs two at a time, determined to distance himself from the calculating gaze of Fenton deMorriss.

He sought refuge among the secluded pathways of the jungle-like garden he'd passed on his way to his meeting. He wasn't ready to return to his ship just yet. Not when he was feeling like this. At this hour the garden was blessedly empty of people. Still he followed a narrow trail deeper into a patch of giant ferns to ensure his privacy.

A short while later he stepped out into a circular opening where several paths met. Although the rest of the garden was ablaze with color and light, here the huge fronds formed a dark, still canopy. The songs of the exotic assortment of birds that inhabited this oasis of green inside the TLC complex echoed above him. Flinging his cape from his shoulders, he tossed it over the nearest of the low stone walls that encircled the small refuge. The useless wig of synthetic hair, designed to hide from a stranger's view the most sensual part of a Dakokatan's body, came off next. Unbound, his hair fell like a flaming trail of lava straight to his waist. Even in the shadows the strands glowed with an uncharacteristic brilliance. He didn't dare touch his hair, though he could feel its fire through the thin material of his shirt, nearly convincing him that he had somehow entered the fire pits of Neraka.

*This can't be happening! Not here. Not now. Yet somehow it is.*

He braced his hands on the ledge of a wall and bent his head, welcoming the coolness of the stones that counteracted the inferno that attacked his body.

Dr. Myrina deCarte. During their talk in the Director's office, her presence had teased his senses, filling his head like a finely spiced wine, drugging his brain and making it nearly impossible to concentrate. He'd answered questions automatically, purposely suppressing any of his body's traitorous reactions. He'd hoped that by leaving he would regain a measure of control and clear his head.

Closing his eyes he breathed deeply, seeking to steady the erratic beat of his heart. *But instead of the heady perfume of the garden, he caught the scent of a female in heat. It was her. Dr. deCarte. Behind him she laughed and he tensed in anticipation.*

*"Did you really think it would be that easy, Ktua?"* Her voice taunted him.

*He swallowed. No, not easy. He'd just never considered such a wildly improbable solution.*

*An instant later her hand settled across his right thigh.*

No! This should not be happening to me. To her. To us. It makes no sense.

*Of their own volition his lips parted and he gulped in air. It did no good. His blood surged southward through his veins to fill his already engorged cock. Biting his lip he endured her slow, sensual stroke along his thigh. Her hand slid round to cup his buttocks before again edging forward to rest inches from his groin. Behind him her body curled against his, so warm and soft.*

*He tasted blood.*

*She was a bold one! Dakokatan women knew better than to caress a man when the flames of lust licked his body like a brush fire across a mountain valley. But she had no such sense. Instead her touch laid claim to him, branding her mark on him.*

A raucous cry of a bird rang through the garden. He looked up in time to glimpse the brightly colored plumes of the bird as it took flight from its perch among the tall fronds of a fern. Distracted, he whirled round, grasping at empty air. The illusion vanished.

In silence Judan stared down at his hands. They trembled slightly, the tremor traveling up his arms to shake his entire body. He clenched his fists, helpless to check the speed and intensity of his reactions.

Slowly, one labored breath at a time, his heart rate returned to normal, though desire still strummed through his body. He threaded his hands through his hair, which was now lukewarm rather than hot. At last some of the electrical energy that ran through the strands had begun to dissipate.

Exhausted, he slumped against the stone wall, memories of his last night at home assailing him. The Three Sisters were surely laughing amongst themselves as they waited for their handiwork to unfold. Especially the Third Moon who hid behind her two sisters, for it was she, Judan's favorite, to whom he'd sent his prayer five months ago.

*He delivered Zane back to his mother's house and stayed to share a meal with them so the table would not seem so empty. Then, at the darkest hour of the night, he donned his cape and walked the five* juhs *from the city center with the other supplicants to the Grove of the Three Sisters. Every evening when the three moons of Dakokata reached their zenith, they appeared here at their closest proximity to each other, like sisters sharing their secrets.*

*Following the novices through a stand of orange trees, he came at last to the small glade, to hear the priestess on duty sing to the moons. Later, he dutifully visited the three shrines, making the standard offering of flower petals to the first two sisters. Amidst the soft murmur and singsong of the other worshipers, he felt like a hypocrite. The priestess believed he offered prayers for a safe mission, a tradition among the* Ktua *and one he'd practiced now for several years.*

*By the time he reached the nearly deserted shrine of the Third Moon, he was seriously questioning the foolishness of his plan. Yet for some time now he'd been unable to deny the fierce longing that gnawed at his heart every time he visited his mother. He wanted Zane as his own son. All the attention and time he gave the boy was not enough. Would never be enough for either of them and yet, by law, any future they had together was inescapably tied to the whim of fate – to* Rakanasmara.

*No child on Dakokata was denied a rightful place within his or her extended family. However, to ensure stability in the face of tragedy, only those family members already bonded by* Rakanasmara *qualified as surrogate parents to orphaned children.*

*And so, illuminated only by the Three Sisters themselves, he humbled himself at the shrine of the Third Moon. Because he didn't dare ask a priestess for advice regarding the offering, he chose it himself. Despite being unsure what made a suitable gift, he knew instinctively that he had to offer her something of immense value.*

*With care, he knelt before the shrine's circle of three sacred stones and lit the small pile of kindling within. Then, before he could question further the wisdom of his actions, he withdrew the knife he kept in a sheath in his boot. Reaching up, he cut off one of the braids in his hair and lowered it into the flames. When his prayer was answered and he'd found his mate, she would weave him another braid to replace the one he'd sent to the Third Moon in the desperate hope of finding her.*

Agitated by the memory, Judan grabbed his cape and wig from the wall only to pause.

*Have I? Have I found her?*

Slowly he made his way through the garden. He needed to get back to his ship and search for some answers. As he retraced his steps along the pathway, his copper hair shone like a fiery beacon behind him.

# Chapter Two

ഌ

Six hours later Myrina entered the Fifth Wheel — she was a woman on a mission. Rested, if not entirely refreshed, she was dressed in her favorite velvety, coffee-brown skirt and T-shirt with matching butter-soft leather boots. The bar was alive with music and it seemed the cacophony of voices spoke just about every language in the universe. She shook her head when one of the waitstaff approached her for her order and scanned the crowd instead.

A moment later she spotted her assistant, Kikki San, who shouted and waved at her. Myrina grinned ruefully, remembering she'd never made it to the lab earlier in the day. And wasn't likely to anytime soon.

Her facial features proclaiming her multiracial background, Myrina's pint-sized assistant dressed with the same flamboyant style she used to approach life. This evening Kikki's dreadlocks were a fluorescent yellow. When Myrina had left for her meeting three days before they'd been purple.

Another colleague, Sonora Austen — Sonny to her friends — sat beside Kikki. Dressed in her TLC-issued jumpsuit, the cultural anthropologist wore her waist-length brown hair in a severe twist. The style aptly summed up Sonny's regally calm, no-nonsense approach to life. A small smile of welcome played across her face when she caught sight of Myrina.

"Have you heard?" Kikki asked when Myrina snagged a chair and sat down.

Myrina suppressed a groan. "Heard what?" She did not need any more surprises today.

"Some green guy was in the lab yesterday looking around." Kikki's voice trembled with suppressed excitement.

"He was in my lab?" Myrina shifted in her seat, causing her chair to scrape across the floor. Damn, she couldn't even say the man's name, though a few other choice terms flitted through her brain. Only invited guests were allowed in the private labs and she'd certainly never authorized his visit.

"You know this man, Myrina?" Kikki asked.

Myrina nodded. "We've met," she admitted reluctantly, then regretted her morose response when she realized Kikki had interpreted it as displeasure toward her rather than the Dakokatan.

"Fenton deMorriss gave him a personal tour," Kikki said, obviously feeling the need to justify her actions. "The authorization came from deVere so I had to let them look around."

*Well crap.* deVere was the Director's Director of TLC and his word was law. If he'd authorized the little green man's snoop around her lab, there was nothing she could do about it.

"Are you talking about the Dakokatan *Ktua*?" Sonny asked. "I'd heard one of their Speedlites was docked at deVere's private port, but I haven't seen any of the crew yet. I was hoping to get a chance to…"

"I'm sure the crew is too busy restocking supplies," Myrina said. "We leave tomorrow morning."

Trust Sonora Austen to go gaga. The woman never turned down an opportunity to study a new culture. Unfortunately, her announcement only made Sonny more curious.

"How… You're going out on a field assignment? Are you okay with that?"

Myrina shrugged as casually as she could. The downside of discussing her upcoming assignment was that everyone knew about her alleged agreement with deMorriss. What could she say? That her stomach still felt tight and slightly nauseous at the thought of stepping onto the Speedlite tomorrow.

Beside her, Kikki looked somewhat dismayed, then grinned. "The Warlord was a bit too intense for my taste," she said. "But what are the possibilities of meeting some other hunky, available Dakokatan on this flight?" If there was a way, Kikki would put a positive spin on the problem.

Myrina gritted her teeth. "None," she said at the same time Sonny added, "Zero."

Kikki frowned at the two women.

"You're not going, Kikki," Myrina explained. "I'm flying solo. Or at least I'm the only TLC employee on this voyage," she amended.

Her assistant looked horrified by the news. "Are you sure you'll be okay, Myrina?"

"I'll manage," Myrina said and just stopped herself from crossing her fingers in the superstitious hope her words were true.

With an uncertain nod, Kikki turned to Sonora. "So what's with this zero, Doc? Are you saying I wouldn't have found true love on this trip anyway?"

"Exactly. The Dakokatans are one of the few humanoid races who are genetically programmed to find their mate."

"Oh, please," Myrina said, frowning at this ludicrous explanation. "Genetically coded love? Give me a break."

"Scoff all you want, but it's true. The genetic marker works like a light switch that turns on when compatible Dakokatan mates enter each other's personal space."

"You mean they fall in love with a stranger?" Kikki asked.

"Actually, from what I can tell the Dakokatan language doesn't have a specific word for love. *Rakanasmara* is the term used to denote the genetic partnership for mating. It's activated in late puberty, so I suppose it's possible for two neighbors to discover they're mates." Sonny shrugged. "It's equally possible that a Dakokatan never finds his or her mate."

"How do you know all this?" Myrina asked, now curious in spite of herself. "The Dakokatans only just joined the Confederacy and I understand they maintained an isolationist policy up until very recently."

Sonora smiled and glanced around the room. A few feet away five lab technicians still in TLC uniforms were engaged in a heated argument. A couple sat behind Kikki, but they were too engrossed in each other to pay attention to the three women.

Satisfied, Sonny leaned forward. "When the Confederacy started negotiating an alliance with the Dakokatans, deVere assigned me to research their culture for TLC's database. Why? Are you interested?"

"Sure," Kikki said with a mischievous smile. "In a certain tall, green alien. Right, boss?"

"Not!" Myrina said. Especially after the weird reaction she'd had to him earlier in the afternoon. She sincerely hoped she didn't have any more adverse symptoms around the rest of the crew. Just the thought of walking onto the Speedlite tomorrow morning gave her the creeps without any added complications. "But I am interested in what you can give me on Dakokatan customs. It may come in handy."

"Are you sure there isn't anything you want to tell us, Myrina?" Sonny asked. Although a smile played across her mouth, her eyes spoke of her heartfelt concern for her friend's situation.

Stubbornly, Myrina shook her head. There was nothing to tell and nothing anyone could do to save her from this field assignment.

"Okay, I'll send you a data-chip on Dakokatan culture before I turn in for the night."

"Thanks." Getting down to business, Myrina quickly explained the portable equipment and programs she'd need Kikki to prepare by morning and then left to search for her next victim.

She had no trouble spotting Parker Brown's wiry frame. He was trying to disengage himself from a couple of Callottas. From the looks of things the two males wanted him to continue drinking the vile resin liquor that left Callottas and non-Callottas alike in a drunken stupor for days. Casually intercepting a grateful Parker, she steered them to a small table near the center of the room. Before she could sit down, he drew her into his arms for a warm hug.

"Nine days is too long," he whispered in her ear, referring to their respective projects, which had kept them apart.

"I missed you too." Myrina happily accepted the warmth and love that were given so freely.

She and Parker had met during their first year at university when they'd been assigned as lab partners in a chemistry class. She'd been little more than a defiant puppy, on her own for the first time and struggling to make a place for herself. Then Parker had suddenly announced one Thursday afternoon he was taking her to his parents' home for the weekend.

Of course she'd refused. She hadn't wanted to give him the wrong impression or lose her chem partner. Instead of taking no for an answer, he'd backed her into a corner. Literally. For all of half a minute—okay, five minutes, maybe ten—they'd explored a certain option. Then backed off, having reached a mutual understanding that, in the long run, the friendship between them was the better choice. He'd still taken her home for the weekend.

The entire experience had been overwhelming, exciting and scary for an orphan who'd never had anyone want her, especially since the rest of the Brown family unofficially adopted her on sight. As strong a person as she was, Myrina considered Parker and his family her saviors because they had provided the unconditional refuge she'd needed from the world.

"Let's go to my place," Parker suggested.

31

"Can't. I just ordered my supplies from Kikki and dropped over to say hello and goodbye. I've been given a new assignment."

With a resigned sigh, Parker released her and plunked himself down on the chair kitty-corner to the one she pulled out for herself. "So much for our dinner date tomorrow night. What's the assignment?"

Myrina shrugged, giving him a half smile that acknowledged her own regret. "It's a long story and a long trip from TLC, courtesy of deVere, I think, although Fenton was the one who gave me the bad news."

Parker sat up straight and whistled softly. "You're being sent off-world? How is that possible?"

"Apparently it's very easy. Fenton had no trouble telling me I was going on a field assignment."

"The bastard. I'll speak to deVere."

"No," she said, grabbing his arm even though Parker hadn't moved.

He shook her off and scowled. "Don't tell me you're okay with this, Myrina. I won't believe you."

"I know." Unlike Kikki and Sonora, Parker was her one friend who knew the whole story behind her anxiety attacks and her work arrangement.

"Do you?" he said, his voice rough with emotion. "I remember when they brought you home."

"Parker." Damn, he was going to get sentimental on her.

"I spent a goddamn month in that hospital," he said as if they both didn't know the story by heart. "Sitting beside your bed talking to you. I didn't know if you could hear me or not, but I kept talking."

"And one day I did hear you and I woke up," she said, reaching over to squeeze his hand. As a scientist she didn't know if that was really true, but sentimentality aside, it was as good an explanation as any why she'd been the only one of the three critically ill team members to survive.

"Sorry, didn't mean to get sentimental. I've had three shots of Callotta resin." He scrubbed a hand over his face. "Must have killed off a few brain cells. So, I talk to deVere, see what's going on?"

"I know what's going on," she said. Once Fenton had informed her of the red alert status code, she'd known. She was going out into the field, no matter how irrational her fear at the time. That didn't mean she liked it any better. She'd done her best so far to ignore the outer space angle of the assignment.

"I can't let you jeopardize your chances at a Directorship," she said. "Besides, I told you, I think the orders came from deVere, so talking to him won't do any good."

Parker didn't look too happy, but nodded to show he'd back off. "Must be big. What happened?"

Myrina wasn't surprised by his question. Parker might not take direct action, but that wouldn't stop him from investigating. And, remembering a certain Dakokatan Warlord, she knew exactly whom she wanted Parker to check out. "A little green man has been playing with environments he knows nothing about and I have to go in and save his ass."

Instead of laughing or, heck, even grinning at her comment, Parker's eyes widened for a fraction of a second before a deep blush stained his face.

"Ah, Myrina…"

Slowly, Myrina let a string of curses flow silently through her brain. She didn't need to look to know who'd just passed by behind them.

With a shock she realized she'd been rubbing her forearm. The tingle was back or had it been there all along only she hadn't noticed it until now? Even her scalp prickled the way it had in deMorriss' office. Since she'd felt perfectly normal when she'd entered the bar, she wondered if her bizarre theory wasn't so off the wall after all. The Dakokatan's presence really did seem to affect her physiologically.

"Shit." She allowed the one word that aptly described what she'd just gotten herself into to escape her lips.

"You're calling a six-foot-three Dakokatan a 'little green man'?" Parker's voice sounded slightly incredulous.

"Don't. Just tell me how close he was." Not that she really had to ask. Her skin seemed equipped with an early warning system where the Dakokatan was concerned.

"Close enough to hear your last comment."

Setting her elbows on the table, Myrina rested her head in her hands and closed her eyes. Fenton would be livid if he found out she'd offended the Ambassador after his little talk with her this afternoon. She sighed. And here she'd honestly thought the day couldn't get any worse.

"I'll have to go and apologize tonight." She murmured the words more to herself but, when she sat up and opened her eyes, one look at Parker told her he'd heard. She shrugged. "I can't go onto his ship tomorrow having him believe I meant what I said."

"After what just happened you want to interact with a pissed-off green alien? Can't you just get reassigned to the Mining Consortium instead?"

She gave him a weak grin. "After our meeting this afternoon, he'd probably like to fly me there himself."

\* \* \* \* \*

Three and a half minutes after leaving the Fifth Wheel, Myrina stood outside the Warlord's door. Given his status as an Ambassador and his preferential docking privileges, she wasn't surprised to find him occupying one of the nicer suites in TLC's guest wing. Of course, since she hadn't yet worked up the nerve to knock on his door, all she'd admired so far were the carpeting and the elaborate silk flower arrangement standing on a replica antique table at the end of the hall.

This was undoubtedly a very bad idea. deMorriss had already issued a warning and even Parker had suggested she take cover after his first look at a Dakokatan. So, what exactly was she doing outside the man's door when the mere thought of an off-world assignment creeped her out?

No, if she was going to humble herself, she needed to be truthful about her reasons. And the answer wasn't too hard to find. Regardless of the Warlord's current opinion of her and her own fears about going off-world for this assignment, she could not sit by and let the Outposters die.

Silently, the door slid open on its own and a voice beckoned. "Weren't you planning to come in, Dr. deCarte?"

Not exactly an invitation, but since he'd opened his door she took it as one. This time she was aware of the Warlord's presence as soon as she stepped over the threshold. In the dimly lit room it took a moment longer to spot him standing with his back to her, fixing a drink for himself at a small table. She knew it was him, even though the man had hair the color of dark copper hanging down to his waist. At intervals around his scalp were thin braids of hair interwoven with silver and black beads.

The flames of a dozen candles set around the room flickered, indicating the door had closed behind her. The candles themselves were beautiful, fat columns of a rich sienna color, their scent containing a hint of vanilla and some unfamiliar essence that filled the room. She closed her eyes and inhaled deeply. The fragrance teased her senses with half-formed visions of what she imagined was the Dakokatan homeworld. *How was that possible?* She knew less than nothing about the Warlord's planet.

"The candle makers add imported vanilla beans to sweeten the bitter scent of the sand from the Tekur desert region."

Her heart thumped a sharp staccato when she opened her eyes and he turned towards her, a half smile playing across his face. Immediately her skin tingled as though an electric current jumped between them. *Damn, how did he do that?*

"Tekur as in tekurilite?" she asked, surprised to learn the candles were made with sand containing a rare mineral, not wax. "When ground into fine dust isn't tekurilite considered…"

"An aphrodisiac?" He nodded, that seductive smile still skirting the edges of his mouth. "Yes. Having second thoughts?" he asked.

Somehow she had the impression he was no longer referring to the distinctive scent of the candles, but rather issuing a challenge. She didn't back away. In fact she needed every ounce of willpower she had to fight the urge to cross the room and touch him. He wore leggings. That was all. No boots and most definitely no shirt.

He made the decision for her, covering the distance between them in a few short steps. Given their difference in height she suddenly found herself eye level with his chest. Make that his hairless chest, leaving her with a clear view of hard, sculpted muscles.

She gulped a breath of air. Warlord indeed. Two faint, ragged lines bisected his left pectoral. She didn't know much about Dakokatan anatomy, but the scars were too close to where a human heart would be for comfort. Her fingers fluttered with the need to reach out and offer comfort. A ridiculous sentiment given the age of the wounds.

"Here." He held up his glass. "You look like you could use a drink."

*Has he noticed my hands? Does he suspect what I want to do?* She nearly shook her head. She didn't need alcohol to cloud her already scrambled emotions.

"It's spring water," he said as if he'd read her thoughts. "Take a sip."

Still, she hesitated. She had the distinct impression he wanted to serve her himself rather than surrender the glass.

Needing to steady her hands, however, she compromised. When he didn't let go, she wrapped them around both the glass and his hand. There were no sizzles of heat or shooting stars or dizzy spells. Only the smooth skin of a firm hand tipping the glass to her lips. She drank, welcoming the cool liquid in her suddenly parched mouth.

*What's happening to me? Between us? With him?*

She suppressed the questions and pushed the glass away. She wished she could shove her wild thoughts away as easily. Before she could let go, however, he drew the cup to his own lips and drank. Just a sip, yet she knew he wanted to share the water with her. She was still holding on when he lifted his free hand and smoothed away the sheen of moisture from her lower lip with the pad of his thumb. It was smooth like the rest of his skin.

Instantly she jerked out of his grasp and dropped her hands. *Get a grip!* Time to remember why she was here. And it wasn't to be intimate with a stranger. Especially one she'd insulted.

"I came to apologize," she said. "My remark at the Fifth Wheel was made in one of my stupider moments."

The Warlord took another sip of water and then set the glass down on a small table beside them. "The man with you told you I'd heard?"

Her face grew hot, a reaction she wasn't proud of. Stiffly, she nodded her head.

"Then you are here to try to, how do you say, dig yourself out of a hole?" Gone was the careful modulation he'd exerted over his voice in deMorriss' office, replaced by blatant curiosity.

Come to think of it, he hadn't once tried to disguise his voice since she'd arrived, any more than he'd disguised his appearance. *So why did he take such deliberate care to hide himself this afternoon?*

"You're right, of course," she said, determined to see her apology and request through to the end. Her simple reasons for coming here had suddenly turned complex. "If you hadn't heard I wouldn't be here, but I can assure you I wouldn't have liked myself any better."

"Tell me about the man you were with."

His request startled her, especially when he gave no other reaction to her admission. "Parker Brown?" How was he relevant to her mistake? "He's the First Assistant to the Chief Medical Officer here at TLC."

"And you've been away from each other for a long time?"

"What?"

"You and this Parker gave every indication of knowing each other quite well."

Just like that her face grew hot again. *Well crap.* Why she should be embarrassed now when she and Parker had been observed together hundreds of times mystified her.

"Yes," she said. "Parker and I are very close." *Period, end of story, butt out.*

"What about deMorriss?"

"Fenton?" No one got close to Fenton deMorriss and after today she knew why.

"Do you like working for him?"

"I like working for TLC."

"Hence your reason for coming here tonight to apologize. Am I right?"

This time he applied the shock treatment without the electrical current. Did he really believe she was that shallow? That desperate? That calculating?

"Is there a problem, Dr. deCarte?"

*Yes, this is a bizarre conversation and to hell with my assignment and my career.* "Not at all, Warlord. I came here to apologize for my rudeness. I'm sorry for the intrusion."

She intended to leave, really she did, but her feet refused to move two short paces to the door and out.

"Warlord is a very inaccurate translation of the Dakokatan word *Ktua*. Say my name, Myrina."

Hearing *her* name on *his* lips jolted her pulse into a higher gear. The slight accent that inflected some of the English words he used made it sound almost lyrical.

"Say my name," he urged again when she was ready to shake her head. He was standing so close they almost touched.

She didn't dare look up at him. "Judan Ringa," she whispered and he groaned, softly.

"Look at me, Myrina."

She looked up as high as his shoulder and stopped, fascinated by the slim lock of copper hair that seemed to reach across the narrow space between them. Her heart skidded to a stop. The man was crazy. *She* was crazy. He'd questioned her integrity, insinuating she'd come here just to save her job, yet she stood here wanting... He stood so close she felt the heat of his breath across her face.

"Are your conversations always this convoluted?" she asked.

"Yes. Myrina, how would you respond if I did this?"

For once Myrina didn't think, analyze or come up with five other possible responses, she simply lifted her left hand and aligned her palm with his. A flame she barely remembered, let alone recognized, licked at her veins and her entire body jerked in painful, exquisite awareness of the man standing before her. It had been so long, too long, since she'd responded to a man this way.

"Yes," Judan growled.

Even though only their hands were joined together there was no mistaking the primitive need in his vivid stare. His eyes were like laser beams capable of burning away her clothing and baring her body to his touch. Her nipples were puckered tight against the lace of her bra and the thin material of her T-shirt. On display. For him.

The sudden ripple in the muscles across his bare chest brought a faint smile to her lips. She realized that if she had trouble hiding her reaction from him, his reactions were equally exposed to her. The sense of power was heady and she took advantage. The fingers of her right hand skimmed across his left nipple. It was already hard, a fact confirmed by his sharp intake of breath. Though she wanted to, she didn't linger. Instead, her fingers sought and traced the two pale lines of scar tissue. Light as her touch was, the faint but steady beat of his heart pounded under her fingertips. Satisfied she held up her right hand and waited.

When his other hand touched hers, she was barely aware of the soft pressure forcing her back one step, then two and she was against the door. All she saw were his eyes. Big and bright and greener than any grass she'd ever seen, they were filled with impossible promises.

Her wrists were pinned securely above her head by one of the Dakokatan's large hands before she remembered it was better not to believe everything she saw. "Stop."

He froze, his free hand sliding away from her arm to his side, but he didn't let her go. And his eyes still blazed with the intense certainty that he'd get what he wanted. And what he wanted was her.

"I can't do this." She never moved this fast with a man. With someone she'd barely met and known for less than a day. If this afternoon's encounter with deMorriss wasn't reminder enough, she could count the number of people she trusted, cared about, on the fingers of one hand.

He frowned, clearly puzzled by her statement. "I know you feel the bond between us, Myrina."

A shiver raced through her and it was all she could do to mask the effect of his blunt declaration. He'd felt the attraction between them, therefore he acted. She'd never had the luxury or been stupid enough to let her life be ruled by lust. She'd never lied either, except by omission. "You questioned my integrity."

The frown deepened, cutting two furrows in his brow and his eyes lost some of their warm glow. "No, I didn't."

Remembering what Parker had said about pissed-off green aliens, she tried to free her arms. They wouldn't budge. Almost imperceptibly he tightened his grip, though not enough to hurt. Her breath hitched when she realized how vulnerable she was. For a moment she fought through an old sense of panic, then reached a state of dead certain calm. Her knee jackknifed up toward his groin. Before it could make contact, his hand shot out and grabbed her leg, shoving it back down. Worse, he didn't let go. He jammed his other leg between her thighs to block any further attacks.

The damn man had barely exerted himself, yet he'd immobilized her but good, keeping his intentions quite clear. The thick length of his erection pressed forcefully against her stomach. Well, she had no intention of making it that easy for him. In fact she'd be more than happy to show him what a pissed off human looked like.

"Let me go," she hissed. "Let me go, you—"

"Little green man?"

*Well crap.* Just like that he knocked the indignation out of her, making her want to laugh out loud. And their full-body contact was initiating so many zings and pings through her system, she'd momentarily forgotten he towered over her by a good eight inches. And, except for his smirk of satisfaction, he hadn't even sounded pissed.

It had to be the candles, or more specifically, the tekurilite in them that was causing her irrational physical and mental responses to the man. The mineral might be rare and only used in very small quantities, but obviously twelve candles' worth could wreak a lot of havoc on a body. Her body.

"Very funny," she muttered. "Now let go."

"You don't smell," he said, before he released her leg and stepped back half a pace. Enough to put a few molecules of space between them, probably so he could maintain his easy grip on her wrists.

"What?" Her head snapped up in amazement. A millimeter of sweat pooled between her breasts and her heart skipped a couple of thuds when she discovered he was studying her again. *What is he looking for?*

"Sorry, I mean you don't wear perfumes or scented lotions. I just smell you."

She wanted to ask what she smelled like in the worst way, but she didn't. The same way she didn't ask, again, if he'd let her arms go. His actions didn't make sense, yet she had no doubt he had his reasons. Besides, now that she had an iota of breathing room, a minuscule amount of common sense actually kicked in. "You were trying to convince me you hadn't maligned my integrity."

"Ah yes," he said and hips lips quirked into a smile. "The convoluted conversation. Dakokatans sometimes have a tendency to…jump all over the place when we talk." He reached out and ran his index finger along her cheek. "I wasn't questioning your integrity, but confirming my earlier judgment that you have some."

"Come again?" she said, well aware he'd dropped his hand before she could move her head away. "Are you telling me your insinuation that I came here tonight because I wanted to save my job was a compliment?"

With an exasperated sigh he shook his head. "I wanted your answers, Myrina. And those answers tell me you are a person of integrity." His gaze softened and his voice became gruff. "Fiercely so. You did not tell me what you thought I wanted to hear, instead you spoke your truth and I am honored."

Maybe it wasn't the candles, after all. Or the glass of water or even his bare chest. These were merely props setting the stage. Maybe it was Judan Ringa himself who'd ensnared her, turning her brain to mush, her insides to jelly and her limbs so boneless it was a good thing he had her pinned to the wall.

For the first time in her life, someone had spoken with pride about her forthrightness instead of labeling it opinionated or worse.

She licked her suddenly parched lips, well aware that he tracked the movement. She shifted, offering just enough resistance that if he'd wanted to he could release her arms. Instead he countered her movements, shifting closer and pulling her arms a little higher. Her midriff was now exposed below the hem of her T-shirt. Then he bent his head until his lips brushed her forehead before drawing back. Even that small contact was enough to heat her blood another half degree.

"If you are satisfied with *my* answer, will you trust me just a little?"

"With what?"

The corners of his eyes crinkled with laugh lines. "With you."

"Jud—"

"Shhh," he whispered. The palm of his free hand cupped the side of her face while his thumb settled against her mouth, preventing her protest. "Let me learn how you like to be touched."

Definitely not the candles. Definitely the man—and his way with her. Ever since she'd stepped into his room she'd been the absolute focus of his attention. She—not the latest test results or lab experiments or even the details of the job he'd "hired" her for. She never liked being so exposed, yet not one of her diversionary tactics had worked.

His had. Every time.

Good thing Judan Ringa wasn't her enemy because otherwise he'd be an opponent to be reckoned with. Especially as he didn't ask for permission, he simply began his lesson.

Smooth and light, the tips of his fingers grazed the side of her face. Moving to her ear, he explored the whorls, then set out to discover her eyes and cheeks and nose and mouth. And everything he touched heated on contact. His concentration was so intense, she closed her eyes to at least keep her soul safe from his scrutiny. An instant later his fingertips glided across the delicate surface of her eyelids.

"That's right," he whispered. "I want to learn everything."

He'd simply taken her gesture as one of surrender, a thought that scared her because she hadn't agreed to that either. Yet his touch felt so good. Another thought that should have her backing away, except she had nowhere to go and he was holding her fast.

His hand slid down to encircle her neck. She swallowed hard, aware that he now experienced every stuttered intake of breath, every rushed exhalation. *Is he learning that, too?* Underneath his fingers, her pulse-point fluttered as rapidly as an insect's wings. And she was just as desperate for his touch as a moth was to reach a bright flame. Unsure, she bit her lower lip to stop the whimper threatening to escape.

"Don't," he whispered.

Slipping beneath the barrier of her T-shirt he settled his large hand on her bare belly. Instantly, she sucked in her breath as tendrils of fire uncurled inside her.

"That's right," he said. "I want to see every reaction your body makes to mine."

*He's asking too much*, her mind screamed. *Not enough*, her body cried out. He inched higher, grazing her rib cage. Each movement painfully, exquisitely slow. Anticipation was sweet torture and her breasts ached for his touch. Answering the urgent demands of her body, she squirmed, determined to end his teasing.

"Hold still." His voice cracked and he gulped in a load of air.

"Why?" she asked, though she knew the answer from the fine sheen of sweat that dampened his chest. His professed lesson about *her* was turning *him* on.

"I need…" He shook his head. "I want to take my time. I give you my oath, I'll take care of you."

What about her taking care of his pleasure? "Then let me touch you, too."

A hoarse laugh burst from his lips. "You don't ask for much, do you?"

Inside her shirt his fingers sought and found her nipple hidden within the lacy bra. His thumb and forefinger claimed the prize, pinching and pulling the nub. A lick of fire hit her womb with such sharp intensity she creamed her panties. She wasn't even aware she cried out until he growled his encouragement.

"Do you see?" he asked. "How did we know you would become so wild when I touched your breasts?"

Startled she looked up. Didn't he understand? *She* hadn't known. This had never happened before.

His thumb rubbed incessant circles over her breast, scraping against the hardened tip before he turned his attention to the other one.

"Beautiful," he said. Already puckered tight, her nipple stabbed against the palm of his hand when he cupped her breast.

Once again a fierce desire built inside her, shortening her breath and tensing her body in anticipation. Betraying her.

"Teaching me," he said as if he'd read her thoughts and was giving her a better answer. "I can smell your arousal,

Myrina. Would you come if I played with your beautiful breasts some more?"

Half sobbing with need, she shook her head. She didn't know that answer either. Wasn't even sure she was thinking properly because, damn it, she wanted to trust him. A haze from the candles or maybe her own desire clouded her vision. All she felt was his hand on her bare flesh and all she saw was a large, muscled expanse of green skin.

"I want to touch you."

"Insistent little thing, aren't you," he said.

She was sure a wealth of affection flooded his voice.

*How is that possible, we've only just met?*

"Yes," she managed to gasp.

"I know." Now he sounded regretful. "And I'm sorry, but not this time."

Protests tumbled over each other vying for ways to prove she was wise to hold back, to keep a little of herself safe. They died the instant his hand moved to her thigh and slid up under the flare of her skirt to her hip. All except one. She struggled a moment to hang on to the single thought and her sanity.

"What do you mean 'not this time'?"

The frown was back. "Because, woman," he growled. "I will obviously need more than one time before you truly accept me."

Isn't that what she was doing? Accepting him?

He shook his head. "Soon. Look," he said, running his fingers along the edge of her panties. "You're already wet for me."

He brushed the back of his hand against her clit. Once, twice, leaving her panting and undulating her pelvis against his lazy strokes. His grin was one of pure male satisfaction. Pushing aside the fragile lace barrier, he slid two fingers along her slit. Slick and smooth, they glided back and forth, teasing the entrance of her pussy, yet never dipping inside. And all the time, his thumb rubbed against her clit while her hips kept time with his strokes. Her eyes closed as she gave herself up to him.

"That's right, Myrina. I can smell how close you are."

Just his words sent another ripple of lust through her limbs and she shuddered. Without a word, he adjusted his grip on her arms until he held her hands instead of her wrists. Boneless, she moaned and curled her fingers tightly around his hand. The small concession wasn't nearly enough. Him touching her wasn't nearly enough.

In one desperate move, she hooked one of her legs around his and tugged. Caught unawares, he grunted and toppled against her. At the last second his free hand, the one that had been doing so much damage to her sanity while it explored her skin, shot out and hit the wall to brace his fall.

*No.* She was not going to allow him any excuse or means to distance himself again. If he wanted to take care of her, he'd better do it right up close and personal so she'd get her share — of him. She hitched her other leg around him and squirmed a little higher for better leverage. In the space of four heartbeats nothing happened. He didn't move and neither did she.

"I don't suppose," he said, his voice so low it barely stirred the air between them, "that I could convince you to let me go."

Her answer was easy. Lifting her head off the wall, she leaned forward and licked his nipple and then continued up the soft, hairless skin straight to his collarbone.

"Mmm," she murmured. "Less salinity than human skin." Delicious though, so she returned for another taste. And another when his breath came in short, desperate gasps and he nuzzled the side of her face.

He muttered some words in Dakokatan and then said, "It's too late, anyway."

His hand slid down the wall to grab her skirt and tug it out of the way. With the barrier gone his erection, still sheathed inside his leggings, nestled firmly between the outer lips of her pussy. She whimpered as his hand took firm hold of her buttock and she rocked against him. Definitely way too late.

"Stop," he growled in her ear.

Pinned between the wall and his big body, she stilled. His hair enclosed them behind a copper curtain. A few tendrils brushed against her body and several strands entwined around her arms. Their hot breath steamed the air.

"Look at me," he ordered.

She lifted her head defiantly. She would not apologize for taking what she wanted. She'd learned that lesson very early in life and no aphrodisiac-induced lust was going to make her forget it. Especially when she saw the stern set of Judan Ringa's face. Yet, despite her determination, deep inside her emotions turned tail and stampeded for the exit.

He simply shook his head, an ancient knowledge mirrored in those vivid emerald eyes of his. "You can't outrun this, Myrina. There's nowhere to go, nowhere to hide. You'll learn that soon enough. Right now I'll give you what you want. But we'll do it my way. I can only be pushed so far."

Before she could think, utter a protest or issue an ultimatum of her own, he lowered his head and his mouth captured hers. The heat and power were like a blast from a fiery furnace, as if she'd been cold instead of very warm only seconds ago. And the taste of him. Rich and oh-so decadent with that hint of sandalwood again teasing her senses.

Trapped and unable to flee, instinctively she fought the invasion. He groaned into her mouth, his tongue sweeping a path across her teeth, daring her to defy him. She couldn't because she couldn't lie, even by omission. Not now.

Her tongue tangled with his and he moved against her. One smooth stroke of his rock-hard cock against her pussy unleashed a blaze within her. She bucked against him but his body held her fast against the door. Instead, he hiked up one of her legs and his hand brushed the entrance to her pussy. Adjusting his hold on her, he inserted the tips of two fingers. And all the while he thrust his clothed cock against her, the hard length of him ground against her clit and his fingers allowed her a shallow, teasing ride.

Consumed, she quickly soaked his leggings with a flood of cum. The slippery slide of the fabric only increased the friction on her clit, bringing her oh-so close to the edge. As if he sensed the approach of the maelstrom, his soaked fingers delved into the crack of her buttocks. The thin lace panties offered no real barrier as his fingers sought and found her hole. Slicking the rim they slowly pushed past her sphincter muscles.

Sobbing because the sensation of fullness overwhelmed her, she screamed into his mouth. He totally surrounded her, filling her mouth and her ass with parts of his own body and yet, strangely, it was the fact that he refused to enter that one sacred place that finally convinced her to fully surrender.

Melting against him, she lost herself in the rhythm he set, welcoming the dual thrusts of his cock outside her and his fingers within. The slow leisure with which he'd established his dominance quickly dissipated. Hard, fast, ravenous, he pounded against her. Desperately she arched her hips, instinctively seeking her release against him. He moaned against her mouth, signaling the keen edge of his own pleasure. Then, just when she thought she'd be riding the high forever, it seemed a gravitational whirlpool caught her in its dizzying grip. She knew she screamed again, probably his name, but she was hardly aware of herself by now. Only him and his own fierce shout as he climaxed against her.

He slumped against her, his hot breath fanning her cheek. Sated, she followed her instincts and turned her head to nuzzle her face against his, purposely delaying any thoughts about the consequences of what had just happened between them. A moment later he withdrew his fingers from her ass. Her legs were still wrapped around him and she wasn't sure if they would support her, but she let him go and he eased her, gently, to the ground. When he would have released her, she shook her head against his chest, reluctant to end the connection between them. He held on.

Had she ever been this close to one single person in her entire life?

She knew the answer before she'd even asked the question. It wasn't that difficult. *Never.*

What was much harder was admitting to herself that *he* wanted more. That he'd been perfectly clear on that point. Even more shocking was the fact that she was ready to say yes.

"So," she whispered, afraid her voice would crack if she spoke in a normal tone. "You, ah, want to have an affair?"

# Chapter Three

Without a word Judan Ringa stepped back and dropped his arms, releasing her completely. Even his hair pulled free of its hold on her, although several strands still floated in the space between them.

Swamped by emotions she couldn't understand, let alone name, she ignored the ache in her shoulders and pressed the palms of her hands against the door, determined she was not going to collapse in a puddle of angst at this man's feet.

*Idiot.* Why had she taken the risk and asked the question?

But she wasn't an idiot and she knew the answer to this question too. It was always better to know where she stood with a man and in this case doubly so because she would be working with him on this field assignment.

Totally absorbed in rebuilding her crumbling defenses, she didn't even notice what Judan was doing until he settled his hands on her shoulders. Startled, she looked up into his green eyes as he set to work gently kneading her muscles all the way down her arms. His impassive expression gave no hint of his thoughts or his feelings.

"Myrina," he asked when he reached the sensitive dip of her elbows, "what does 'have an affair' mean?"

Praising the solid mass of door behind her and her shaky but stable legs, she laughed out loud. *Well now, isn't this embarrassing?* And yet it made perfect sense. She rested her head back against the door, closed her eyes and took a deep breath. Judan's English was excellent, almost idiomatically perfect, but it was his second language and she didn't suppose he'd ever had cause to discuss "having an affair" with anyone while negotiating the Dakokatans' membership into the

Confederacy. Which also meant she really had been a bit of an idiot interpreting his actions using her own cultural norms.

She opened her eyes and cleared her throat. "It means that we...that on our way to Hitani we're... Well, dammit, you said 'this time', which implies a next time, which means you're asking me to have an affair while we go to Hitani and rescue the Outposters."

"No, I'm not."

Thoroughly exasperated, especially since the fatigue had returned, making it impossible to think straight, she tugged her arms out of his grasp and pushed him away. He stepped back far too quickly for her peace of mind.

"So what was this then, a cheap thrill?" she asked, idioms be damned.

He shook his head, his face registering his obvious confusion over her reaction. "I don't understand what you just said, but I'm sure the answer is no. And I don't want a cheap thrill affair either."

The man was a quick study and he obviously wasn't about to let her use any difficulties he had with the English language to baffle him.

"Then what was this..."

"Myrina, I want you."

Stunned, her fingers curled against the smooth surface of the door seeking a firmer grip. She found none and turned away, unwilling to leave herself so exposed to the man despite their recent intimacies.

"It's late," she said, absently smoothing the edges of her skirt. "I'd better go to my apartment. We leave early in the morning."

"Myrina."

She hesitated. She did not want him to explain or coax or persuade or to even talk to her right now. "Yes?"

"Wait for me. I'll change and walk you home." He turned and strode purposefully toward the bedroom.

As soon as he was out of sight, she walked the few short steps to the little table and checked her appearance in the oval mirror that hung above it. Just as she feared, her face was drained of color, her eyes definitely betrayed signs of fragility and her hair was spiked every which way. In other words she was a mess outside and in.

*I want you.*

Three little words she'd spent her entire life waiting to hear. She closed her eyes against the pain and the impossibility, only to open them again because she never hid from herself.

Dropping her gaze she spotted the glass of water on the table. However, when she reached out for it, her hand trembled so badly she snatched it back into the familiar, comforting folds of her skirt. Her fist crushed the plush velvet while she steadied her nerves and blinked back the salty tears that threatened to spill from the corners of her eyes.

She'd cried only once since she was five years old. Back then one of the older girls at the orphanage had expropriated her single toy, a doll much older than herself that no one else had wanted because of its faded eyes and the three bald patches on its head. The second time, she'd been mourning a deep loss. This time she didn't have an excuse. She would not cry.

She smoothed her skirt and went through the motions of straightening the rest of her outfit. All the while she watched the glass of water. It wasn't going anywhere. And neither was she until she'd taken a drink.

Resolutely she reached out and picked it up, two-handed but without the shakes, lifted it to her lips and took a sip. She glanced into the mirror when she felt a prickle along the back of her neck. Sure enough, Judan Ringa, dressed in his black boots and a loose, black tunic-style shirt that hung over a new pair of leggings, stood a few paces behind her. Watching. Studying.

She turned and held out the glass. "Would you like some?"

An odd mixture of pleasure and amazement transformed the angular lines and planes of his face, making them appear far less stern. He stepped forward and encircled her hands and the glass with his before bending forward a little so she wouldn't have to reach so high. When he'd taken his fill he smiled at her, his eyes blazing with renewed desire.

But all he said was, "Thank you, Myrina," before he released her hands. "Are you ready to leave?"

She nodded. Turning to put the glass back on the table, she paused. It seemed the height of silliness to seem so unsure about such a simple action, yet she had the strong sense she'd left something unfinished.

"Are you all right?" he asked.

"Yes. I'm sorry, I'm ready." She took another quick sip of the water and set the glass down. Only then did she remember that he too had taken a sip of the water after serving her. Before she could consider the oddity of her actions mimicking his, the door slid open and she followed him out into the corridor.

He held out his hand, an invitation that surprised her. His position, hers, the crisis on Hitani and the job they had to do together—all good reasons to discount what had happened between them tonight inside the privacy of his room as an aberration of both their behaviors. Besides, her personal priorities wouldn't normally allow her to jeopardize her career by accepting such a blatant public acknowledgment of their intimacy.

*I want you.*

The memory of his words echoed in the silence around them, beckoning her with those impossible dreams. Yet there he stood ready to walk her home, his outstretched hand offering her a place at his side. She was a crazy idiot to trust this—him—any further than she already had, yet the tiniest seed of longing that had lain dormant for longer than she cared to remember stirred inside her heart.

She'd never risked working with a lover before and entangling her security with the intense bursts of carnal satisfaction she'd occasionally sought for herself. She hadn't exactly planned to gamble her future this time either. But fate in the guise of Fenton deMorriss had already cast the dice and she was heading out on a field assignment tomorrow. So right now seemed as good a time as any to take a personal risk.

She accepted his hand and together they walked down the hall to the bank of escalators that would take them to her floor. Moments later they stood outside the door to her apartment. He was still holding her hand and he seemed somehow disinclined to release it.

"Well, good night, Judan."

"Good night, Myrina." He tugged her around to face him and for a moment she thought he might kiss her again. "I'll meet you just before seven at the *Ketiga Bulan*."

A part of her brain noted that this was the first time she'd heard the name of his ship. The rest of her held back. A name made the ship more real. Which made the voyage a tangible reality too. Unable to nod, she could only hope for the best.

He turned to go, but, at the last moment, she tugged his hand, halting his progress.

"Judan."

He turned those laser eyes on her, focused, intent.

Intimate impetuosity had never been her strong suit, but she seemed to be in a risky mood this evening. Standing on tiptoe, she brushed her lips across his.

"I like your smell, too," she whispered before letting him go.

\* \* \* \* \*

Absolutely no way. She could not do it.

She'd passed through the docking checkpoint without a hitch. She'd even entered the docking bay itself. The utilitarian room was no more than five or six meters long, but she'd taken one look and come to a halt.

Illuminated by harsh lights, the Speedlite's hatchway looked like the gaping mouth of some fiendish monster ready to swallow her whole—an image that set her body shaking so hard she clutched herself for support. Her heart banged loudly against her chest, setting off reverberations in her head and, despite the cool shower she'd taken only forty minutes ago, her entire body was coated in a sheen of sweat.

If standing inside the doors of deVere's private docking bay gave her the willies, walking on board the ship was expecting the impossible.

Of course, early last evening Myrina would have claimed having a hot and heavy sexual encounter with a Dakokatan Warlord was an impossibility too, so what did she know?

She knew. The symptoms were unmistakable. And as if the other physical sensations weren't bad enough, her throat seized up threatening to choke her every time she even thought of taking another step forward. She'd always considered it some sort of diabolical joke when, years ago, her psychiatrist had identified her reactions as a "limited symptom attack". *Limited, my sweet petunia!*

Every time she so much as looked at a shuttle, let alone a ship the size of a Speedlite, nausea overcame her. Over the years she'd tried all the standard cures for her anxiety attacks and a few nonstandard ones as well. Nothing had worked, unless she wanted to try the drug route, which she most emphatically did not. She'd managed to survive a childhood that was dependent on the whims of others, she was not about to hand over her adulthood to a harsher master.

Since Fenton's pronouncement she'd cocooned herself in a state of denial. And last night she'd effectively managed to suppress her worst fears and proceed with plans for the job as if she were heading to the lab rather than out into The Field. Even this morning she'd taken her shower and convinced herself she was dressing for work, as usual. But face-to-face with the hatchway into the Speedlite she knew she hadn't really fooled herself. Her brain was way too smart to let her fool it into thinking they were merely taking another quick trip to a satellite meeting station, which was the main reason she'd never asked either Fenton or Judan just how long it took to reach Hitani.

The truth was, it would take more than guts or a keen desire to save the Outposters to get her aboard the Dakokatan Speedlite.

In self-disgust she flung her duffel bag onto the floor. It whizzed across the smooth surface like one of those shiny black pucks her friends used to chase in their hockey games at the rec centre, coming to rest with a soft thud against the hatchway. Traitor. If even her bag could head in the right direction, why couldn't she?

"Welcome to the *Ketiga Bulan*," a low, deep voice said from behind her.

She whirled around so fast she felt lightheaded and came face-to-chest with Judan Ringa. She hadn't sensed his presence at all, or maybe she had but the tingles had been hidden by all her other symptoms.

He was dressed in the same black outfit she'd first seen him in, minus the cape and wig. With his copper hair flowing sensuously around the fine cloth of his shirt—a garment she knew from personal experience hid an amazingly smooth-skinned, muscular frame—he made for an infinitely more appealing sight than the Speedlite's hatchway. Except, of course, for the fact that now he would expect her to follow him through that cavernous hole onto his ship.

"Um, hello. I, ah, arrived a few minutes ago." *Well crap.* Not only were her nerve signals confused but so, apparently, was her ability to tell the truth, because she'd gone and lied to him. She'd been standing in the docking port for a good ten minutes at least.

He frowned down at her. Given his track record so far with reading her mind, she wouldn't be at all surprised if he could tell she was fibbing.

"What are you wearing that for?"

"What?" Startled by his hyperjump in their conversation, she checked her jumpsuit. It looked okay to her. "I always wear this to the lab."

"You aren't going to the lab."

"Fine," she said, waving her hands in exasperation. She did not need to be arguing technicalities right now. "I always wear it to work."

If anything his frown deepened. Once again his response reminded her of a pissed-off green alien or at the very least an annoyed one. *What is his problem this morning, anyway?*

"I didn't like it yesterday afternoon and I like it even less this morning."

*Well tough!* She immediately bristled at the insult. This was definitely not the sort of meeting she'd imagined having with him the morning after. Where was the tender but assertive lover? The man who only last night had asked her to trust him?

"It's comfortable," she said and instantly hated herself for defending her wardrobe choice.

He shook his head. "It's ugly. Take it off."

"I beg your pardon?" She took two steps back. He followed, looking if not exactly pissed off, then at least determined as hell.

"You heard me," he said. His voice sounded deceptively casual, with a hint of seduction. "The begging part is optional."

A rush of adrenaline zinged through her veins, sending a shot of heat straight to her pussy. No way would she ever actually beg the man for anything, but the suggestion alone was enough to turn her on. Big time.

"Yeah, I did hear you," she said, overcome by a wild desire to push back. Test his limits. Maybe even tease him a little. She straightened to her full height. He still towered over her by a good eight inches, but she wasn't about to let that stop her. "And what if I don't? Are you going to make me?"

He didn't bother to disguise the answering flare of lust in his eyes at her challenge. In less than a heartbeat his hands curled around her lapels. An instant later he ripped open the snaps of her jumpsuit clear down to her crotch.

"Now just a damn minute," she screeched, abruptly aware they were still standing in the middle of the docking bay. She tried to back up, only he wasn't letting go.

"And that's another thing." With no effort at all he hauled her to within inches of his face. Immediately the faint smell of sandalwood tantalized her senses. "While you're on my ship you'll watch your language."

"Watch my language?" she sputtered. "Are you nuts?"

More to the point, was she nuts? Except for her panties she wasn't wearing anything underneath the suit. The cool air instantly caused her nipples to tighten to hard points that jutted towards him as though in offering. Which meant she was bared to his view and anyone else's who happened to pass by. *Well isn't this just dandy. I'm turned on by the idea of being a freaking exhibitionist!*

"By the Third Moon you are beautiful." His voice cracked on the word "Third" and his eyes glazed over as he gazed down at her nearly naked body.

All the indignation drained out of her as she sensed the transformation within him. The visible signs of his anger dissolved so quickly she could hardly believe they'd been real. In their place, though, was something much more dangerous.

*I want you*, he'd told her last night. And suddenly he looked hungry enough to back her up against another wall and help himself. She shuddered under his fierce stare, which was akin to the bolt of lightning that had struck her the first time they'd met.

Totally mesmerized, she saw the harsh lights, even the docking bay itself, fade, replaced by the proximity of hot breath and hotter bodies. She reached up to steady herself against him, only somehow her hands tangled in the silken copper strands of his hair. They seemed to be alive, twisting around her fingers and she reveled in the almost ticklish sensation across her palms.

"That's right, Myrina," he said, his voice rough and scratchy. "You cannot hide this from me."

*I'm not trying to hide*, she wanted to tell him but couldn't because maybe it wasn't true. Maybe she'd spent the last eight years hiding behind her jumpsuit. In her lab. Tucked away from the world. Then again maybe she was just full of psychobabble bullshit.

"Already I can smell the moisture gathering, waiting for me."

She whimpered because this time what he said was true. Whatever arguments she might have with herself, she couldn't deny the lust that lit up inside her, like a shooting star zooming through the sky, every time she was in close proximity to the Dakokatan.

He bent his head closer. "What would happen if I touched your pretty nipples, Myrina?"

She sucked in a breath. His hands were only a millimeter or so away from her bare skin. *Please touch me.*

Yet he didn't, though his hands shook, forcing him to tighten his grip on the cloth of her suit. Taking advantage of the tenuous leash he seemed to have on himself, she brushed her lips against the edge of his blunt chin. He shook his head as if denying the force of her touch, then stopped and nodded, more to himself than her.

"Just one taste," he murmured.

Judan gently rained tiny kisses from one corner of her mouth to the other. Each one promised more, teased her with the expectation that eventually he'd claim her. Yet he worked so slowly, savored each kiss and murmured his pleasure again and again against her mouth. She waited, honestly she did, but she just couldn't hold back and finally darted her tongue out for a taste of her own. He nipped her lower lip in response. She grinned and nipped back. He growled and counterattacked.

She'd never dared to be so playful before, so spontaneous. Life had always been too serious to stop just for the fun of it. But this she enjoyed immensely. Especially the unexpected discovery of her feminine powers. She alone had stoked the hunger that consumed him. Barely leashed, the tension that ran like a taut cord through his body was as tangible as the tongue he slid inside her mouth. And each time she responded he couldn't seem to stop himself from taking more.

The kiss ended so abruptly, she was sure she would have collapsed to the floor if he hadn't been holding her up. Then, as suddenly as he'd grabbed her, he released his hold on the jumpsuit. She staggered back two paces, stunned.

With a calculated grin he eyed her. By now she should have been used to his near constant scrutiny. She wasn't, even though her body was now partially hidden by the flaps of her suit. She doubted she'd ever feel comfortable being the object of so much attention.

"Definitely ugly," he said to no one in particular. "I'll find you a new outfit."

Before she could process his comment, he strolled past her to the hatchway and picked up her duffel bag. Hastily snapping the front of her suit together, she hurried after him. The two tasks weren't so easily accomplished in tandem though and she left more skin bared than covered.

"Hey," she cried indignantly when he opened the bag and pulled out a shirt.

He ignored her protest and tossed the garment onto the floor. Abandoning her snaps, she dove for the shirt. It was olive green, which definitely clashed with his skin tone. Okay, bad choice for this trip, but it was still one of her favorites.

"Where's the little shirt you were wearing last night? And the skirt? I liked them," he asserted, shaking out another neatly folded garment for inspection. This too was tossed unceremoniously at his feet. A third item of clothing quickly appeared in his hand.

"None of your business," she muttered, grabbing her spare jumpsuit in midair. "Now give me my bag."

"Not until I find that shirt," he said, backing away from her groping hands.

"Judan!"

This was a damned outrage! And if she let him get away with it, he'd unpack her entire gear because that T-shirt he liked so much was at the bottom of the bag, along with the velvet skirt. They just damn well better not meet any of his crew until she'd cornered him and given him what for. Especially since behind the steadily growing pile of clothes in her arms she was still half exposed. Yet, try as she might, he always managed to stay one step ahead of her. Usually because she was forced to abandon pursuit every few meters or so to retrieve a discarded item. When he rounded his fourth or fifth corner, she sagged against the wall, clutching the bundle of clothes.

*What the effing hell does he think he's doing?* And if he didn't quit soon, she'd be mad enough to tell him that to his face, edicts about language usage be damned.

"Myrina?" He sounded as though he were standing right around the corner.

"Yeah?" She stayed right where she was. No way was she falling for that old trick. Once she looked around that corner he'd be gone again.

"Come here."

"Why? You'd just toss my unmentionables onto the floor and potentially embarrass me in front of your crew."

Silence. So much silence, in fact, she got nervous.

"Judan?"

"I'm looking."

"For what?"

"One of those 'unmentionables'."

*Argh.* She shuffled forward and peered around the corner. "Don't play innocent with me, Judan Ringa."

He stood in front of a doorway looking totally unruffled. She wished she could say the same about her current condition.

"My English is good, Myrina, but you know I sometimes have trouble understanding you. I have never heard of 'unmentionables' before," he said, still peering into her bag. "Do you mean this black lace you forgot to put on this morning?"

*That did it.* At the sight of her bra dangling from one of his large hands, she stormed round the corner and followed him straight into a modestly sized bedroom.

"Oh."

The exquisite brushed metal and wood decor brought her up short. A gorgeous, russet-colored bedspread dominated the color scheme of the room offset by a beautifully carved headboard and a pair of matching side tables. Against one wall she spotted an ornate cabinet, to her left a cozy chair next to a floor lamp and to her right a workstation. A shelving unit of sorts stood beside the workstation. Constructed of five slim, floor-to-ceiling metal poles, none of the shelves or cupboards fitted between each pole were lower than waist height—Dakokatan waist height.

"Welcome to your quarters, Myrina."

"My…what?" she stuttered, trying to wrap her mind around what he was saying.

Fenton had warned her that the Dakokatan had the authority to do what he wanted. Get whom he wanted for a job. Judan also obviously hadn't had any qualms about doing whatever he had to to get her aboard his ship. No wonder she'd been surprised by how quickly he'd shut off his anger. He hadn't been angry at her at all. From start to finish the entire episode in the docking bay had been staged.

"I hope you'll be comfortable here," he said.

"Yeah." She tried to sound upbeat and failed miserably. "This is…" She hesitated. After last night she hadn't expected subterfuge or… The man obviously came from a well-connected family and, given the furnishings in this room, not to mention the size of the ship they were on, was filthy, stinking rich to boot. "It's really elegant."

*Well crap, why not just spill your guts and tell him the truth.* She didn't do elegant. Or, more correctly, she'd never done elegant.

She'd only just stepped aboard his ship and already she was out of her depth. She walked over to the bed and dumped her armload of clothes on it before hastily snapping her jumpsuit closed. Then she picked up a pair of her pants, methodically shook them free of wrinkles and refolded them. As usual, Judan watched her intently.

"Elegant is not to your taste?" he finally asked. He spoke slowly, suggesting he'd searched for the correct words.

She blew out a little breath, shrugged then continued folding her clothes.

"The ploy to get me aboard your ship worked. You didn't need to bribe me with this," she said, waving her hand around to indicate the room. She knew her remark was probably unfair, but she didn't care. The guest room did seem awfully lavish for a TLC scientist on assignment. Besides, she hated the ease with which he'd been able to use her body against her.

Last night when she'd surrendered to the zings and pings zipping through her system, she'd thought he was along for the ride. This morning she'd learned the truth. He might have reacted to her, but he now seemed perfectly fine, yet his presence had set off one hell of a shit-disturbance in her body.

To avoid any further discussion she picked up the pile of clothes she'd folded, turned away and walked over to the cabinet. Judan immediately appeared beside her and, without a word, slid open a drawer for her. Her senses were immediately assailed by a faint odor akin to sandalwood. One she recognized. Inside the drawer, the smooth, light colored wood lining was studded with dark, tiny twiglike shapes.

"The dark inlay comes from the bark of the alam tree," he told her. "It's very common on Dakokata and nearly everyone uses it to scent their clothes."

*Including you.* She nodded and set her pile on one side of the drawer. Uncertain if she was about to make a fool of herself or not, she cleared her throat.

"So, this." Again she gestured to indicate the entire room. "These furnishings, they're standard on Dakokata?"

Those vivid eyes of his didn't so much as blink. "Probably above average," he answered. "But yes, many people have this kind of furniture. It is, how do you say, a point of honor to welcome one's guests with the best one can afford."

*Okay, so he answered honestly.* But that didn't excuse his earlier behavior. Or hers, falling for his ploy so easily. They stood in awkward silence—at least it was for her. Her dread of moments like these was one of the many reasons she'd always kept her personal life totally separate from her professional one.

"Myrina?"

"Yes." *Now what?* Somewhat startled by her thoughts, she realized she was curious rather than annoyed by the fact that she didn't know what he'd say or ask her next. Suppressing a wry smile, she acknowledged she was becoming accustomed to Dakokatan ways, or at least this Dakokatan's way.

"Why do you call your underclothes unmentionables?" he asked.

*Well crap.* Half embarrassed, half ashamed, for the second time in as many days she felt a warm glow of a blush creep up her neck.

Might as well tell him the truth. It wasn't as if she could keep her past hidden much longer anyway. Heck, if he'd done any kind of background check on her—and why wouldn't he if he expected her to save all those people—he'd know most of it already.

With a casual shrug she said, "One of the matrons in the orphanage was very straitlaced. She used all sorts of euphemisms to avoid certain subjects and words."

And right now she couldn't think of a single one to describe what Judan had done to get her onto his ship.

"Don't overanalyze what happened, Myrina."

Annoyed, she glared at him. "What are you now, a mind reader? How do you know what I'm feeling? What I'm thinking? That I even care about what you did?"

Abruptly she swung away from him, cutting off her words before she said too much. Revealed too much.

"No, I can't read your mind, only your face. It is very expressive, Myrina, and shows me what is going on inside that head of yours. Right now it assures me there's been a misunderstanding."

Refusing to look at him, she shook her head. "I don't think so. You needed me on your ship and you found a way to get me here. Good for you."

"I used the clothes to distract you."

"Like I said, it worked." She took one step forward only to feel his hand on her arm holding her back.

"Myrina, you were never in any danger of meeting the crew and being embarrassed."

"That's good to know." A sharp, matter-of-fact statement. It didn't ease the stiffness in her spine to know that he really had planned the whole charade, right down to commanding his crew to stay out of the way.

"Is it? You don't sound too happy."

"I'm on a ship about to head out into deep space to visit a hostile planet, what do you think?" Sarcasm, as her friend Sonora Austen loved to point out, was her usual last stand of defense against anyone who tried to push her too far too fast. Even the Dakokatan couldn't miss her acerbic tone and fail to understand.

"I think it would be nice," he said gently, his thumb caressing her arm through the sturdy fabric of the jumpsuit, "if you didn't…slam the door in my face every time I take one step forward with you. Yes, I distracted you. But everything else between us was quite real."

Disconcerted by his continued insights, she instinctively wanted to pull away. To protect herself. Yet his words reminded her too sharply of her psychiatrist.

By mutual choice she hadn't seen Dr. Smith in four years. Despite the anxiety attacks and the nightmares that still haunted the fringes of her dreams, she'd needed to move on, to be on her own and Dr. Smith had concurred, with one piece of advice—*Myrina, make sure you have a door somewhere along those walls you've built to protect yourself. You need the walls now to keep you safe but one day you might want a way out.*

At the time she'd heard the words, but the message hadn't meant anything to her beyond the usual cryptic statements Dr. Smith uttered at the end of a session. Yet Judan had just said she'd slammed a door in his face, so maybe she had listened after all. A door meant she could open it and at least invite him in, even if she herself wasn't ready to leave the safety of her walls just yet.

"So," she said, facing him at last with a lighter heart and a teasing grin playing at the corners of her mouth. "Do you usually go to this much trouble to get your lovers aboard your ship?"

"Never," he said, catching her in a fierce embrace.

With a yelp, she wrapped her arms around his neck to steady herself. When she tilted her head to look at him, his brilliant eyes shimmered with pleasure and the unmistakable glint of desire. A fact confirmed by the bulge pressing against her abdomen.

"I have never brought a lover aboard my ship. You are the first."

Heady words that made her want to ask if she'd be the last.

*Slow down. Take your time. Enjoy him.*

Sensible advice for a woman who didn't believe in moving too fast.

"I want you, Myrina."

The silky smooth texture of his copper hair beckoned to her. She adjusted her hold on him, entwining her fingers around one of the braids to play with the beads that held it fast. His long hair softened the harsh planes of his face, but this up close and personal she could study his features to her heart's content. His face was more square than oval, his cheekbones high enough to cast shadows in a certain light, making him look more severe than he was. He had a proud, intelligent face and his eyes didn't miss much. Nor did they seem capable of lying.

"Okay," she said. "I'll trust you a little."

Big words and a bigger risk.

His eyes flared with pure masculine triumph. Last night he'd asked for her trust. And while she'd surrendered to his touch and then taken his hand when he'd walked her home, she'd never made any promises. Until right now.

She didn't do nebulous time frames or relationships, yet she'd just committed herself to a non-affair affair with this man. It didn't make any sense. She didn't make any sense. And frankly she didn't care.

Before she could pull him down for a kiss, his hand slid up her back to cradle her head, holding it steady for his mouth. That subtle smell of alam bark, mixed with the masculine scent that was Judan's alone, was as powerful as any tekurilite candle. And his kiss… It was neither teasing nor tempting nor slow seduction. His tongue plunged deep inside her mouth until their breaths mingled and fused, sustaining them both during his bold invasion.

Only she had no intention of being swept away on the tide of his passion. He might have accepted her invitation, but she was the one who had opened the door.

Obviously, Judan Ringa was a powerful man, one used to storming in and taking what he wanted. And while his dominance attracted her, she knew enough about herself to recognize that if he didn't surrender at least part of himself when they met like this, then she could never respect him. And never totally surrender to his control.

By now his other hand was firmly holding her ass, pressing her body along the rigid length of his erection. Their tongues tangled, then hers brushed the edge of his teeth before it stole deeper inside his mouth. His low groan convinced her that this counterattack had evened the playing field.

Yet while their tongues dueled with each other, eventually blocking out rational thought and consuming her senses, their bodies remained locked in stasis. As if they were both afraid that this time, if they took it too far, they wouldn't be able to stop.

Abruptly, as though by mutual consent, the kiss ended and they pulled away from each other, panting. His eyes had turned predatory and his hair swirled and snapped aggressively. That now familiar tingle she'd felt when they'd first met was back, sending a wave of goose bumps across her skin. Exhilarated, her entire body felt alive.

"This is dangerous," he said.

"Yes," she replied.

"I should get to the bridge."

"Yes."

This pretense at a normal conversation was idiotic, yet it was the safest thing she could think of doing. "Where's my equipment?"

"In the lab. I'll take you there now if you like."

At the mention of the Speedlite's lab, the tension inside her broke and she laughed.

"You cheater," she cried. "You told me I shouldn't be wearing my jumpsuit because I wasn't going the lab. But I am."

Judan shrugged. "That outfit of yours is still ugly."

"Then maybe I should change into something more comfortable," she offered, her hands reaching up to open the snaps on the suit.

His fingers moved restlessly against his sides until he forcibly halted their movement by clenching his fists so tight his knuckles turned white. Yet his eyes continued to track her every move as first one, then two, then three snaps came free. With a gruff sound he swung away from her.

"I'll wait for you outside."

# Chapter Four

ဢ

Judan didn't activate the comlink until he reached the end of the corridor. There was one three paces outside the guest suite, but he'd forced himself to put some necessary distance between himself and the pale-faced temptation he'd left inside.

"How long until our first jump?" he asked without preamble.

While he'd been coaxing Myrina deeper inside the ship, his small crew had, at a prearranged signal, started the launch sequence. By now they should have decoupled from the TLC docking port and left the planet's gravity to await permission to leave the Confederacy's restricted airspace.

"We've received permission to power the propulsion system to FTL2 for the first jump, Captain." The voice of his navigator, Hylla, reverberated along the walls of the corridor.

"Fine," he said with a sense of relief.

Usually, ships weren't allowed to leave Confederacy space above a faster-than-light configuration of one, which was barely enough power to wrap space-time beyond a ten planet solar system. His ship, a sleek, tubular craft, was the most sophisticated FTL Speedlite model available. When the *Ketiga Bulan* powered up to full FTL capacity, panels unfurled along the slimmer outer edge and shutters slid over the bulge in the center of the hull, encasing the ship in a protective metallic shield. Right now, with clearance for an FTL2 jump, they'd move directly into free-space. This would enable them to power up to full FTL4 capacity in less time for their next series of space-time jumps.

"I'm awaiting priority status clearance," Hylla confirmed.

"Excellent," he said. Despite the fact the ink wasn't yet dry on the treaty between Dakokata and the Confederacy, the Council hadn't hesitated in expediting the *Ketiga Bulan's* departure.

"What's the latest from Hitani?" he then asked, knowing his Second-in-Command, Chiara, who for this trip doubled as the communications officer, would also be on the bridge, listening.

"I received a short-power-burst communiqué from the Outposters' base just before we left the docking port, Captain," Chiara reported. As usual her voice carried little inflection, so he couldn't guess whether the content of the message was positive or negative.

A competent woman, Chiara was a stickler for protocol. She'd now served as Second-in-Command on the Speedlite for three years and Judan depended on her good sense to keep the ship running efficiently. In return, Chiara had learned to accept some of Judan's more unorthodox approaches to mission operations.

"The situation on Hitani remains unchanged. The status code remains critical," she reported.

"Thanks," Judan said. At this point, no change was better than the alternative, another dead Outposter. "I'll be up as soon as I've escorted Dr. deCarte to the lab."

Shutting off the comlink before either Chiara or Hylla could question him, he strode back down the hall. All he'd succeeded in doing was postponing the inevitable. Yet a part of him welcomed any excuse to keep Myrina to himself for just a little longer, even if a door—and what little common sense he still possessed—stood between them.

Back in front of the guest suite he rested a hand on the door. He wanted nothing more than to go in and...what? A sense of elation rippled through him at the thought of seeing her. Stepping away from the door, he leaned against the wall and closed his eyes.

His mission was a desperate one. Already one man was dead and the lives of the other seventy-seven Outposters now depended on the success of his plan. He'd been coping with a potent mixture of grief and tension in which this sense of excitement by rights had no part. And yet, when he faced the truth of his feelings, a definite state of euphoria beat a rhythm in tune with his heart.

At the age of thirty-three, Judan Ringa was experiencing *Rakanasmara*. And, he was certain, *Rakanasmara* had come to Myrina deCarte as well. A human female who should have been biologically incompatible as a mate.

And yet the signs were unmistakable, despite the lack of a reasoned explanation. When he'd returned to his ship yesterday, he'd accessed the archives, searching the ancestral data for some bit of history that would confirm the impossible. He'd found nothing, but Chiara had guessed the truth and the news had spread through the crew like white summer smoke. He'd have to wait until he returned to the capital to visit a more extensive archival collection. Nevertheless, he knew, Dr. Myrina deCarte was his.

Opening his eyes, he pulled aside the fabric of his shirt and dipped his hand beneath the folds, where his fingers grazed the scars that marred his left pectoral. It wasn't the puckered lines he cared about, but the faint traces of her imprint on his skin. Her touch yesterday had threatened his sense of control.

*Liar. You've never had any control as far as she's concerned.*

It was true. Last night he'd been overwhelmed by Myrina's scent. Despite pinning her hands so she couldn't touch him again, despite his own focus on her pleasure, he'd fought every moment he'd been with her for control over himself.

Humans, he'd once read somewhere, described themselves as hairless. An erroneous myth he'd happily disproved the previous evening. The sensitive pads of his fingers and his ultra-responsive palms had delighted in the fact that every millimeter of Myrina's skin was covered with superfine hairs. A shudder of desire racked his body at the memory and he adjusted his position against the wall. Even now his fingers itched to weave themselves into the short strands of her brown hair, as soft as any Tigalian silk. But the immense pleasure he'd derived from touching her was only half the potent mix that stirred his blood and kept his cock harder than the trunk of the alam tree.

What he hadn't anticipated was that he'd also have to subdue her. Or that doing so would only inflame him further, bringing him greater pleasure. Her fierce warrior nature intrigued him. Made him want both to fight her and tame her at the same time, a paradox that made no sense, yet the fantasy of doing just that ignited his desire and threatened to cloud his brain altogether.

He glanced at the door. Except it wasn't the door that obsessed him, it was the woman behind it. His sleep, at least what little he'd had early this morning, had been haunted by the sound of her voice, urgently pleading with him to free her hands. No woman had ever challenged him like that, so determined to keep her autonomy while demanding his own surrender as he pleasured her.

A thin layer of perspiration covered his already hot skin. Judan stared down at his hands. They trembled slightly, the way they had the day before, in the garden. In the confines of his leggings his cock throbbed with an intensity greater than the one he'd experienced as a young man suffering through the plague of sex dreams.

For a year he'd endured the teasing of his older brother and the embarrassment of stained sheets. Eventually he'd been driven from his bed to the privacy of the forest. But the sex dreams had been little more than the awkwardness of an undisciplined boy heading into manhood. For the next fifteen years he'd kept a tight rein on his physical needs, taking what he needed but never again letting his cock have control. Until yesterday afternoon in Fenton deMorriss' office when he'd met Myrina.

Later that night, his own defenses had been powerless against her. Her scent, the taste of her and texture of her skin had overwhelmed him. In truth, he hadn't much wanted to resist her. The need for his own release had consumed him as much as his desire to satisfy her.

*Will it be this uncontrollable – this all-consuming – every time we come together?*

He closed his eyes and breathed deeply, seeking and then sensing the kernel of sexual energy that sat at the base of his genitals. A white-hot flame licked its way up inside his body. Now that he'd found his life partner, the only way he could harness his growing desire was through the mating. He would have to be very careful the next time he touched her or he would have her backed against another wall, the *Rakanasmara* initiation ceremonies completed before the day was done.

Despite the fact that he'd always known what would happen, at least in theory, he hadn't expected *Rakanasmara* to be this intense. Nor had he expected to want a woman the way he wanted Myrina.

He settled down on his haunches, his back still against the wall. Since the age of three or four, he'd accompanied his father most evenings up a hill behind their house and they'd sat, hunched like this, discussing life. Even after he'd grown older and left home, he'd still made the time, whenever he could, to visit his father and talk on their hill. Now that his father was gone, only the hill and his memories remained.

"Do you see, Judan, how the Hunter's patience has been rewarded?" his father had asked, gazing at a quartet of bright stars in the sky. "For five months the Hunter has chased his quarry across the sky and now he is ready to make his capture."

Judan, twelve at the time, wasn't impressed. He didn't really see a Hunter or his prey in the sky, just a bunch of stars. But, for his father's sake, he'd pretended an interest in seeing for the first time in his life, the Year of the Hunter. Every evening for the last five months he'd trudged up the hillside with his father to watch the progress of the celestial phenomenon that occurred every twelve years. While they watched, his father had told him stories of the mythical sky hunter.

"And so," his father had continued, ignoring Judan's silence. "Tonight concludes the Legend of the Hunter. What do you see in the stars?"

Startled, Judan looked first at his father and then at the sky. He knew better than to mumble just any answer. Either a man had something to say, or he kept silent.

"It is up to you to decipher the true meaning for yourself, Judan," his father had said when the silence between them stretched as far as the night sky. "I have found the answers that satisfy me. Whatever you decide, your actions from this day forth will influence your life."

Judan blinked at the blank, tan-colored wall in front of him and shrugged the memory away. But his father's question still lingered between them. He hadn't been able to answer it all those years ago. He glanced at the door and wondered how far his actions in the Grove of the Three Sisters really had determined events.

*I have my answer,* Bapa. *I am the one who's been searching like the Sky Hunter all these years. I am the Hunter and I want her,* Bapa.

The irony was, wanting Myrina wasn't enough. His genetic bond was with a human woman who didn't know the first thing about *Rakanasmara* or Dakokatan traditions. And, after their awkward discussion last evening over the word "affair", he was convinced any explanation about the initiation ceremonies, which would make Myrina his life partner, would be met with skepticism. His gut knotted at the thought that she might consider *Rakanasmara* a "cheap thrill affair" despite his declaration that he wanted her.

Whenever he'd thought about *Rakanasmara*, he'd thought first of Zane's needs and his desire to be the boy's father. He wanted the right to nurture Zane's young mind and teach him how to be a man. Not once had he given any consideration to the woman who would be his life partner. Indeed if he'd given any thought to his mate at all, he'd assumed she would know her duty. And, once he'd introduced Zane to her, she would want the boy as much as he did. But would Myrina?

What he needed was a plan, like the one he'd used to negotiate the alliance with the Confederacy. Then he'd used every resource at his disposal, every iota of strategy he'd learned from his father, to fulfill the new destiny that he, and others like him, had envisioned for Dakokata. Unfortunately, with Myrina, he was hampered by his lack of knowledge of human mating customs.

After delivering Myrina safely to her apartment last night, he'd visited the TLC archives. All his research had yielded was an ancient human ritual called "wooing". Apparently it involved the bestowing of flowers and chocolate, along with something called a "dinner date" as tokens of "love", another equally unintelligible human concept. If you'd found the right woman to be your life partner why did you need to "woo" her to "win" her love? It made no sense. Besides, from what he'd learned about Myrina, he doubted any of those gifts would impress her.

Dr. deCarte was an unpredictable force who'd stormed into his life, knocking him upside down and sideways. In the process he'd developed an insatiable hunger for her. He rather liked that peculiar English phrase, "knocked upside down and sideways". It accurately described the powerful effect *Rakanasmara* and Myrina had on him.

"You can wipe that grin off your face, I'm not wearing a skirt to the lab."

Startled out of his thoughts, Judan looked up into a pair of eyes the color of high meadow grass after the first thin sheet of ice had crystallized it. A potent reminder that, while the

*Rakanasmara* was far stronger than he'd ever imagined, he was faced with an even more compelling challenge. Yesterday morning he would never have considered taking such an unimaginable gamble with his and Zane's future. But now, their future was inexorably Myrina's future, too.

He would "win" Myrina deCarte by wooing her. Only forget the chocolate, the taste of which he didn't much care for anyway. The initiation had already begun. And Myrina had responded. Henceforth, like the Sky Hunter, he would pursue her and woo her, Dakokatan style.

The decision made, Judan allowed his lazy grin to turn feral as he examined her outfit.

Skirt or no skirt, Dr. Myrina deCarte was worth the wait. She wore beige pants made from a loose fabric that caressed her legs with each tiny movement and emphasized the gentle curve of her hips. Above the waistband he caught a generous glimpse of skin where she'd left three buttons undone on the short-sleeved brown shirt that otherwise hugged her slim frame.

Her expressive face, surrounded by golden brown spiky hair, was reminiscent of a drawing he'd once seen. The picture claimed to be an accurate depiction of the indigenous hill dwellers of Dakokata, said to live in the Gunun Mountains. But despite the numerous reports, to his knowledge, no one had actually seen a hill dweller for seven cycles of the calendar, a period of over eighty years.

He stood, keeping the wall at his back. Then he reached out and pulled her a little closer so he could trace the edge of her shirt with his free hand where it gaped open. Deliberately he brushed his knuckles across her exposed skin. A tiny flare darkened the pale green of her eyes, sending a signal straight to his cock. As if she suspected the effect her appearance had on him, her eyes roamed down the front of his shirt straight to the bulge in his leggings. Her tongue darted out to moisten her lips.

"Glad you approve," she said, with a wink. Her tone dropped into the sultry range that pulled him dangerously close to sweet temptation.

*Soon, but not yet.*

Beneath his feet, he sensed a very faint rumble signaling the final shift in the propulsion system's calibration. The ship was preparing to jump. Instantly Myrina tensed and her hand gripped his like a prickle-thorn sticking to clothes. Her awareness surprised him. Not many people were that attuned to the subtle displacement of a spacecraft this size, especially as no two ships reacted in exactly the same way before a jump. For a woman who hadn't done much flying, it should have been impossible.

He studied her to make sure she was all right. Under the bright corridor lights, her already pale skin appeared nearly translucent, emphasizing the tight, tiny lines around her eyes. And the pulse at her wrist raced beneath his thumb.

He didn't comment on her anxiety, simply eased his big body away from the wall. Intentionally he moved close enough to brush his erection against her hipbone. "Thanks for changing," he said. "This outfit looks much better. Matches the walls, too."

She tipped her head back and huffed. "After a few days, Captain, you'll be just as bored with my civilian attire, which is almost as limited as your basic black."

He laughed, pleased rather than annoyed that she'd held her own against him. It made the prospect of "wooing" her an exciting challenge. One he greatly anticipated. But, more importantly, while he'd distracted her, the *Ketiga Bulan* had made its jump.

Gently tugging her hand, he set off down the corridor toward the modest onboard lab. He matched his pace to hers. However, she pulled him up short once they'd turned the corner past the comlink he'd used earlier. He turned toward her.

"I can look after myself, Judan."

"I know."

Instead of accepting his statement, she shook her head.

"I don't expect or want special treatment and I don't want you trying to rescue me every time I…"

"Have a panic attack?" he said when she hesitated.

She immediately pulled her hand out of his. "All right, how do you know that?

"Your service record is listed in the data-chip we received outlining your credentials. You haven't gone on a field assignment in eight years, Dr. deCarte."

He'd noticed the oddity in her work record when he'd investigated her personal history for a clue explaining *Rakanasmara*. The incident that had caused the attacks had obviously occurred eight years ago and explained how a TLC scientist with Myrina's specialization in colonization dissonance had avoided field work for so long.

"How did that tell you anything?" she demanded. "I know damn—darn—well my service record doesn't mention my panic attacks."

He suppressed a grin and decided it best not to mention right now that his edict against her expressive use of language had also been part of his plan to distract her.

"I, ah, 'put two and two together'. I didn't *know* anything until I met you in the docking bay this morning. I recognized the symptoms, you were wearing that ugly jumpsuit and I wanted to kiss you, so I improvised." And took advantage of the fact that he'd already arranged for his crew to be busy elsewhere so he could welcome her himself.

"Right. You just happened to recognize the symptoms." She guffawed and waived her hand dismissively. "Somehow I can't see you suffering from anxiety attacks."

"I don't, but my oldest brother does. Many years ago he was trapped inside a chamber of a cave for nearly a week.

Over the years I've learned how to distract him when the memories become too strong. To this day he avoids dark, enclosed spaces, always goes to bed in the largest room in the house and sleeps with a light on."

"Lucky him, he can sleep," she muttered.

With a gesture in the direction of the lab, he indicated they should keep walking.

She followed him, but kept arguing her case. "I mean it, Judan. I'm sorry you know about the panic attacks, but that doesn't change the fact that I can do my job and I don't need you holding my hand every time I get nervous."

Evidently the trust she'd given him a short while before didn't extend past the bedroom. Fortunately, he was a patient man. He could wait.

In a way he understood exactly what she was up against. Deep down she had trouble trusting the unexpected, yet undeniable, attraction between them. He would probably feel the same way if he hadn't had centuries of Dakokatan tradition and experience behind him. As it was, he still planned to look for an explanation for the *Rakanasmara* between them. In the meantime he would keep Myrina safe—even from her own nightmares if necessary.

The back of her hand brushed against his. The fine hairs tickled his skin, sending a vibrant strand of energy arcing between them. He caught hold, lacing their fingers together. She glanced up at him and arched an eyebrow. He shrugged. He wasn't about to apologize. It felt too good.

Besides, he needed this woman. Not just as a life partner, but for her skills as a scientist. And while her anxiety attacks had obviously restricted her field work, her work record itself indicated a remarkable dedication to her job. It was one he shared.

"The Dakokatans are a race of explorers. That is how we came to live on our current homeworld," he said. "So despite your assumptions yesterday, we weren't playing with

81

environments when we chose Hitani for further exploration. But there's no explanation for what's happening down on the planet. There's no explanation for why the Outposters are sick in the first place."

He stopped, unable to articulate fully the sense of accountability he felt towards the Outposters. He'd already lost one of them. He, she—*they* had to save the rest. Failure was not an option.

Her nod was brief, her smile even briefer, then her thumb brushed along the back of his hand.

"I'll save those people, Judan," she said, her voice quiet but confident. "You have my word."

* * * * *

Growing up in an orphanage, Myrina had learned to guard her food and her few pieces of clothing, because neither were replaced if she lost them. She'd learned how to act tough and, eventually, become tough. And she'd learned that the only thing of value she could call her own was her word.

So, until about two minutes ago, she'd never made a promise she didn't know with one hundred percent certainty she could keep. Why, then, had she uttered such a rash statement? It wasn't as if she'd been trying to impress the green guy. His impromptu stunt to get her aboard the ship all but told her he was a man impressed by actions—even crazy, spur-of-the-moment ones—not words. A credo she herself believed in.

When it came to saving environments and people, mostly from each other, her colleagues at TLC would be the first to attest that her methods were often audacious. Once she had her proof she never hesitated in voicing her opinion and she was always brutally forthright about her findings.

And therein now lay her problem. She'd skipped a couple of steps, bypassing the proof altogether and rushing straight past ruthless honesty to paint a rash fairy-tale ending for the

Outposters. What was more, Judan had accepted her word without question.

Myrina had never had that kind of naive faith in another human being. It was a little awe-inspiring to realize the Dakokatan apparently had. In her.

She glanced at the man standing beside her in the elevator tube. Despite having witnessed her panic attacks, he still wanted her for the job. He hadn't judged her and found her wanting. She was far less generous with herself.

Not that she doubted her own abilities. She did not need a lab report to know the ecosystem on Hitani was seriously pissed at the Dakokatan "invasion". Like any sentient being, however primitive, threatened planets and moons could become highly protective of the indigenous life forms they sustained. A hypothesis she'd proved time and again.

No, the trick was in locating the one small factor that turned the seemingly benign planet hostile. Even there, she was sure of herself. Within the micro-world of her lab she maintained absolute command. Whatever was making the Outposters sick and keeping them stranded on Hitani, she'd find the answer. What she couldn't guarantee was that she could rescue them, because sometimes all the dedication in the world just wasn't enough. A lesson she'd learned the hard way.

Judan's large green hand enclosed hers in a steady warmth that sent tiny, pleasant ripples up her arm. And, once again, his hair seemed to have a peculiar affinity for her. Several copper locks had wrapped themselves around her upper arm, binding her close to his side. What was even more amazing was that she calmly tolerated all this touchy-feely stuff between them. After less than a day, her personal boundaries seemed shot to hell—make that heck—around this man. Geesh, she was even trying to adhere to his damn—darn—edict about language usage.

But she had to do better than that. Fenton hadn't been far wrong when he'd said her job was on the line with this assignment. Sure he'd intended to scare the crap out of her, even if he hadn't meant the threat literally. She hoped. In spite of their deal, she'd known that eventually she'd have to accept an off-world mission. Her job demanded it, whether she had anxiety attacks or not.

And TLC wasn't just a job or a place where she lived. It was the only place she'd ever really called her home. But while she cared about TLC, her career wasn't what drove her.

Her job provided her with the means of preventing the unnecessary abuse of ecosystems and the ability to save people from colossal, potentially life-threatening mistakes. Judan's mission was to save the Outposters and, from what he'd just said, he *would* hold himself accountable to those seventy-seven stranded Dakokatans. She was no less committed. And now, with her promise, she'd placed herself squarely in a position of being accountable to them, too.

Not a smart move when the final outcome was so unpredictable. Because deep down she knew the truth. In accepting her promise, Judan Ringa also expected results.

*Will he still want me if I can't save those people? Will I still want him?*

Bottom line, she never wanted to be in a position to find out either answer. She could not fail. She did not want seventy-seven souls on her conscience. Two were more than enough for one lifetime.

# Chapter Five

ℰꙄ

The tantalizing smell of rich coffee assailed Myrina's senses the moment the door into the mess room opened. Good thing the science lab was located four decks below, deep within the bowels of the ship, otherwise she might have been lured out sooner.

The lab itself was about a quarter of the size of the one she had at TLC, but the equipment was state-of-the-art. And, once Judan had shown her around, she'd worked steadily all morning bringing herself up to speed. If he hadn't come along a few minutes ago and insisted she join him for a meal, she'd probably still be there reviewing data logs.

She hunched her shoulders to work out the kinks, then sniffed the air, positive she was hallucinating the suspiciously familiar aroma. "Wow, that smells good. Reminds me of home."

A place she hadn't thought of all morning. Not that she'd spent her time brooding about being aboard the Speedlite either.

A challenging mystery always absorbed her attention and in this case the Hitani crisis had done double duty holding her anxiety attacks at bay.

"I made a, how do you say, fresh pot," Judan said.

She glanced up at him when she heard the familiar catchphrase that suggested Judan was still testing out an English idiom. Coffee must be new to Dakokatans and she wondered if he'd acquired a taste for the brew during the negotiations with the Confederacy.

"Would you like a cup?" he asked, steering her into the room.

She enjoyed the feel of his hand on the small of her back, though his proprietary interest still had the ability to surprise her. Curious, since other men had certainly desired her and actively shown their interest, too. Except she'd never reciprocated with the same intense feelings towards any of them the way she did with this man. There was something about Judan that drew her attention and, quite definitely, her desire. She still wasn't certain what to make of the fact that he didn't want an affair, simply her. There was nothing simple about that. Or about what she wanted in return. Him, for a start. Already she could feel the sexual hunger stirring in her womb.

"Sure," she nodded, turning toward him. Why not? She was already living on the edge. "It smells a little strong for my taste, but I think my system could use the wake-up call."

Judan frowned. "Too strong? I followed Dr. Brown's instructions precisely."

Shoving a braided strand of copper hair off her arm, she looked up at him. So the smell wasn't a delusion wrought by an anxious mind, then, but an equally improbable reality. "You're joking, right? When did you see Parker? And how did you persuade him to part with some coffee? He guards his stash of beans like a rare metals merchant."

"I believe Dr. deCarte just called you a liar, brother."

*Brother? His brother is a member of the crew? Well crap.*

"And here I thought you were running a ghost ship," she whispered up at him.

While she'd been just as happy not to meet members of the crew in a state of semi-undress, she had begun to wonder about the total absence of a crew. A ship this size generally had between fifteen and twenty crew members. Gritting her teeth and ignoring Judan's low growl of exasperation, she twisted around to face a man and two women.

Behind her, Judan said, "I'm operating what in English you call a 'skeleton crew'. There are five aboard, six including you. Does that qualify?"

She shook her head at his lame joke, though secretly she smiled. He might not be entirely comfortable with English idioms yet he was adapting to them. To her.

"You can't keep her to yourself forever, Judan. Aren't you going to introduce the esteemed doctor?"

Myrina quirked her eyebrow. The comment was rather pointed, bordering on outright rude. The small size of the crew explained why she hadn't met any of them until now. Likewise the crisis on Hitani explained why *they* hadn't bumped into *her*. She wasn't exactly here to socialize.

The man, Judan's brother, stood near a sideboard laden with food. At least two inches taller than Judan and at least two years younger than she, his blond hair was tied back from his face. Only the blunt lines of his cheek and jawbone declared him a Ringa, along with the laser-sharp green eyes that looked her up and down with open curiosity. Then he winked at her. A challenge of sorts because he had to know Judan had seen him. And sure enough, Judan settled a large, warm hand on her shoulder in a primitive show of possession. Reflexively, he rubbed his thumb along her shoulder blade, but whether it was to soothe her or him, she didn't know.

*And here I thought the Dakokatans were a highly civilized culture.* Yet Judan had clearly staked his claim to her. Just how primitive was he planning to get?

"I think Myrina meant I received a valuable gift from Dr. Brown when I met him earlier this morning. Isn't that right?" he asked, squeezing her shoulder lightly in case she didn't get the hint.

"Right," she said to no one in particular.

She deliberately ignored the brother's wolfish grin. Something more than sibling rivalry was going on between them and she wanted no part of it. Judan's assessment, however, was fairly astute. While she wondered what kind of meeting Judan and Parker had had early this morning, Judan really must have made an impression for Parker to part with even a single coffee bean.

"My brother, Vand," Judan said by way of introduction. "He was the medical officer aboard the reconnaissance vessel sent to assist the Outposters on Hitani before he joined the *Ketiga Bulan*."

Judan's words were stark and emotionless, just as they had been the other day in Fenton's office. So Vand was the one who wrote the report on the dead Outposter. The report had been competent, if uninspiring in its conclusions. Sensitive to Judan's sudden change in mood and her new insight, she studied his brother and wondered, again, what was going on between them.

If he noticed her scrutiny, Vand chose to ignore it and Judan. Instead he quirked a smile and bowed low in her direction. "Welcome aboard, Dr. deCarte."

Out of innate politeness she sent a protracted nod toward him. At that moment several strands of copper hair cascaded across her arm. The stuff seemed to have a mind of its own and a definite affinity for her. Unconsciously she shifted when the fine hairs tickled her skin. Four pairs of emerald eyes intently watched her reaction.

*What's with these people?*

First Judan and now his crew. They acted as if they expected her to do...what? It was all a big mystery to her and one she didn't particularly like. She did not want to spend the trip as though she were under a microscope.

"This," Judan said, gesturing toward the older of the two women, "is Chiara, my Second-in-Command and the Communications Officer. Beside her is Hylla, the navigator. The systems engineer is still working."

Myrina dutifully smiled and nodded toward the two women. Both topped six feet, which made her the little white human among the tall, green Dakokatans. Used to growing up, living and working in multicultural environments, she experienced an odd sense of disorientation coupled with the inexplicable urge to back into Judan's embrace. No wonder everyone was staring at her. She truly was the alien aboard the Speedlite.

"They won't bite," Judan said, pitching his voice low so only she could hear his words. He released his grip on her shoulder. "Sit and I'll get you something to eat."

Normally, she would have protested his high-handedness or simply followed him to the sideboard. And she didn't doubt he somehow knew that, hence his diversionary tactic. *They won't bite, my – sweet petunia!* Better not to tempt fate or the all too calculated gaze of the Second. Myrina was now just as curious about the other Dakokatans as they were about her.

If there was a dress code among the crew, she couldn't spot one. Unlike the Confederacy, no one wore a rank or insignia. Like his brother, Vand wore skintight leggings and a belted tunic, only his were a warm rust color that matched his boots. The two women wore a looser pant and smart, three-quarter-sleeve jackets in shades of brown. Myrina made a mental note to ditch her skirt and stick to pants, so she wouldn't stand out any more than she already did.

Casually she glanced around. The room could easily accommodate sixty people, but the small crew had elected to sit at a table closest to the galley. The large mess room was decorated in soothing shades of red and brown. Not quite as ornate as the furnishings in her room, the sideboard, chairs and tables were, nevertheless, beautifully carved.

She sauntered over to the women's table, choosing a chair opposite them. Both women sat back down in their seats when she did. A pitcher of water sat in the middle of the table, next to a basket of cutlery. She poured herself a glass and took a sip, taking the opportunity to study the women surreptitiously.

Hylla, who looked to be about Vand's age, gazed in utter fascination at Myrina's short hair. She also seemed self-conscious of her own because she kept patting it with her hand. Myrina guessed short styles weren't common among the Dakokatan. Both Hylla and Vand had secured their hair in a long braid behind their backs. Chiara, on the other hand, wore one of those ugly, wig-like hairpieces that Judan had worn in Fenton's office. The coarse sticks of synthetic hair did nothing to enhance nor soften the no-nonsense lines on the older woman's face.

By the time Judan returned to the table with two steaming bowls of food, Vand had joined the group, three seats to her left. Close enough to appear sociable, but definitely his own man.

Following the brothers' example, she took a spoon and a fork from the basket and began to eat, using the fork to shove the food onto her spoon. Her first taste of the grain, meat and vegetable concoction burst into a riot of flavors inside her mouth. Burning heat vied with exquisite pleasure, causing her eyes to fill with tears. Her entire body was infused with a short blast of energy and her stomach gave a low rumble of approval.

She suspected she'd just been introduced to one of those high-powered protein sources used on long distance voyages. Both the natural and synthetic varieties of the food were intended to counteract the stressful effects of space travel while maintaining a healthy balance of nutrients. She'd eaten the synthetic variety years ago, but this tasted like the real thing. She took another sip of her water before cautiously filling her spoon again.

"Do you like the taste of giant sand lizard or do you find it too...spicy?" Chiara asked, hesitating slightly over the last word. Her accent was heavy but her English was good.

Myrina really wished the Second hadn't specified the exact food source, but guessed the older woman was testing her. She obviously knew nothing about life in an orphanage. Myrina had learned quickly enough to simply be grateful for any food put in front of her.

"It's delicious. Thank you," she said and took another mouthful to prove it.

The five of them ate in silence. When the meal was finished, Vand and Hylla cleared away the plates while Judan collected the pot of coffee from the sideboard. Myrina, used to chores, offered to help but was waved back into her seat. The other Dakokatans, for the moment, lost their interest in her as they watched him pour the dark liquid into ceramic mugs. Used to a wide range of reactions to Parker's personal blend, Myrina sat back, fascinated as each of the Dakokatans coped with the new experience.

Vand, determined not to be outdone by his sophisticated brother yet intent on appearing nonchalant about the whole matter, sniffed the brew before taking a hefty slug. His face lit with pleasure, evidence that he enjoyed it. Hylla clearly hated the taste, but feared offending the Captain. Myrina had no such qualms.

"You definitely followed Parker's recipe," she said. "Do you have any milk or cream to cut the taste?"

Not offended in the least, Judan smiled and looked rather pleased with himself. The damn man thought she was giving him a compliment. Across the table, Chiara sent her a stern glance, but Hylla rushed off to the galley, clearly relieved at being offered a solution to the strong flavor. Myrina suspected from the older woman's own tentative sips that the Second didn't much like the coffee either.

A few minutes later Myrina poured a healthy shot of what Hylla called *santan* into her coffee. The white, milky substance, Hylla told her, came from a Dakokatan fruit, *kelapas*. Myrina found it both diluted and slightly sweetened the strong brew. She set the jug on the table. As for the consequences facing the Outposters, she had no intention of diluting the truth or sweetening the facts. If a solution wasn't found soon, the men and women could all end up dead.

"Before he died, Lorre was a walking pharmacy," she said. She purposely used the man's name, listed in the report, to give her statement more impact.

And she sure as hell succeeded. For a second, everyone at the table froze, then Vand set down his mug with a bang. Coffee sloshed over the side, staining the table. His jaw clenched and he stuck his hand under the table, probably in an effort to control his temper. On the other side of her, Judan resumed sipping his coffee as though he were completely indifferent to her news. Still, she sensed the tension radiating from him. He'd gone into alert mode.

"That information was in my report," Vand said at last. "I recorded all the meds Lorre was taking. Nothing was hidden."

"I know," she said, gently. "I didn't say you or anyone else was hiding information, Vand. I was simply stating a fact."

"Facts," Vand spat out. "I already know the facts. Lorre is dead. You're supposed to give us the solution. A way of getting those people off that damn planet before they're all killed."

A thin line of perspiration broke out across her brow, but Myrina stared the young man down. She suspected his lack of specific conclusions in the report was a result of ignorance, so she didn't take the accusations personally. Vand had obviously been deeply affected by the Outposter's death.

"Didn't you find it odd that a man of twenty-three had so many ailments?" she asked.

Across from her Hylla gasped. "My cousin is on Hitani," she said. "He's twenty-five and..." She choked on her words and her voice trailed off. She darted a glance toward Judan who'd remained conspicuously silent.

Seconds later his hand rested on hers. A restraint of sorts which he tempered with a brief caress, so she kept silent. Across from her, Chiara shifted in her seat. Like Myrina, she obviously sensed the strain between the two men.

"Vand?" Judan said, looking straight past her to his brother.

Vand stood so abruptly his chair tipped backwards onto the floor. "Of course I thought it was abnormal!" he shouted. With some effort he reined in his emotions. "When I checked my findings with the information on the medical data-chip, it appeared the symptoms kept accelerating exponentially on an almost daily basis."

Myrina nodded. "The meds he was taking gave him a measure of relief and slowed the rate of progress down some, but not enough."

"All the Outposters are being treated for one ailment or another," Chiara said.

"Yes I know," Myrina said. "That's the problem."

"Explain." Judan's voice was pitched low so the others had to strain to hear him.

"The meds being prescribed are intended to treat real medical conditions," she said. "But the illnesses afflicting the Outposters are phantom manifestations."

"Bullshit, Doctor," Vand said. His voice had turned hard as he struggled to suppress all emotion. "Lorre's arthritis was very real. He couldn't even greet me properly when we met, his hand was so twisted and inflamed."

The keen edge of frustration laced his every word or maybe it was plain old garden variety fear. Myrina certainly detected the fear in Hylla's eyes and the sense of grave uncertainty in Chiara's frown. Even Judan, who'd kept his face impassive as he'd listened to her, couldn't quite hide his concern despite his apparent trust in her.

Oh yeah, he trusted her all right. To find a solution and, as Vand put it, get those people off the damn planet. She was glad she'd chosen to wear light fabrics to combat the higher temperatures aboard ship. Even so the cloth stuck to her skin, which felt itchy. She stood, hoping to ease her discomfort. This was the part of her job she hated the most. None of them wanted to hear that the Outposters' situation would get far worse before it got better.

"You saw for yourself," she finally said, directing her comments to the medical officer in the group but well aware that the other crew members were listening just as intently. "The meds aren't doing their job because the various illnesses are symptoms of a greater problem. They may appear real enough, but if you conduct a deep physiological scan on Lorre's body you'll discover there are great inconsistencies with the progress of each of his conditions."

Vand righted his chair but remained standing. As quickly as his temper had flared, he'd turned contemplative. "I'd like to see those results," he said. "I didn't consider running a deep scan. How did you know what to look for?"

"Experience," she said, not in the least offended by his desire to check her work. She respected a person who was willing to learn from his mistakes. "And I still don't know exactly what I'm looking for, just where to look. In the meantime the Outposters have to stop taking their meds immediately."

"But they could die," Hylla said.

Before Myrina could respond, the shortest Dakokatan she'd seen yet rushed through the door. He stood a shade under six feet tall and had a much stockier build than the other crew members. Even his slightly disheveled appearance was out of character for a Dakokatan. At least the ones she'd met so far. Bags rimmed his eyes which were shot with red. Not a flattering color combination against the deep green. He carried a rag in his hand and used it to wipe the fine traces of sweat soaking his flushed face. He looked as if he'd been working under the hot sun instead of inside the bowels of a ship.

"I did it, Captain," the man said. In his agitated excitement, he was blithely unaware of the strained silence in the room.

"This is Dr. deCarte, Biali. What happened?" Judan stood beside her, his fingers caressing her arm. His voice reverberated with a sudden excitement.

Biali barely glanced in her direction. "It took a few reconfigurations of the propulsion system following Stinn's Notations, Captain, but the simulation worked. A hyperslide is now possible on the Speedlite."

"How many times did you test the scenario in the simulator?" Chiara asked. "I'm not endorsing multiple hyperslides based on recommendations from your space trader friends."

"Ideas, yes, I took those from my friends," Biali said. "Endorsements, no. I did the testing myself. Seven sequential simulations with a time lapse of no more than five minutes between tests. The *Ketiga Bulan* will take much longer to recycle between jumps."

Chiara nodded in obvious satisfaction. "Captain."

"Yes, Captain," Myrina said. She had no clue what a hyperslide was, except both Judan and Biali looked mighty pleased with themselves. "Would someone mind telling me what, exactly, a hyperslide is?" she asked.

Above her, Judan chuckled. "I wondered how long it would take for you to, how do you say, get in the act. Explain it to her, Biali."

"By adjusting the propulsion system, I've enabled the ship to continue its accelerated momentum *after* it comes out of a space-time jump, hence the term hyperslide."

"How soon until we've powered up for the next jump, Hylla?" Judan asked without waiting for her comment.

Myrina hadn't even noticed the navigator had joined the little conclave. She stood close enough to Biali that their arms brushed against one another.

"Ten, fifteen minutes tops, Captain. And I've also been studying the chapter on navigational techniques from Stinn's Notations, sir."

"Then you feel confident you can maneuver us into a hyperslide after the next jump?"

"Yes, sir," Hylla said, sending a quick smile in Biali's direction. Obviously a hyperslide was the sort of navigational challenge she enjoyed, whereas the current routine tasks of powering up and maintaining course speeds until jump time could be left to the Speedlite's computer system.

Myrina looked around for Vand, the only crew member who hadn't voiced an opinion, yet. He'd moved close enough to listen, but maintained his distance. He caught her staring at him, though, and winked.

"You want my opinion, Doctor?" he said, then gave it before she could say yes. Or no. "The Captain makes a regular habit of risking his ship by pulling crazy stunts like this."

*Risk the ship? Didn't that mean risking the crew? Wonderful.* She didn't much like being on an FTL flight into deep space to begin with and now she discovered she'd hooked up with an extreme sports enthusiast.

Gently but firmly, Myrina pulled away from Judan's half-embrace to face him. "And this enormous risk to the *ship* is a good thing because?"

He quirked a smile and shook his head. "Calculated risk. And a few hyperslides will cut our travel time to Hitani. Instead of five days we'll be there in three."

Which meant she had far less time to conjure a miracle to save the Outposters.

"Then I'd better get back to work," she said.

She wanted to reassure him she would find the answer, but kept her mouth shut. This time she didn't plan on making any rash promises until she had irrefutable proof.

* * * * *

Back at the lab, Myrina slid a powerpack into a slot, flipped open the lid and pressed a button to activate the GCS.

*That's right, baby, come on.*

A couple of blips and bleeps later the screen blinked. She typed in a few keystrokes and the GCS program ran its start up routine. Myrina sighed. The Genetic Code Simulator allowed her to create and test hypothetical scenarios using a variety of variables such as environmental conditions, ecosystem impact and genetic responses. However, despite its ability to produce results in half the time of other testing options, she often wished the inventor had installed an instant activation code on the damn machine.

"All these sound effects give me too much time to think," she muttered to herself. "And I don't want to think about the hazards of hyperslides. I don't care about hyperslides. They aren't my problem. Unless of course we don't come out of one and crash into an asteroid. Or something bigger.

"But I'm not allowed negative thoughts, so erase that last remark. Besides, seven simultaneous simulations sounds pretty impressive, doesn't it? Of course it does. Sounds downright safe to me. And Judan knows more about this sort of thing than I do. Of course the fact that I've discovered he's a closet space jockey in no way influences my confidence in the man."

A firm set of hands encircled her waist. "I am glad to hear that, though I would like to know what a 'closet space jockey' is so I know whether or not you gave me a compliment."

# Chapter Six

**℘**

Myrina jumped as a now familiar lock of hair draped itself over her shoulder. "Hey!"

Wasn't he supposed to be on the bridge overseeing this "calculated risk" of a hyperslide? He sure as heck wasn't supposed to be invading her space right now.

"Hands off and hair out of my face," she said. "I'm working." She shoved the strand of hair away and made a half-twist to look behind her. "And I was not giving you a compliment."

Judan instantly released her and backed away, a puzzled look on his face. Flustered, Myrina turned back to the computer and stared at the GCS menu. The simulation would take some time to run, so it wasn't as if she couldn't afford an interruption. Her hands shook so badly she had trouble selecting the correct option to set up the test scenario. In desperation she clasped them around the framed screen of the computer case. That helped, some, but did nothing to still her thudding heart.

*Crap. This is what comes of getting involved with a client. He's now been introduced to the obsessive, working bitch side of my personality. Make that neurotic, obsessive working bitch.*

Though she tried to focus, the data blinking past her on the screen blurred. Aside from the fact that she did become so totally absorbed in her job she frequently forgot the world around her, her self-talk therapy had been strictly intended for her ears only.

"Sorry," she said with a halfhearted wave of her hand. She didn't want to face him yet, until she'd collected herself.

At least her voice sounded normal. "I was being unfair. I'm just feeling a little…"

"Anxious."

She started to shrug then gave a slight nod instead. She was feeling tense. While she wasn't thrilled about hyperslides, she did understand, even applaud, Judan's determination to reach the Outposters as quickly as possible. But, yes, that increased her anxiety levels, though not enough to throw her. Thanks to her psychiatrist, self-talk therapy was an automatic habit that allowed her to keep her restless energy focused until the task absorbed her.

"I sent a communiqué to Hitani informing the Outposters about our new estimated time of arrival," he said. "I also sent instructions that all but the ten Outposters on life support should stop their meds immediately."

"Oh," she said. Given his dedication to the mission she wasn't too surprised he'd made a decision so quickly. "Well, thanks."

"I didn't do it for you, Myrina. I did it to save them. I'm a pilot turned politician. You're the scientist, the technical expert on the mission. I need you."

She blinked. *I need you. I want you.* Heady words. Words she'd dreamed of hearing. Imagined hearing a thousand times in a thousand different ways. Yet this was one scenario she'd never, ever anticipated. Whatever daydreams she'd spun for herself, not a one had come packaged as a tall, green-skinned sexy stranger.

"A pilot, eh?" She looked over her shoulder. For some reason she'd expected him to be on the other side of the room, not less than a foot away from her. Where were those warning tingles when she needed them?

"Years ago I was an Outposter," he told her. "I became, as you call it, a 'space jockey'. My mother didn't mean it as a compliment either when she had to explain that her son was a pilot."

Myrina puffed out a breath and licked her lips. "What did she want you to be?"

His stark features shifted until he appeared almost amused. He shrugged. "She always maintained I was so…headstrong, I should be a member of the *Ktua*."

She grinned at his confession. Damn, but the man looked good, even when he was admitting to his daredevil, bad-boy streak. He… She quirked an eyebrow in surprise. "What did you do to your hair?"

He shrugged and turned his head to give her a better view. Like every other member of the crew except Chiara who wore that awful wig, he'd braided his hair down his back. Two of the beaded strands were wrapped around the bulk of hair at his nape. He'd worked fast because she hadn't been turned away from him for long, which meant he'd worked from experience. Yet, ever since their first meeting he'd worn it loose.

A slow, sexy smile played across his lips. "I did as you asked. I'm keeping my hair out of your face, and mine, too."

Her eyes widened in disbelief. Who was he kidding, anyway? The man had followed his own agenda since the second they'd met, yet suddenly he was complacently following her orders. She crossed her arms, certain he was up to something, but his face had that look of stubborn sincerity she was coming to recognize all too well. She saw the exact same look in the mirror every time she gazed in one, too.

"Sit," she commanded, deciding she'd go for broke and throw her weight around a little.

He took two steps back and sat on a stool. Instantly, her suspicions grew. Then he crossed *his* arms over his chest and quirked *his* eyebrows. Watching her again. Definitely challenging her. That was the only word for it. His eyes twinkled. Teasing her. Flirting with her?

*He wants to play? After I told him off?* It didn't make sense, but then, not much about this relationship did.

100

"Do I look better now?" he asked.

She pretended to seriously assess him again. He didn't so much as blink under her scrutiny. Just sat there patiently letting her look him over. Like he didn't mind in the least if she took her time. That was new, too. He hadn't let her take her time last night.

Was it only just last night? Their entire relationship seemed to have moved at FTL speeds until a moment ago. But if he was going to give her this moment, she'd take it.

He sat on the stool with ease, one booted foot planted firmly on the floor, the other propped on the metal rim that circled the chair legs. Even though he came across as a no-nonsense kind of guy, the relaxed look suited him somehow. Or could it be that he was now comfortable with her.

A little voice inside her head suggested that maybe she was the one who'd become comfortable with him. The idea startled her. Except for Parker, who'd worked at it for years, she rarely let her guard down around a man, or anyone for that matter. Okay, so she'd agreed to open the door and let him in. She simply hadn't realized how far beyond a kiss he'd take it. Or she'd let him take it.

She circled behind him. At ease or not, he was a solidly built man. The sleek contour of his leggings accentuated the ripple of muscle along the length of his extended thigh. Her hand dropped down and oh-so slowly her fingers traced a lazy pattern along his leg. Even through the fabric his body was hot to the touch.

"My hair, Myrina."

His tight, slightly sardonic command made her laugh. Gave her a heady sense of power. Her simple touch affected him. Unable to resist, she caressed his arm next, smoothing the already taut cloth of his shirt.

"I'm getting there," she whispered next to his ear and thought she heard an answering groan.

"What's your assessment, Doctor?" His voice sounded hoarse, belying the casualness of his question.

She spoke her mind, blunt as always. "The braid doesn't suit you," she said. With his hair pulled back, his exotic features looked too stark.

A rough laugh rumbled out of him. "Then undo it," he said.

Pure temptation. Which was odd because she couldn't ever remember being this fascinated with a man's hair before.

Without hesitation, her hands unraveled the twist of beaded strands that held his hair fast. Starting at the narrow end she then began releasing the skeins. Liquid fire threaded its way through her fingers and brushed against the sensitive underside of her wrist. She shivered and her breath hitched in her throat as she bit back a moan of pleasure. The man might have a sexy-as-sin body, but his hair was truly gorgeous.

She reveled in the gloriously sensual feel of the coppery strands that came alive under her touch. This kind of play was downright decadent. Unwinding the last of the bonds, she gathered his hair in her two hands and then set it free. A glittering waterfall cascaded down across her palms and she frowned.

Tied tightly together, Judan's hair had appeared a sleek column of deep red, but this close she thought she noticed an entirely different shading. Separating a thick lock of hair, she held it close. She blinked in frustration, but it was no use. Her eyes, the lights in the lab, something must be playing a trick on her brain because she could swear she saw golden-brown strands interspersed with the copper ones in Judan's hair.

"Don't ever tame your hair again," she said, smoothing her hands through the silky locks. "I like it better loose."

He shook his head.

"Don't move." Carefully she untangled her fingers.

He chuckled. "I didn't realize a human woman could be so contradictory."

She swatted his shoulder. "Then you regret taking up with one?" she asked, only half joking.

She didn't even see him move. One minute she was behind him, the next she was on his lap and in his arms. Caught off guard, she yelped and her arms locked around his neck. Heat radiated off him in waves that crashed over her. The faint odor of alam bark teased her senses and her entire body tightened in anticipation.

"What do you think?" he asked, glaring down at her.

Actually it was more of a stare, because his eyes were focused on her lips, making her mouth go dry. Or maybe it was the naked desire surfacing from those green depths that mesmerized her. This close to him, her insides liquefied and she very nearly melted against him. Only the severest willpower kept her upright.

"I, ah, think this seems vaguely familiar," she said. *Damn right it did.* She'd told him hands off and he'd promptly found a way to put his hands back on her.

He shook his head. His tousled hair framed his face, softening the intensity of his gaze. He was assessing her again, or at least her statement, with great seriousness. "I don't think so."

"You're sure?"

"Yes. I would have remembered this." He palmed her ass and hoisted her a little higher in his lap. Right on top of his erection.

Her eyes widened at his audacity, but she stayed where he'd put her.

"And this." His hand slid over the curve of her hip and ducked under her shirt.

She gasped at the heated brush of his fingers across her belly.

"But I do remember this," he said and settled his big hand over her breast, confined in her lacy "unmentionable". She wasn't sure, because her eyes were kind of out of focus, but she thought he had a superior masculine grin on his face.

Barely swallowing the next gulp of air, she nodded. She remembered, too. His hands made her body go crazy.

Gently, he massaged her breast. At first the rhythmic squeezes lulled her into a pleasant sense of lassitude. So much so that she was caught unawares when a fine line of sweet fire coiled itself through her body from her breasts to her pussy. Lazily, his finger flicked back and forth across her nipple until it peaked. The tension tightened inside her and she squirmed, her butt rubbing against his engorged cock.

He growled and the green in his eyes heated another degree. Hot enough to burn.

"Judan."

She never got the chance to say another word beyond his name. His thumb stroked the bare curve of her breast and slid over the lace. Then he clamped her stiff nipple between his thumb and forefinger.

A heady dose of desire slammed through her and she bit her lip to stifle a moan. He shook his head, increasing the pressure just enough. With a tiny whimper of pleasure, her body arced towards him, begging for more. He obliged, twisting the nub and sending another signal flare straight to her womb. Convulsively, her fingers clutched the strands of hair she'd so recently freed.

"That's it," he whispered. "Show me everything, Little Warrior. I definitely remember your responses."

She could barely breathe, let alone think, yet she remembered, too. "What about your responses?"

His supporting arm gripped her waist before she could so much as wiggle. She frowned her displeasure. He definitely needed a lesson in cooperative play. The suggestion died on her lips when she met his feral stare.

"Don't." The command was a bare whisper of breath between them.

It was on the tip of her tongue to argue when he shook his head.

"Please," he ground out the single word as if it cost him a measure of pride. "One more move and I'll explode."

He was not feeding her a line. She didn't know why this articulate thought intruded in the midst of sensual incoherency, but it did. And she trusted it. And him. In fact, she respected him all the more for admitting such a weakness where she was concerned.

"Okay," she whispered, caressing the back of his neck to ease the tension there. "But you need to slow down, too."

His eyes closed and he drew in a deep, shuddering breath. In the next instant his hand left her breast to settle on the curve of her hip. Far enough away not to cause havoc, but close enough to still disturb her presence of mind because he made sure his hand remained under her shirt, maintaining the skin-on-skin contact.

Eyes open now, he was back to studying her. Was he wondering whether she was wet for him, or did he know? Could he smell her scent? She licked her bottom lip, teasing it between her teeth while she waited.

"I remember," he said. "I remember this."

He didn't give her time to think before he bent his head. After all their fiery passion, his lips felt like cool drops of rain against her mouth. The sensation and the promise of more were brief. Before she truly had time to taste him and savor the unique flavor of man mixed with coffee, he retreated.

"Judan?"

His lips brushed against her forehead. "I think it's best if we talk."

The request was so unexpected she fell against his chest in a fit of giggles.

His back stiffened in surprise. After a moment of pained silence, he asked. "This is funny?"

"Yes," she said. "And it will certainly slow things down."

Since he didn't object, she kept her head where it was and wrapped one arm around his waist. The other hand followed a trail of skin past the collar of his shirt and down the seam, coming to rest in the region of his heart.

"Not if you're going to do that."

"Shh, unless you want to remove your hand from my person, again."

His thumb drew lazy circles on her skin. "No." His whisper was decidedly emphatic.

"Didn't think so," she muttered, nestling closer. He made a very comfortable pillow. She stifled a yawn, not surprising since she'd woken early and hadn't had much sleep the night before.

For someone who'd wanted to talk he didn't seem to have much else to say to her after that. Beneath her, Judan's body felt warm and solid, enveloping her with a sense of safety. The whole experience was a novelty. Cuddling was something she'd never really done before, yet Myrina was strangely content to sit in silence, nestled in this man's arms. Despite growing up with two hundred other children and care-workers at the orphanage, intimacy had been in short supply. And love had been practically nonexistent.

*Love.* Now where had that word come from?

Next to "I want you", the three little words "I love you" had haunted her dreams for years. Still did a time or two, though she'd never met them in real life.

Oh, she loved her work, no doubt about it. Then there was Parker. Every few months or so, the rumor mills at TLC would churn out yet another speculative piece on her "affair" with Parker, or his with her, depending on who was doing the talking. What no one seemed capable of understanding was, yes she loved Parker and he loved her, but like a brother and a sister would. Yet, nice as they were, neither kind of love was the one she'd ever spent time building daydreams about.

Then, eight years ago she'd come face-to-face with a cold, hard reality that didn't care one bit about dreams or hopes or a wayward, unpredictable emotion called love. Some people were meant to find it, have it, give it. For Myrina it remained an elusive dream.

Her hand dipped lower. Judan had such fine skin. Except for the two lines of scarring it was as soft as she imagined a newborn baby's to be.

What would it be like to love this man?

Pretty damn dangerous. After one relatively short lesson, he'd learned her skin. Gotten under it, too. That scared the shit out of her. Primarily because she wasn't quite certain how he'd done it. Though she did know one thing for sure. The way the heat sizzled between them, she was playing with fire. Trouble was, now that she'd touched a living flame, she didn't want to stop. Wasn't sure she could.

"Myrina." Judan's rough voice rumbled over her head as he drew another couple of circles on her belly. "Why were you talking out loud to yourself earlier when I came into the lab?"

*Shit.* Myrina's pleasant lethargy evaporated the instant the question mark appeared at the end of his inquiry and she shot to a sitting position. The L-word be damned along with her raging hormones. The Dakokatan *Ktua* Judan Ringa wasn't just dangerous to her senses, he was positively lethal to her peace of mind.

True to his stubborn, persistent hide, Judan only let her get so far. His arms encircled her in a steely grip, meant to steady her and keep her in her place. On his lap. While he waited patiently for her answer.

"None of your damn business," she said, her defensive shields dropping swiftly into place. She suppressed a shiver, the heat from the bare, skin-on-skin contact having cooled to subzero-degree temperatures.

A swarm of bees took up residence in her stomach, buzzing angrily. There was no way in the collective hells of whatever cultures you wanted to pick that she was going to tell Judan what had happened to her eight years ago. A jumble of memories surfaced along with one clear thought. Judan wasn't just stubborn, on this he would be inflexible.

"If it helps," he said, "I'm guessing it has something to do with your anxiety attacks."

Slowly she nodded, grasping at the one fact he already knew.

She might owe him an explanation, but maybe, just maybe, she could keep her secrets while telling him a truth of sorts. What had happened to her *was* her own business, no matter what Judan said. Next to Fenton deMorriss and a couple of doctors, Parker was the only one who knew, and that was because he'd been the one to give her the bad news.

"It's called self-talk therapy," she finally admitted, once her stomach had settled down and she could think more rationally. "My psychiatrist taught me how."

He nodded without breaking his intense stare. "You are seeing a…a head doctor?"

"You mean a shrink. And no. Not anymore."

"A shrink." He muttered the word to himself, undoubtedly memorizing it. "Yet you still have anxiety attacks."

"Yes," she said. "This self-talk therapy is a way of controlling them."

"Is it working, or do I need to distract you, again?"

Incredulous, her mouth fell open. "What?"

He shrugged and pulled her a little closer. "You are the scientist," he said. "You tell me which is more effective. This self-talk therapy or…"

"You?" she asked, realizing with a sense of relief he was satisfied with her explanation. That he did not want to know more.

"Exactly," he said and kissed her.

Several minutes or hours later, she wasn't sure which, the door of the lab swished open. She paid no attention, her focus totally on the man holding her in his arms. Except he must have heard it too because he raised his head slightly. A moment later a loud cough cut through her sensual haze. The noise sounded totally fake and filled with embarrassment at having caught them in an intimate act.

*Damn.* "Tell whoever it is we don't want any."

Judan chuckled. "Whoever is already in the room, Little Warrior."

"So? That's the point, maybe they'll leave."

"I don't think he wants to."

*Well crap.* Three guesses who it was. Surreptitiously, Myrina peered over Judan's shoulder before settling back against his chest. She'd been perfectly comfortable and totally distracted, thank you, and resented the intrusion.

"It's your brother," she said.

# Chapter Seven

**ဆ**

Judan shifted his position on the stool to better shelter Myrina from Vand's view. With her rumpled hair, slightly wrinkled shirt and swollen lips she looked like a woman who'd been well-kissed. And while her responsiveness to his touch and his lips pleased him immensely, causing his shaft to strain against the confines of his leggings, he had no wish to cause her further embarrassment.

Still using his large body as a shield, he set her on the floor, where she immediately started straightening her outfit. Her neck and face had turned a dull shade of red and he regretted his brother's lack of judgment. But he hadn't come this far in his career not to recognize when it was best to confront a problem. And, at this moment, Vand was the problem he had to deal with.

"I am sorry, Myrina," he said, pitching his voice low so his words would remain private between them.

She glanced up at him, her eyes wide with surprise. "Why? You can't help it if your brother has lousy timing."

Yes, there was no denying Vand had, as she said, "lousy timing", but she was wrong in her other assessment. He could help it. And right here, right now, Judan was going to do just that.

"I mean," he said, caressing her cheek, "that I am sorry I have to end our time together so abruptly to deal with Vand. We will finish this later."

She licked her lips and flashed him a sultry smile. "Which, our discussion or the kiss?"

"What do you think?" he asked with an answering grin before turning to face his brother.

"You will apologize to Dr. deCarte for barging into the lab," he said. "Your quarrel is with me, not her."

Vand had always been brash, but since Lorre's death, he'd subtly challenged Judan at every turn. At first, Judan had believed his brother was suffering from acute grief. Vand was the more emotional of the two, and the one closer to Lorre in age.

"Like hell I will. I sat there and listened. We all sat in the mess room and listened to what the good doctor had to say about Lorre. And then I realized you hadn't told her," Vand said.

"Told me what?" Myrina asked before Judan could respond.

"About Lorre," Vand said.

"The dead Outposter?" Myrina turned to Judan. "What is your brother talking about?"

"Our brother is lying dead on a slab in the clinic across the hall." Vand's tone was dark with anger. "But the Captain didn't tell you that, did he, Dr. deCarte?"

"Lorre is your brother?" she asked, stepping closer to face him, turning her back on Vand. "Why didn't you tell me the other day in Fenton's office?"

Judan placed a thumb against her lips, silencing her. "Leave it, Myrina. I'll explain later," he said. The pain of the loss still circled like a vulture above his heart. Until now he'd managed to mourn in private and do what he had to do in public to keep the rest of the Outposters alive.

No more. Vand's rash behavior had exposed their grief, forcing him to face it head on. But he would not subject Myrina to the hostility festering like an open wound between them. Abruptly he turned to his brother. "We're leaving. Turn around and walk out that door before you say something you regret."

"Like hell I will," Vand yelled and charged, cursing loudly in both Dakokatan and English.

Judan made no attempt to block the attack or protect himself. His single thought was to safeguard Myrina. He shoved her out of the way seconds before Vand's body checked him, ramming him backwards.

He let his body go slack to absorb the blow. They still hit the counter with the force of a rampaging wild ox. The impact momentarily knocked the wind out of both of them and sent the machine Myrina had been using skidding across the counter. It hit the wall with a resounding bang.

"Hey, watch it, you two!" a voice shouted. Myrina. He prayed she had the sense to stay clear.

Neither he nor his brother moved. Jarred by the blow, for an instant they simply stood facing each other gulping air into their lungs.

His brother grabbed hold of Judan's shirt with both hands. Only then did Judan's instincts take over. Before Vand could use the cloth as leverage to smash Judan against the counter again, Judan hooked his foot behind his brother's. One swift yank and Vand's leg flew out from under him, toppling them both to the floor. They rolled, Vand's extra height and bulk giving him the initial advantage. A healthy shot of adrenaline mixed with the sexual high from his encounter with Myrina, though, gave Judan the strength to overpower his brother. By the time he'd pinned Vand to the floor beneath him, they were both breathing hard.

"Stop!" a voice yelled above him.

*Stay back*, he wanted to warn her, but the words didn't form fast enough. A pair of slim hands grabbed his arm and tugged.

"Stop, I said!"

Sure enough, when he took his eyes off Vand a second later and turned, he looked straight into a blazing pair of pale green eyes. His Little Warrior knelt beside him and she was furious.

"Get back," he ordered.

"No."

She defied him without hesitation and tugged harder, even though both he and Vand outweighed her by more than a few *pauns*. He couldn't risk having her hurt, so he let go. Shoving himself up off the floor, he rose, pulling Myrina to safety with him. His brother still lay on the ground staring at them both in open-mouthed shock.

Vand swallowed and nodded at Myrina. "Is she always like that?" he asked.

"Yes," Judan said.

"Like what?" Myrina demanded, looking from one brother to another. "Level-headed, non-pugilistic and intelligible? I realize you're both speaking English, but would one of you mind telling me what in the—" She paused and gave Judan one of her level-headed looks. "What is going on?"

"Vand blames me for Lorre's death."

Silence. While Myrina contemplated his revelation, Vand averted his gaze and scrambled to his feet. So Judan had guessed correctly then. An impotent rage welled up inside him, burning his gut and he clenched his fists in frustration. It was one thing to carry the burden inside himself, it was another to learn that his brother also blamed him.

"So that's what you believe?" Myrina finally said. He sensed a rock-hard core beneath her quiet, almost calmly spoken words. Almost immediately she gave him a dismissive waved of her hand. "Forget I asked."

Instead she pierced Vand with a no-nonsense stare. "Perhaps you'd care to explain where you got such a dumb-ass idea that Judan killed your brother."

Despite the seriousness of the accusation, Judan bit back a grin. Her earthy sayings were, he guessed, a product of her upbringing and she tended to use them when, like now, she was in full warrior mode.

"Vand?" he prompted.

"Lorre would still be alive if he hadn't left the planet," Vand said.

"So?" Myrina asked as if his statement of fact were inconsequential.

Judan flexed the fingers on one hand, but the action did nothing to release the tension. How could she so easily trivialize Vand's words when he'd told himself the very same thing every day since Lorre's death? His brother didn't appear any happier with her apparent indifference.

"I was serving aboard the reconnaissance vessel sent to investigate the crisis on Hitani. We were handling the situation just fine when the *Ktua* decided we needed help from the big guns and Judan arrived on the scene."

"The *Ktua*?" Myrina asked with a glance in Judan's direction. "But I thought you were a *Ktua*."

"The word is both singular and collective. Although 'Warlord' is the English translation, it more accurately means 'Chieftain'," he explained. "The *Ktua* is the governing body in Dakokata. And yes, they voted to send a representative to rendezvous with the reconnaissance vessel. Even before Lorre's death many people were worried we couldn't handle the situation and get the Outposters off the planet safely." He paused. Not once during the emergency meetings had anyone questioned whether the proposed evacuation strategy would cause far worse repercussions than the illnesses the Outposters were already dealing with.

Myrina nodded, then turned back to Vand. "So what happened?"

"Big brother happened. Our ship was orbiting Hitani. Another Outposter was scheduled to deliver the medical data-chip to us, but Judan asked Lorre to come aboard instead." As he talked, Vand's voice lost its sarcastic edge and ended up sounding slightly bewildered. Judan felt a small pang of compassion. They'd never talked about what happened. About the choices each of them had made.

"We rarely had a chance to meet these last few years," Judan said. In the midst of a crisis he'd manufactured an opportunity for three of the four Ringa brothers to be together—and paid the price. Was his admission now a way to rationalize his own actions or seek forgiveness?

"I can't believe this," Myrina said. "Neither of you could predict the Outposters would die if they left the planet. It's not exactly a common consequence. Illness, yes. Devastating environmental impact on indigenous species, definitely. Death, only very rarely."

Vand leaned against the nearby counter and crossed his arms, but he wouldn't meet Myrina's stern glare.

"He would still be alive." His whispered words sounded like a plea.

"Quite possibly," Myrina said. "There are no guarantees in this business. But if that other man had died, would you feel any better about it now? Carry less of a burden? Feel less of a responsibility?"

She glanced between them and shook her head. "I don't believe that. Of either of you."

An awkward silence descended upon them. For his own part, Judan couldn't so easily shake off the burden of responsibility. And yet, Myrina's professional and unbiased opinion brought some perspective to his view of the day Lorre died. Lorre had eagerly accepted his suggestion to bring the data-chip himself. To visit with his two brothers, despite his crippling pain and the uncertainty on Hitani. Even the top scientists among the Outposters hadn't guessed the tragic results of his visit. How could he?

He felt the light touch of Myrina's hand on his arm and he looked down at her. Behind the concern, he caught a glimpse of the softness he'd seen earlier when he'd held her in his arms. She glanced quickly in Vand's direction before standing on tiptoe. He bent forward, ignoring his brother's glum expression.

"Grief can do funny things to people," she said. "Cut yourself some slack."

Her low-pitched voice sounded as if she spoke from experience and he wondered again about the incident eight years ago. He understood her idiomatic turn of phrase perfectly. But, until the other seventy-seven Outposters were off Hitani, he had no intention of cutting himself any slack. They were his responsibility.

"I'll handle it," he said.

She sighed, but didn't argue the point. "Okay, then. I better check the GCS and see if it's still running the simulation."

Before she could walk away, Judan reached out and threaded his fingers through her hair. She let out a yelp of surprise when he hauled her to within inches of his face, her hands reaching across the space between them to steady herself against his chest. Her touch sent a wave of heat storming through his body, but he tried to ignore the reaction.

Bestowing a chaste kiss on her forehead, he whispered for her ears alone, "I admire your warrior spirit, Myrina. I don't wish to tame it, but if you ever try to break up a fight again you will answer to me."

Myrina's eyes first went wide with pleasure, then darkened with a touch of indignation before settling to a soft shimmer. She swallowed hard, but kept her chin up and her eyes on his face.

"When I was growing up I'd have given my soul for a brother or a sister to stand with me. You've already lost one brother, Judan. I...I didn't want to see you lose another."

"By the Third Moon, I am doing my best not to," he said, amazed by her loyalty to a relationship she'd only ever imagined. "In the meantime, stay out of a fight. I will keep you safe."

Together he and Vand left the lab. At the door, however, Vand paused and turned back.

"Myrina," he said.

She was, he noted, already retrieving and restarting her machine. When she turned, her brow was lined in concentration. "What?"

"I'm sorry for barging into the lab."

Her face lit up in pleased surprise and she smiled at him. In Judan's opinion, though, his brother still had a long way to go to deserve such a reward. To emphasize that fact, he pinned Vand against the wall no more than two steps beyond the lab.

"Do not ever disrespect her again," he growled.

"She accepted my apology. She understood."

More false bravado. Judan wasn't in the mood. He felt raw. *I'll handle it.* How? By slamming his brother against the wall. He released Vand and stepped back.

"You are now serving aboard my ship, Vand. I suggest you tread carefully from now on."

Vand pushed himself away from the wall and paced down the hall, putting some distance between them. He wheeled back to face Judan.

"I sometimes go in and talk to him, you know."

Judan hadn't known, but he wasn't surprised. Vand had shared a room with Lorre when they were growing up. According to their mother, the two boys had spent more time talking to each other than sleeping at night.

Vand gave a helpless gesture, then slumped against the nearest wall. Despite the mess his own emotions were in, Judan recognized the confrontation in the lab had released Vand's pent-up feelings. He walked over and hunched down beside his brother. For a long time neither of them spoke, but it felt good to sit together.

"I blamed you so I wouldn't have to blame myself," Vand said.

"What are you talking about?" Judan seriously regretted not talking to Vand sooner. It had been a mistake to keep his own grief to himself. Neither of them had coped well and with each day the pain had shifted like a sand dune, widening the distance between them.

"I talked him into becoming an Outposter. You'd left to become a *Ktua* and I…I wanted a brother out here with me."

Judan nodded. Despite the bond between all four brothers, he and Wyn, the eldest, were both fiercely independent. Even Lorre, the youngest in the family, had chosen his own path as soon as he was old enough to leave home. Vand was the one who craved the company of his brothers, who lamented the loss of their weekly visits when they would climb the hill at the back of the house and sit like this and talk. It was precisely because Judan knew how Vand felt that he'd suggested Lorre come aboard the reconnaissance vessel.

He stood and offered a hand to his brother. The Three Sisters twisted fate to suit their purpose. Perhaps he'd been foolish to visit the shrine of the Third Moon without proper guidance. He'd offered his gift, one of great personal value, and asked for what he most wanted. But, like his daydreams of *Rakanasmara*, not once had he thought of the consequences of his prayer.

He didn't believe in the random coincidence of events. If the Outposters hadn't been in trouble, if Lorre hadn't died, he never would have gone to TLC in search of Myrina. In his efforts to create a family through *Rakanasmara* had he unwittingly destroyed the family he already had?

"Myrina was right," he said. "Neither of us could have predicted what happened. Lorre's death wasn't anybody's fault."

It was time to heal the rift between them. To leave their regrets in the past. To mourn Lorre and move on. He had seventy-seven Outposters to save and a woman to "win".

"I have to get to the bridge," he said. "You'd better get to work, too." He turned away and started walking down the corridor.

"Judan."

He turned back. "Yes."

"I...I was as shocked as the rest of the crew when you came back from your meeting with the Foreign Affairs Director without your wig on. I don't understand how it's possible, but now that I've met her... I'm glad you found Myrina deCarte. She is worthy of a *Ktua*."

Judan shook his head. Vand still had much to learn. As did he. This was no longer about him and his needs. He saw that plainly now. In Myrina, the Third Moon had sent him another orphan. A fact he'd discovered when he'd researched Myrina's personal history. The knowledge that she'd been abandoned and been forced to live out her childhood in a Confederacy-run orphanage horrified him. Small wonder she was wary of placing her trust in others.

How would he teach her to trust him? More importantly, how would he set about making her believe he could be trusted? That he would protect her, as was his duty. That he would give her a son and any other children she wanted. Children who would have the security of the Ringa family name.

"My status doesn't matter, Vand. My only wish is that *I* prove worthy of being her life partner."

# Chapter Eight

ം

The lights in the guest suite were turned low. From her position in the middle of the bed, her arms wrapped around her knees, Myrina surveyed the unfamiliar shadows.

She'd been sitting like this for at least an hour. A retreat of sorts from the lab and her work and the empty corridors. For all she'd seen of the rest of the crew since the midday meal, the Speedlite might as well be a ghost ship. The vessel echoed with emptiness and urgency. A strange mix, which made her restless and had finally forced her to retreat. At least here she could call the dark corners her own. And by the time the environmental controls signaled the start of a new day, the shadows wouldn't hold any secrets.

She sincerely wished she could say the same about the data she'd downloaded onto the GCS. After Judan and Vand had left the lab, she'd sat for hours reviewing charts, comparing stats and running a few more preliminary simulations.

Nada. Zip. Zilch.

Day one done and she had more questions than answers. Even the few answers she'd found had only led to more questions. The one angle she'd confirmed was a link to Dakokatan genetics. She'd found markers predisposing most of the Outposters to the illness they'd subsequently contracted. But even with a map of Dakokatan DNA, it could take her a long time to work through the double helix and pinpoint the marker that had triggered the planet's malevolent reaction.

She glanced at the door. Although Judan had dropped by the lab a couple of times, there'd been no repetition of the intimacy they'd shared earlier. With the mission underway, both of them had instinctively pulled back and gotten down to business.

That hadn't stopped her from replaying every glance, every touch and most definitely their kisses. They'd shared three so far today and each one had left her mildly disoriented and majorly horny. During his so-called scientific experiment, comparing self-talk therapy against his kisses, Judan's technique had won hands down.

But it wasn't just the kiss itself that was compelling. It was the man. He honestly seemed to view her anxiety attacks as a problem she struggled with rather than an impediment to her job or her competency at it. Absently, she rubbed her arm and smiled. What's more, he seemed determined to help her. With kisses. A strangely endearing quality for a Warlord politician to have.

She scrubbed her hands through her hair, massaging her scalp. She needed to turn her mind off, let her subconscious or maybe even her unconscious take over for a while and work on the Hitani puzzle. She needed to…look at the door.

She was going to feel awfully foolish if she was wrong, except she didn't think she was. Wrong.

"Aren't you going to come in?" she called out.

The door slid open and Judan Ringa stepped inside.

Immediately, the temperature in the room shot up a couple of degrees. Felt like it, anyway, because there he stood in his leggings and his boots. His shirt was open, flashing her an expansive view of his broad chest. And, surrounding him like some halo-effect, his coppery hair danced in the slight breeze made when the door swished close behind him.

"Hi," she said.

"Hello, Myrina. I knew you wouldn't be asleep."

How had he known?

She'd told him—one throwaway line when he'd mentioned his eldest brother's anxiety attacks. *"Lucky him, he can sleep."* And he'd remembered. Pretty impressive.

"So you decided to drop in and distract me, huh."

"Yes."

She was a little stunned by his bluntness. Not that she'd expected him to be coy, exactly. She just hadn't thought he'd be this focused. But one look at him told her he was most definitely focused. On her.

She scrambled to her knees and the sheet fell away, baring her legs. He sucked in his breath, the sound echoing in the quiet room. For the longest time they simply stared at each other. Neither spoke and yet the communication between them was as electrifying as a bolt of lightning in a storm.

His eyes bore into hers and her lips parted in anticipation of another kiss. Her breathing slowed, matching her own lazy perusal of his bared torso, straight down to the waistband of his leggings. About the time her eyes fastened on the thick erection straining against his leggings, his fingers flexed. Her breasts tightened, aching for his touch. And, when he shifted slightly, her pussy clenched.

A wicked sense of delight zigzagged up her spine and then back down again.

*Nothing would distract* me *more than to distract him.*

Crooking her finger, she beckoned.

He came. Slowly, steadily and perhaps wisely, considering her sudden mood, with a wary expression on his face. He stopped less than an arm's reach from the end of the bed.

*Close enough.*

Shoving the silky sheets aside, she crawled forward, without once breaking eye contact. The muscles along his jawline clenched, his laser green eyes riveted on her body. Her lips parted and she caught her breath.

She enjoyed being the sole focus of his attention. Enjoyed knowing her body teased and tantalized him. Since meeting this man, she'd definitely developed a rare streak of impetuosity where he was concerned. She was not a gambler by nature—look how long she'd managed to avoid field duty. For her, life had proven to be a big enough gamble without actively seeking risks. Yet some unseen force inside her yearned to take just such a chance. Perhaps because he always made her aware of herself as a woman. His woman. Even this afternoon in the lab when they'd acted all business, the knowledge had been there between them.

At the edge of the bed, she rose to her full height on her knees, bringing her almost to eye level with him.

*What's happening to me?*

She hadn't even realized how much she'd missed the sight, the touch, the taste of him until she'd picked up on her skin's warning tingle. She reached out and brushed one side of his shirt off his shoulder. Instinctively her fingers sought and traced the length of the twin scars. His skin was hot to the touch. Already on fire, for her.

"Judan, I want my turn tonight. I want to learn you."

She wanted to give him pleasure. To seduce him.

A fierce growl rumbled deep in his chest and she thought he said, "You don't ask for much." Words he'd spoken last night. She hadn't been capable of thinking about what he'd meant by them then. Yet clearly he was implying she was asking a lot.

Still on her knees, she shuffled back a pace and straightened her shoulders against the bite of disappointment.

*The man wants me. Why couldn't I leave well enough alone?*

But she couldn't. Perhaps in her childhood, being wanted had sustained her dreams. In reality, being wanted was only the tip of a polar ice cap.

"Myrina?" His voice sounded hoarse.

"Yes," she whispered, steadying herself for rejection.

"Do men of your world…" He paused, frown lines marring his smooth forehead while he searched, she guessed, for the correct word. Finally he shrugged. "Do men of your world permit women to learn them?"

She was so surprised by his question, she nearly toppled onto the mattress. Catching her balance, she exhaled slowly, recovering her wits. *Well crap. I walked right into that one, didn't I?*

Her thoughts were immediately followed by one of his. *I'm sorry, but not this time.*

His apology from last night—was it only last night?— came back to her. The implication was clear. Dakokatans seemed to observe strict customs surrounding women touching their men. Yet, by asking about her customs, he seemed willing to—what?—negotiate.

"Yes," she said. "Many men sometimes enjoy a woman taking charge."

"And you would enjoy this? With me? You asked to touch me before."

He sounded a little shocked. But whether it was the idea that she would enjoy touching him or that she wanted to touch him in particular, she couldn't be sure. Either way, she'd committed herself to answering honestly, however strange it might sound to him.

"Yes," she said with a nod. "I'd very much enjoy touching you. Learning you," she added. Somehow it was important he understand she wasn't making a casual offer. She'd wanted men before and had taken them, too. Only this time was different. This man was different. She just wished she could understand why. Could understand what was happening to her. To them.

Instead of answering, he tossed a small, oblong box she hadn't noticed he'd been holding before, onto the bed. Then he stepped back two paces. She ignored the box in favor of keeping her eyes on him, still unsure what he meant to do. He toed his boot, loosening it, then pulled first one then the other off and tossed them both toward the door.

"All right," he said, stepping forward again.

She grinned at the words left unspoken. She voiced them herself, unwilling to leave anything to chance. If he was giving himself to her, he needed to tell her, plainly and clearly. "Does this mean you are giving me permission to touch you, Judan Ringa?"

He shook his head. "You asked to follow your customs." Then he shrugged. "I think," he said. "That I am giving myself permission."

Stunned, she reached out to caress his cheek, oblivious to the strands of copper hair that immediately twined themselves along her arm. He'd willingly compromised his own customs to respect one of hers. She felt honored and humbled at the same time. Arching upward, she brushed a kiss against his lips.

"Thank you," she said.

She didn't waste any time. She pulled her T-shirt off and threw it aside. His breath came in a harsh rasp when she stepped off the bed to stand just inches away.

"Myrina."

"Shh," she said. "Right now I need you to turn around."

He obliged and they shifted positions so that now his back was to the bed. His easy acquiescence ended when her hand came to rest on his bare chest. He captured it in one of his large hands. The green of his eyes glinted like crystals.

"There is something you should know before you begin," he said. "When you are done, I *will* have my turn, the way I planned when I came here tonight."

"That's fine, Judan," she said, biting back a shiver of anticipation. She was certainly willing to exchange mutual pleasure for mutual pleasure. "As long as you understand that I plan to take a very long time."

The muscles under her hand twitched, the only sign he gave that her promise affected him. Otherwise he was strangely impassive. It occurred to her he was uncertain of his role now that he'd surrendered himself to her care. Since he'd definitely driven her wild last night and again this morning, she decided to tease him back just a little.

He stood complacently while she eased his shirt over his broad shoulders, letting it fall to the ground. She stroked his arms. The solid muscle automatically flexed under her hands. With his chest bared, she was free to satisfy her craving for the feel of his smooth skin against her own. Skin-on-skin contact at last. She leaned forward and rubbed her breasts against him. Her nipples, already taut and aching, stabbed his skin.

"Show me," he whispered.

She whimpered and clutched his arms, kneading the flesh. Her breath came hot and fast against his skin. The friction was impossibly arousing sending tiny flashes of heat straight to her pussy.

He groaned and tipped his head back. Eyes closed, he looked ready to howl in frustration.

"Myrina." He uttered her name like a fervent plea.

"Shh," she whispered along the sensitive edge of his collarbone. His pulse danced against her lips. "Tonight, I'll take care of you."

Yet he wasn't the only one who needed looking after. The continual friction of her breasts across his heated flesh sensitized her already hardened tips. A tiny moan of frustration escaped her lips.

His reaction was immediate. His head snapped up and his eyes opened, pinning her with feral intent. Maintaining body contact, she stood on tiptoe. He bent his head to meet her. Their kiss was filled with as much hunger as it was passion. Their tongues dueled, gained entrance and explored. Then retreated and surrendered.

Denied a healthy dose of oxygen, she finally broke away. Gasping, she rested her forehead against his chest. Beneath the surface of his skin, his heart thudded an erratic beat. She was sure hers gave an answering call and shivered with the intensity of her emotions. He truly was different from other men she'd been with. None of the kisses she'd shared with him were the least bit simple or tame and each of them left her wanting more. Wanting him.

Yet, although he too trembled slightly, he stood a little stiffly within her half-embrace.

"Judan," she whispered, "you're supposed to relax and enjoy this."

"I am enjoying this," he assured her. His voice sounded hoarse with desire. "I will try to relax if you wish it."

She laughed. Her hot breath fanned his skin. "Judan."

"Yes, Myrina?"

"Just because it is my turn doesn't mean you can't hold me. Would that help?"

His head shook, almost imperceptibly. "I do not think it would help, no. But, I'm happy to learn I can touch you, too."

He wrapped her in a fierce hug. Since her body was free of clothing, his hands roamed at will up and down her back. This was nice, too. She rarely took the time to share quiet intimacies. With a contented sigh, she snuggled closer. And that was the moment Judan asserted his will. One of his hands strayed past the small of her back to palm her ass.

"Judan!" Her cry was one of pure lust. Her pussy was pressed firmly against the enormous ridge of his erection. With a slow purr her body revved, heat rushing through her veins.

"Yes, Myrina?" he said in a gruff whisper.

"I said hold, not cop a feel."

"But I'm much more relaxed."

"Not yet," she said with a hoarse laugh, delighted he had relaxed enough to tease her in return. "But I assure you, you will be."

Gently, she pushed away and he, reluctantly, released her.

Enough teasing.

She knelt in front of him. Then, one by one, she undid the tabs on his leggings. He held himself rigid, barely drawing a breath each time her fingers brushed against his hard length. She worked quickly, aware that his near constant state of arousal since they'd met brought a measure of pain with the pleasure. She shoved his leggings down to his thighs, releasing his cock into her waiting hands.

He cried out and stumbled like a man drunk on desire. He bumped into the bed and toppled backward. The mattress caught his fall while the pillows she'd piled around her in the middle of the bed cushioned his head. Assuring herself he was unhurt, she hastily stripped off his leggings, baring his entire body for her sole enjoyment.

"Damn, you're beautiful." And entirely hairless. His cock jutted magnificently into the air. His balls, two round globes drawn tight to his groin. And neither was hidden by any pubic hair. Even his legs, she noted absently, were as bare as his arms and chest.

She wasn't aware she'd spoken aloud until he laughed.

"Beautiful," he said, his tone rough. "Isn't that word used to describe women, not men?"

Through hooded eyes she meet his half-lustful, half-curious stare. He rested on his elbows, which propped up his upper body so he could see her.

"You want to argue semantics or watch?" she said with a sultry smile.

Sure enough, with one question she *had* distracted him. He blinked, his eyes darting to his erection then back to her face.

"Yes," he said. "I want to watch."

*Well crap, I have turned into a damn exhibitionist. I want him to watch me. Watch what I do to him.*

She was on display for him. Naked and aroused herself, she was the one kneeling before a man ready to pleasure him. At once dominant and submissive.

A heady sense of power swept through her and with it a healthy dose of responsibility. It hadn't taken a great leap of logic to figure out that probably no woman had ever touched Judan the way she was about to touch him. To do the things to his body that she was about to do. Why else would he have asked about her customs and given himself permission to accept them?

Another reason this man was different. This time more special.

Settling herself between his legs, she rested her hands on his thighs. His legs twitched and he voluntarily spread them wider. She accepted his offer and slid her hands to the juncture of his hipbone. She sat there checking him out.

Fully erect, his cock was definitely above average in size, but then maybe not given his height. The head flared wide over the thick shaft. A perfect mouthful. She licked her lower lip, anticipating the taste of him.

He hissed and she glanced up at him through hooded eyes. A thin sheen of sweat glimmered across his green skin. His eyes were wide with apprehension. His nostrils flared. He'd caught her scent. Already fully aroused, he wouldn't last long. Especially as her own body answered each and every one of his signals. Her pussy was dripping.

"I can smell you, Myrina. You're ready for me." He broke eye contact to glance, once again, at his cock. "See what you do to me."

A little bug-eyed, she watched in rapt fascination as the bulbous tip of his penis pulsed and the tiny hole expanded, doubling in size. The muscles under her hands tensed and his entire body stiffened. He gave a sharp guttural cry. His head tipped back and his eyes closed, as his cock shot a small load of cum.

*Well, hot damn. Now that was cool.* And he was right. She was more than ready to impale herself on his still-stiff shaft. Except this time she'd dedicated herself to his pleasure.

She cupped her thumbs underneath his balls, her fingers still flanking either side of his genitals. His creamy ejaculation had soaked his shaft and dribbled down to his testicles, offering her a ready-made lubricant.

Gently, she stroked upward, careful to maintain a firm, but light pressure. His balls bunched tighter against his shaft and he moaned, pushing himself into her caress. She massaged the twin sacs before releasing them to grip the base of his cock.

Slick from his juices, her hand slid easily up his shaft to fondle the head. By alternating hands, she maintained a steady stroke.

For a man who'd allegedly never had a woman touch him like this before, Judan turned pro fast. He instinctively caught her rhythm and began pumping his cock. His evident pleasure of tactile sensation was awesome to behold.

After two more successive strokes, she lifted her hands away, bent her head and took him into her mouth. Anticipating his heated reaction, she only encompassed his head, licking it with her tongue. He screamed and shoved his shaft as deep as she would allow. Because he was big and thick, she could only accommodate about half his cock, but he didn't seem to mind. And because he didn't try to gag her, she allowed him to set the rhythm.

Knowing he was ready to blow any moment, she didn't worry about her technique. *Damn.* Probably anything would feel fantastic about now and her tongue certainly loved the faintly ribbed texture of his shaft.

Her concentration on his pleasure was so acute, she didn't realize what he was doing until his fingers threaded their way through her hair. He didn't demand more, still allowing her to control how much of his cock she took into her mouth. Then he signaled his intent by tightening his hands on her hair.

She drank him dry, savoring the slightly sweet taste of his cum. Then she licked him clean before grabbing a corner of the sheet to clean her hands. Sometime after his triumphant shout and his last spurt, Judan had released his hold on her. He now lay sprawled on the bed, his eyes closed, his chest heaving.

She crawled up the bed and leaned over to kiss him. Almost immediately he captured her, pulling her down and opening his mouth to taste himself on her lips. When she lay beside him, he turned toward her. His big body shook when she gathered him into her arms, but then she was none too steady, either.

Judan had blown apart. Willingly given himself up to her hands and her mouth. Sought and trusted his pleasure with her. Just because she'd asked him to.

Even as she savored the responsibility, a part of her stood back, wary. Because what had just happened with Judan here on her bed didn't feel like an affair, where each person shared and claimed pleasure for themselves. When she'd made her offer she'd thought about this one time. This one night. But now she wasn't so sure. Judan wasn't a casual sex kind of guy. He'd made it clear he wanted more. Wanted her. But, beyond this one desire to learn him, she didn't know how to take care of anyone else but herself.

She shifted and he collapsed on top of her, pressing her against the mattress. The oblong box he'd thrown onto the bed earlier jabbed her in the back.

"Ouch."

She wiggled, trying to get into a more comfortable position. He rolled over, carrying her with him.

"I've got it," he said.

A pillow sailed over their heads and he shifted their bodies again as he searched for the box. But they were too close to the edge of the bed. When he reached out to grab the box, they slipped. She cried out in surprise and clung to his neck as they tumbled over. He managed to tuck her tight against him, taking the brunt of their fall.

When they hit the ground, he deliberately used the momentum to roll them across the floor. Totally disoriented, she had no idea which direction he was taking them or why. What's more, she didn't care. Tucking her head into the curve of his neck, she started to laugh and hung on for the ride.

He stopped as suddenly as they'd started with him on top of her. Lying beneath him gasping for breath, she was acutely aware of their full-body, skin-to-skin contact. His flaccid cock stirred and lengthened along her stomach while his balls were wedged against her mound. It had been a long time since she'd felt the pleasant weight of a man on top of her. Then he pulled away, far enough to allow her to catch her breath. Only the air lodged in her throat when she glanced up and met his savage gaze.

"My turn," he said.

# Chapter Nine

ဆာ

Already aroused from the touch and taste of him, her body craved its own release. Yet, while she'd agreed to a mutual exchange of pleasure, she wasn't willing to surrender so easily to his command.

"What if I'm not finished?" Myrina asked. Her thumb brushed across his nipple and skimmed down his rib cage.

His growl was fierce. His eyes blazed at her challenge. Within moments her hands were secured above her head, the full weight of his heavy body pinning her to the floor. She bucked against him, literally gasping for breath. He immediately shifted his weight. Then, before she could protest, he pulled her arms apart.

"Hang on," he said.

Dazed, she didn't understand him at first until she looked up at the underside of a cabinet. They were lying between two of the poles that held the shelving unit.

So, he wanted to go back to the no touching rule. For a brief moment, the urge to struggle overwhelmed her. She'd resisted last night, too. Not that it had done her any good in the end.

"You can't pretend you didn't enjoy what I just did to you. That you didn't like my hands on your body."

"I pretend no such thing." He sounded affronted.

She blinked and looked away. *Okay, so you enjoyed everything I did to you. Then why hang on to the stupid custom?*

But of course she couldn't ask that and insult his traditions. Especially not after he'd compromised and accepted one of hers. She flexed her hands and grabbed onto the poles. Only to frown at the masculine look of triumph that lit his face.

"Don't go away."

Three deep breaths later, she nodded. She had, after all, agreed to trust him a little. "I won't."

"Good," he said and sat up.

He wasn't gone long. Soon he knelt over her, the oblong box he'd snatched up before they'd rolled off the bed in his hand. The box was red and looked like it could contain a pair of glasses.

"On Dakokata, a man usually presents this to his woman before he has her spread naked on the floor."

The possessive pronoun warmed her straight to her core. *I want you. His.* It seemed a little unreal to hear someone actually say those words.

She licked her lips. "We aren't on Dakokata."

He grinned. "A very good thing," he said. "Now I won't have to wait to use this."

Before she could ask, he snapped open the lid. Nestled inside the case lay a teardrop pendant on a chain. Even within the protective canopy of Judan's hair, the multifaceted yellow stone sparkled.

*Hot damn, it's the most exquisite piece of jewelry I've ever seen.*

Unable to resist, she wanted to reach out and touch it. Only her arm wouldn't cooperate. In fact, neither of them would move. And the man's damn hair was in the way so she couldn't see what was wrong.

"Judan!" She panicked. "I can't move." Choosing to hold onto the poles was one thing. Not being able to let go was quite another.

He bent and nuzzled her cheek. "Shh, it's all right," he said.

He set the still-opened jewel case on the floor, then gathered his hair in his hands, holding it aside for her to look.

She quickly discovered that two of the braided and beaded strands, one on either side of his head, had wrapped themselves around her wrists and the pole, holding her fast.

She gulped in some more air. His hair certainly seemed to have a mind of its own. Given his height and the length of his hair, the braided strands made an effective rope. Given her proportionally smaller size, she was definitely at his mercy because he would have no trouble reaching any part of her body he wanted to.

"Why?" she asked. Her body already knew the answer. His possessive dominance made her hot, hot, hot.

"Once I start learning you, teaching your body to respond to my touch, it will be difficult, if not impossible for you to hold on."

She shivered at the certain knowledge in his voice. Knowledge that said quite emphatically he could, would make her lose control.

"Judan."

He lifted the pendant from its case before shoving the box away. The chain didn't appear to have a clasp. Obedient because she had chosen to surrender herself to him, she lifted her head. With one hand still holding the pendant, Judan slipped the chain over her head.

"This pendant was made for you, Myrina," he said. "It reminds me of the color of your hair."

The stone lay warm and heavy between her breasts.

"It's beautiful," she said.

"No." He straddled her, his hands on either side of her face. He bent and licked the pulse point at her throat. "You are beautiful, stretched out like this, offering yourself to me."

"Yes," she whispered, as he trailed kisses down the center of her body. Towering over her on all fours, his cock fully erect again and straining toward her, he was the one who looked magnificently beautiful.

"You will show me everything, Myrina." He kissed her navel, causing her stomach to flutter madly.

"Yes," she said, again.

"You will hide nothing."

She shook her head.

"Then, Myrina deCarte, I will show you how the necklace makes you mine."

He'd barely touched her and yet his hot words scorched her body. Every millimeter of skin ached for him. But he was taking his sweet damn time about seeing to her needs. She was wearing his necklace, dammit. She —

Saw his finger touch the rim of the pendant one moment, and the next three slim chains were shooting out of the rounded bottom of the stone, landing on her belly. She cried out in surprise. After all that heat, the chains were cool. Judan grinned.

"What?" she gasped.

"Your breasts are so pretty, Myrina," he said. "They deserve to be on display."

He plucked a nipple in his thumb and forefinger. She gasped, arching her body up, offering herself to him. He nodded, more to himself than to her and selected one of the chains. Releasing her nipple, he slid a thin hoop over the nub. She tensed in anticipation. Gently, he tugged on the chain, tightening the hoop. She cried out again as fire licked at her, coursing through her system straight to her pussy.

"That's right," he said.

He rubbed her stomach, soothing her. Lulling her into a state of semi-relaxation. He paused once to check the tension of the first chain, then, satisfied, he set to work harnessing her other nipple.

By the time he was finished, her breath came hard and fast. The pressure wasn't painful. Still, she was intensely aware of the tiny hoops and the chains' hold on her. Aware of the constant lick of flame feeding the growing inferno inside her.

He crawled backwards until his head was level with her thighs.

"One more," he told her.

She couldn't help it. She tensed again, imagining where the third and longest chain would go. He adjusted his position, so that now her legs were draped over his thighs, exposing her. To him. The pillow he'd tossed onto the floor earlier was within reach and he grabbed it, lifted her bottom and stuffed the pillow underneath her, displaying her pussy for his viewing pleasure.

And all the while his hands roamed over her heated flesh. Caressing, kneading, exploring. He bent his head low over her body and licked her navel. He had to hold her hips to keep her from rearing up off the floor.

"Do you see this small stone?" he asked holding up the third chain.

There, along its length, glistened a small, round stone. She nodded. Like a jeweler, he fitted the stone into the setting of her navel. He laid the remaining length of chain on her stomach. His fingers tickled her mound.

She rolled her head back and forth, trying and failing to control the spasms that pulsed in her pussy. He'd spoken the truth. Her hands were slick with sweat and she doubted she would have been able to hold onto the poles if his hair hadn't bound her in place. The undersides of her breasts were damp, too, from the constant pressure of the hoops keeping her nipples erect.

Digging her heels against his thigh, she bucked against his hand. His fingers dipped through her curly hairs to part the walls of her labia. She caught her breath and cried out when his thumb scraped across her clit.

"Please," she whimpered, wanting, needing more.

Apparently satisfied she was ready, he lifted the final length of chain. She shook her head, not sure she could accept more of this exquisite torture.

"Show me everything," he said, fitting the final thin hoop over her clit.

A mini orgasm rocked her body. He slid two fingers inside her and her hips immediately bucked against them, her sheath clamping them tight inside her. He held his fingers still, letting her ride out the sudden storm. His free hand continued to caress her, soothe her.

When it was over, he pulled his fingers free. But it wasn't over. Bracing his arms to hold her legs wide, he bent his head and licked the length of her pussy.

She screamed, tried to buck, her arms straining against the restraints. *Too much.* The tension was back, strumming though her veins. Her body cried out for immediate release as if she hadn't just come.

He continued to lap at her juices, careful to avoid the ultra-sensitive nub. His tongue delved deep inside her, mimicking the thrust of a cock. The walls of her pussy clenched, desperate for the hot, hard length of him filling her. Thrusting inside her. And still he continued to enjoy his feast. Bringing her close to ecstasy, but never over the edge.

In her mindless haze, she vaguely realized the little loops around her clit and nipples somehow prevented her final release.

She started begging long before her body went into convulsive spasms. And each time he'd simply whisper two words—"Show me." When her entire body clenched, straining for release, he reared up on all fours, which caused her legs to slide further apart. An offering he didn't seem to be in any hurry to take.

Instead, he crawled on his hands up the length of her body, surveying his handiwork. She melted under his sensuous gaze. Digging her heels against his thighs, she bucked, begging him to take her. He pulled back just enough to prevent her from taking what she wanted.

"My turn," he whispered and bent down to nuzzle her neck.

She groaned when he allowed his cock to dip low enough to scrape against her mound.

"Please."

"Soon." He kissed her collarbone, working his way steadily downward and around the curve of one breast. Then he set to work gently removing the hoop before he sucked the nipple into his mouth, hard.

*Too much.* Her body cried out in pleasure-pain. She was super conscious of the remaining chains and hoops keeping her aroused. Preventing her release.

When he moved to the second breast, she tensed. Anticipating. Waiting. For him. How could one man do this to her? He bent over her, allowing his hot breath to fan her engorged nipple before he touched it with the tip of his tongue.

"Ahh!"

Her breath came hard and fast. Her exquisitely sensitive nipple tightened further against its restraint sending a flare of liquid heat straight to her pussy. The second hoop was off and her nub was in his mouth before she'd recovered. His wet mouth did nothing to douse the flames rising within her.

Slowly. Ever so slowly, he kissed his way down her body, past the curls to the hoop encircling her clit. By now anticipation rode her.

*Please. I need to come so badly. Please. Please. Please.*

He removed the hoop and sucked her clit into his mouth.

She screamed. Her legs would have thrashed violently if he hadn't been holding them down, too. Shock waves surged out across her entire body sending it into total orgasm. Wave after wave after endless wave. She lost all sensory contact.

Each upsurge consumed her and was rapidly followed by the next one.

Minutes, hours, days later, she didn't know and didn't care, the sensations died down until they were only tiny ripples echoing across her body. Boneless, exhausted, she lay on the floor unable to move. Barely able to think.

Judan's face appeared above hers.

"You were magnificent, Little Warrior."

Magnificent. Hadn't she called him that?

"Don't leave."

He had to bend low to catch her words. She tried to shout but only a whisper of sound escaped. She was so limp, so helpless, she couldn't move at all when his hair released its hold on her. Oh-so gently, he gathered her in his arms and carried her to the bed. The last thing she remembered was his body curling around her own. Giving her permission to sleep because he would be there, protecting her.

* * * * *

Myrina woke slowly, reluctant to open her eyes. How could she look around her elegant room without thinking decadence, sensuality, seduction?

Languidly, she stretched her limbs. *Lazybones*. A favorite term of the matron at the orphanage whenever Myrina or some other child was slow to get up in the mornings. But that's exactly how her body felt today.

Lazy and deliciously sated.

Peeking through her eyelashes to the other side of the bed, she discovered it was empty. He'd left her then. But only very recently because she could see the indentation of his big body on the bed. She reached out a hand. The spot was still warm. Just as her body was. Still warm from his touch.

The scent of alam bark mixed with male sweat lingered in the bed with her. She rolled over, savoring the satiny texture of the sheet beneath her skin. A soft moan escaped her lips when the sheet, tangled in her legs, tightened against her pussy.

Sated? She was no such thing. The banked embers from last night's inferno sparked to life. Her hips rocked against the sheet increasing the pressure.

Damn, she needed Judan here with her this morning!

She reached up and cupped her breasts. Both of them ached for his touch. Her thumb and forefinger searched and found her nipple jutting proudly from her areola. The other was the same. Anticipating their submission to him. She pinched and pulled them and her hips rose in answer.

Slowly, she trailed a hand down her rib cage and across her stomach. The bed wasn't the only place where Judan had left his imprint. Maybe he had set out to learn her body, but it was her body that had learned his touch. Her legs parted and her hand dipped lower. Two fingers slid beneath the folds of her labia already slick with her juices. The tiniest brush of her finger against her clitoris forced her to cry out in pleasure-pain. Her entire womb was over-sensitized. Marked as his.

With each stroke the exquisite tension built. She sobbed and her body bowed as the flames fanned higher. It didn't take long. When the orgasm hit she clutched the sheet, burying her mouth against the mattress to muffle her scream.

Myrina pushed herself into a sitting position, shaking her head to clear the grogginess. She glanced at the clock beside her bed. She'd already slept late when she'd woken the first time. After her self-induced orgasm she'd actually dozed off. Since sleeping at all aboard a spaceship was a minor miracle, she wasn't sure how she'd rate dozing. A healthy round of orgasmic sex was the one cure to anxiety-induced insomnia she'd never tried before.

No, that made what had happened last night between her and Judan sound like a prescription cure-all, rather than... She glanced at the rumpled sheets. The outline of his body was still visible. Proof he'd kept his promise and held her all night.

While, incidentally, she'd been aboard a ship traveling at faster-than-light speeds and doing crazy hyperslide stunts.

She scrambled to the edge of the bed. The first thing she saw was the pendant he'd given her last night lying on the side table. He must have removed it after he'd carried her to bed. She picked up the necklace, clutching the teardrop-shaped stone. When she ran her finger around the faceted edge she found the tiny lever that released the chains he'd adorned her with the night before. She was careful not to trigger the catch. Even without the secret compartment, the necklace was an exquisite work of craftsmanship. By far the most beautiful and, without a doubt, the most expensive piece of jewelry she'd ever owned.

*Owned.*

She now owned this necklace. The morning after was a bit late to decide she couldn't accept such a gift. Besides, she'd accepted a lot more than a hunk of stone, gorgeous as it was, when Judan had surrendered himself to her. Yet she was the one who'd been overwhelmed by the primal honesty of his reaction.

Lifting the chain over her head she put the pendant around her neck. The rounded end of the teardrop sat nestled between her breasts. She would wear it today. A gift from her lover and a potent reminder of her gift to him.

Ten minutes later she was showered and dressed in the same pants she'd had on the day before plus a T-shirt. She'd never been one to waste time on the routine chores of daily living when she had somewhere else to be and other things to do. Picking up her towel from the counter, she gave her nearly dry hair another rubdown. Gorgeous—and talented—as Judan's hair was, she preferred easy care. She hung up the towel and turned back to the mirror, then leaned closer for a better look. Sure enough, the dark circles under her eyes really were gone. With quick, light strokes she feathered her hair into some semblance of a style.

142

*Strange.* She turned her head for a better look. She must have Judan's amazing hair on the brain because she could swear she was seeing reddish highlights among the golden-brown.

*Right. Time to quit fantasizing about great sex and get to work.*

She spent the morning in the lab, after a short detour through the deserted galley for her morning meal. This time she focused on Lorre and an intense study of Dakokatan DNA, tracking the changes that had occurred in the dead Outposter until his death. The task was like searching for a needle in the proverbial haystack. Since she'd spent many a summer working on one of her patroness's farms, she knew firsthand how seemingly insurmountable the task was.

But the job absorbed her thoughts and virtually blocked out the minute tremors that vibrated through the floor of the ship when the Speedlite took another space-time jump and then shuddered into the third hyperslide of their trip.

Judan visited her in the lab around midmorning. His eyes lit with pleasure when he saw she was wearing the necklace. Her heart did a crazy flutter when he reached out to hold the pendant and the back of his hand brushed against her. For a split second the push and pull of lust stirred between them, a remembrance of their night together. It was a little crazy, this madness they shared for each other in the midst of a crisis. And Judan must have felt the same way, too, because he gave Myrina—by their usual standards—a chaste kiss hello.

Then he asked for a status report, making the request sound almost routine. Only it wasn't and they both knew it. Each hyperslide took them closer and closer to Hitani. Her time was running out. And with all but the most critical patients off their meds, the Outposters' chances were running out, too, unless she had a solution in place by the time they arrived above the planet.

By midday frustration ate at her optimism. Each time she looked at the data she saw exactly the same information and knew she was missing a vital link. The key that had turned on the steady, intense breakdown of the Outposters' bodies.

Figuratively throwing her hands in the air an hour later, she stalked out of the lab, intending to go to the mess room. Except when she reached the elevator, she rode it all the way up to the observation lounge on the top deck. The one, maybe the only, good thing about being aboard a spaceship was looking at the stars any time of the day. And suddenly she wanted to.

She'd started watching stars when she was little. Not because they were pretty but because they offered innumerable potential avenues of escape from the restrictions of life in an orphanage. She'd planned an imaginary trip through the stars each night for years and never followed the same route twice. A person could get lost among the stars.

When she had finally started traveling in space, her first few times out she'd been like a kid on a thrill ride, never wanting the adrenaline rush to end. It was only after she had gotten lost, just that one time, that she'd learned it was sometimes better not to get what you wished for.

Despite the severe reality check, she still liked stargazing. The sky provided a large enough canvas to puzzle over and work out problems on. She didn't need the numbers and the facts about the Outposters anymore. Her instinct told her she had the pieces in her head. She just needed to figure out how they fit together.

She stepped into the observation lounge as soon as the elevator doors slid open and looked up. Big, black, vast. All she could see through the plexi-bubble was the universe rushing past. She lowered her gaze and turned, taking in the panoramic view.

Chiara stood on the other side of the room, clutching her wig in her hands.

# Chapter Ten

## ❧

"Oh," Myrina said at the unexpected sight of the Communications officer. "Hi, there. I'm sorry. I didn't realize anyone else was here."

"What are you doing here?" Chiara asked.

*Okay. Not the most friendly of welcomes.* And under the circumstances she did not feel obliged to explain. Given the Second's dedication to duty, she might not understand how stargazing would help solve the Hitani crisis.

"Like I said, I'm sorry. I'll leave."

"You shouldn't be here," Chiara said, as Myrina turned to press the button for the elevator.

Myrina frowned, turned back and leveled her best no-nonsense stare at the older woman.

"I beg your pardon? I wasn't aware there were restricted areas aboard the Speedlite." *In fact, I know there aren't because* the Captain *gave me the run of the ship. So, unless the observation lounge was suddenly declared your personal quarters, I can be here if I damn well please.*

The Second blinked. "My English is perhaps not the best," she said, waving her hand in the air. She still looked serious and none too happy. "I did not say you *could* not be here, only that you *should* not be here. I come here every day before the midday meal to do my exercises and I have not yet finished dressing."

Since all her clothes were on, Myrina wasn't quite sure what the woman meant. Then she noticed Chiara worrying the edge of her wig. She couldn't help it, even though she was in clear violation of the other woman's ethnic rights. Curiosity compelled her to raise her eyes and take a second look. Chiara's hair was piled on her head, ready for the wig. It must originally have been a rich, copper color like Judan's, but now it was liberally shot through with white hairs. Quickly, Myrina averted her eyes and turned away, but not before she noticed Chiara studying her necklace. Feeling as though she'd violated some taboo, she apologized for a third time.

"I'm sorry I disturbed you."

She didn't turn around again until the elevator doors had closed. Her chance for quiet contemplation among the stars gone, her stomach strongly suggested she should think about food.

Hylla and Biali were in the mess room when she arrived and, in her humble opinion, they'd been sharing a lot more than food. Although the engineer was considerably cleaner than the last time they'd met, he hastily tucked his T-shirt into the pants he favored over the leggings worn by Judan and his brother. Nor was the navigator's uniform as crisp as the one she'd worn the day before.

Considering Myrina had hardly seen anyone the day before, it was a little disconcerting to be bumping into the crew right and left. At least Hylla's and Biali's greetings were warm and friendly. She poured herself a cup of semi-fresh coffee from the sideboard, evidence that Judan had been here recently, and liberally laced it with *santan* before joining the couple at the table.

Hylla was in the middle of braiding her hair. Although neither she nor Biali wore a wig, Myrina was extra-sensitive about respecting whatever Dakokatan hair custom she'd transgressed with Chiara. Just because the Second's manner had bordered on rudeness—after all she appeared to be gruff with everyone—didn't mean Myrina could ignore her own discourtesy. She might be here to help these people, but she was still a guest.

"Would you prefer if I left?" she asked, gesturing to Hylla's hair. "I don't mean to be disrespectful."

146

"Oh no," Hylla said, her eyes shifting to Biali who grunted his agreement. "You aren't. It just takes a little getting used to, that's all."

Myrina raised her eyebrow at that, but concentrated on her coffee rather than ask. She had no clue if she or Hylla was the one who was supposed to get used to something. Biali must have seen her puzzled expression, though, because he attempted to explain.

"We weren't expecting this to happen," he said.

*Well, that certainly clarifies things, doesn't it?* Given her innate curiosity, Myrina decided to take the plunge.

"You weren't expecting what to happen?" she asked.

This time Biali exchanged glances with Hylla. The look seemed to say, "Your turn to answer this one." Hylla's eyes flickered to Myrina's necklace, then back to the task of fixing her hair. Myrina tried to shut off the slow burn of a blush that threatened to creep up her neck. Evidently in choosing to wear the necklace, she'd become a walking advertisement for her tryst with the Captain. Based on the previous conversation then, it didn't take too many skills to figure out what the crew hadn't expected. She wished she'd at least kept the necklace hidden under her clothes rather than on display.

After she'd finished braiding her hair, Hylla cleared her throat and looked across the table.

*Oh boy, here it comes. And I had to open my big mouth and ask.*

"The *Rakanasmara*, of course," the navigator said. "No one expected it to appear while on a mission. Especially not with a…a foreigner."

Myrina set her coffee mug down before she choked or burned herself. *Rakanasmara*. She'd heard the term before, but couldn't immediately remember where.

"*Rakanasmara*?" she said, half to herself.

Her memory of the conversation with Sonny and Kikki returned at the same time Hylla explained.

"You and the Captain are life partners."

Somehow, some way, Myrina managed to drink her coffee, keep her mouth shut and smile pleasantly until Hylla and Biali left. She couldn't do anything about her accelerated heart rate, though. Or the trouble she had breathing past the lump in her throat. Her appetite was shot, but since her body needed fuel regardless of her emotional confusion, she filled a bowl with nuts and dried fruit. Snack food she could munch on while she did some long neglected research.

Of course, she wasn't going to find the answer to her question by consulting Sonny's data-chip. No, she'd have to go to the source for that one. The source being, of course, the big green guy himself. The question being, of course, why the freaking heck he hadn't informed her of this little complication called *Rakanasmara* between them. A Dakokatan term for what in plain English meant marriage.

Myrina muttered several choice words, courtesy of a Situsian boy she'd grown up with at the orphanage. She had to wipe her hands twice on her pants before her fingers were dry enough to snap Sonny's data-chip into the GCS' port. It didn't take her long to find what she was looking for. Sonora Austen's organizational abilities were legendary and the data she'd compiled on Dakokatan culture was no exception. Myrina clicked the "Mating Rituals" icon and the word *Rakanasmara* flashed onto the screen.

She couldn't read past the definition. *Rakanasmara* wasn't simply a marriage between two Dakokatans. It was a genetically imprinted identification device that could only be triggered by one person. A mate or life partner.

Swift and fierce, an emotional tidal wave swamped her, forcing her to grip the edge of the counter for support. For the longest time she simply stared at the screen, reading and rereading that single word.

*Rakanasmara.*

Unable to contain her agitation, she shoved her stool aside and stood.

*Rakanasmara.*

The notion that she was experiencing a genetically triggered mating signal was ludicrous. Ridiculous. Preposterous. And any other "-ous" words that might apply. Yet, try as she might, she could not deny the "symptoms" associated with the onset of *Rakanasmara.* She studied the list. The instant, heightened awareness, the sensation of electrical impulses across the body and especially to the hair, the almost hypnotic pull — she'd experienced them all.

Damn, her hand — her entire body — was shaking like a piece of paper fluttering to the floor. Abruptly, she sat again before her wobbly legs gave out and she landed on her ass. If this was true, the implications were astonishing.

*If. Hylla and Biali could be wrong... There could be a more rational explanation for what's happening between me and Judan. Like lust. I've been attracted to men before. Why not a tall, green-skinned Dakokatan?*

Only it wasn't the lust part that needed explaining. That she could handle. Heck, she had been handling it right up to and including a full-body orgasm, the like of which she'd never experienced before in her life.

*My life.*

She was here to save a group of stranded Outposters. She was here to do her job. Not come face-to-face with her own damn destiny.

A couple of deep breaths later she stood, shut down the GCS and walked out of the lab. She'd taken care of herself for twenty-nine years. Now that the initial shock had passed, she would damn well handle this situation, too.

But she'd do it in private. A few minutes later she stood in front of the elevator and contemplated her destination. No way was she going to confront Judan on the bridge in front of crew members or worse, roam the ship like some pathetic creature searching for him. Finally she opted for his office, situated next door to his bedroom and two doors down from her own room.

He wasn't there. Not that she'd expected him to be waiting for her. She didn't particularly mind. Unlike most of the Directors' offices at TLC, Judan's actually reflected the personal side of the man, not just the Captain of a Speedlite.

His office was as big as her stateroom, with furniture that tended toward cleaner, less ornate lines. He favored wood and minimal metal accents and appeared fond of water images. Even the walls were painted a light shade of blue, a sharp contrast to the earth tones that dominated the rest of the ship. And the wall behind his large desk was filled with a space view of a large lake bordered by palm trees. His shelves were lined with books—some in English—and a few knickknacks. She recognized a water jug from Uppanat. A rare gift? It must be since the Uppanatians guarded their water vessels as zealously as their wells. In addition to the bank of lights above the lake picture, two cubic-shaped floor-to-ceiling glass tanks adorned the two corners of the office nearest the door. Filled with gently bubbling water, plant life and fish, they were illuminated with powerful beams of light set into the ceiling.

She wandered over to one of the columns and watched the fish for a while. They paid her no attention and she wondered if they were as indifferent to the hyperslides as they were to her.

Deciding she might as well sit down while she waited, she walked over to the chairs near the desk, which was seven feet long, over five feet wide and virtually empty. Shades of her own smaller-scale office at TLC, which was just as neat.

She picked up the single picture frame that adorned the desk top and turned it over to take a look. The frame itself was studded with seashells, continuing the watery theme of the room. Inside was a picture of a smiling boy. He was young with dark brown shoulder-length hair and a dimple in his right cheek. The angle of the picture was such that he appeared to be staring right at her. Or Judan, whenever he sat at his desk. His green eyes were bright with a hint of sun and his smile was one of pure delight. And unabashed love.

Myrina didn't doubt the boy had indeed been looking at Judan when the picture had been scanned. She checked the back of the frame but found no clue to the boy's identity. The only thing she knew for certain was that he wasn't one of Judan's brothers. The boy looked nothing like the dead Outposter or Vand and she didn't think Judan would keep a picture of his eldest brother without also displaying images of the other two.

"That is Zane," a familiar voice said as if he'd heard her silent question.

Myrina spun around, the picture still clutched in her hand. Sure enough, Judan stood just inside the doorway watching her.

"Oh, he must be someone very special to you," she said and could have kicked herself. Surely she could have said something more intelligent rather than stating the obvious.

"Zane is an orphan," he said, meeting her gaze and holding it. "My cousin's child. My mother is raising him."

With care, she placed the picture back on the desk, in part to hide her tumultuous feelings. She was familiar enough with Judan's quirks by now to know that his stark answer and the presence of the picture on his desk hid some deep, special connection to the boy. Yet for all that had passed between them, he hadn't trusted her enough to share. The knowledge hurt and made her wary.

"You have a habit of collecting orphans then?" she asked.

He gave a hoarse laugh, making her wonder if he'd entertained the exact same notion. "Yes, it would seem so," he acknowledged.

Myrina's heart sank. If he saw her as an orphan, and one "to be collected" at that, what did this say about the attraction between them? About his feelings for her?

"Why didn't you tell me?" she asked. That wasn't really what she wanted to know, but it was a place to start.

"Would you have accepted *Rakanasmara* if I had?"

For a man who specialized in enigmatic shifts in conversation, he had a bad habit of being painfully direct. Nor was there anything like hearing him utter that particular word to make it real. A stark fact to be dealt with.

"Dammit," She glared at him, ignoring his answering frown. "Don't you dare answer a question with a question. Why didn't you tell me?"

He strode towards her then, his hair swirling around him, his face an impassive mask. He wasn't giving her a single clue about what was going on inside that head of his.

"This has never happened before, finding a life partner outside our race," he said, coming to stand in front of her, forcing her to look up to meet his gaze. "I thought it possible you would deny what was happening between us."

*I have never denied the attraction, the connection between us.*

"Is that what you think, now? That I'm someone outside your race who wouldn't understand?"

He reached out and rubbed his thumb against the side of her cheek. It took every ounce of willpower to hold her head steady and not lean into his softness. The smoothness of his hands still amazed her, each and every time he touched her, even as her body remembered and yearned for more.

He smiled down at her and for a moment he appeared highly amused. Then he shook his head. "It is a fact, Myrina, that growing up within the Confederacy you are not familiar with Dakokatan customs. The wooing seems to be going well, though."

"The what?" she asked, biting back an astonished laugh.

He hesitated and she tried desperately to sober the grin that threatened the corners of her mouth.

"Wooing," he said. "Dinner dates, flowers and chocolate. Though I didn't think you'd be interested in the last two ideas so I chose Dakokatan rituals instead."

"Which include hot and heavy sex, huh? That's some technique you've got there, Judan Ringa."

A slight frown marred his forehead and she almost regretted teasing him. He must have consulted the TLC database to come up with his archaic ideas of wooing. Which was actually kind of sweet, but still didn't answer her question. If this *Rakanasmara* between them meant he viewed her as some sort of charity case, she wanted no part of it.

"Then you like flowers and chocolate?" he asked, still stuck back on first base.

With a sigh, she nodded. "Wildflowers and dark chocolate," she said, seeing no reason to complicate matters and admit that no man had ever actually wooed her with these items. "As for dinner dates, I like to eat, too. And I'm not complaining about the sex, which has been pretty fantastic, but so far it sounds like we're having an affair."

At the word affair, Judan scowled. "I thought we'd established that already. I want you, Myrina deCarte. We are not having an affair."

"Why not? Hylla and Biali are."

He shrugged, apparently not surprised at all by her revelation. "*They* are having a "cheap thrill" affair. They do not have what we have, Myrina. There is no *Rakanasmara* between them."

"How do you know? They look very happy together."

"Because, Little Warrior, all crew members aboard this ship, now save one, are single. It is a requirement of service before a mission for a crew to gather to determine whether or not they have found their life partner. If so, neither person can serve.

"And before you ask, no, this rule does not apply if life partners meet, as we have, while on a mission."

She laughed and shrugged off his ability to read her objection before she'd voiced it. However there was a bigger issue that went beyond their admittedly mutual captivation with each other that needed to be dealt with.

"Okay, I get it, no affair. But since you didn't tell me about the *Rakanasmara*, what did you expect me to think?"

His hand slid around the back of her neck, holding her fast. His thumb traced the edge of her jaw, sending shivers down her spine. Then he pushed her head up a little so he could look into her face.

"I did not expect a dissection of Dakokatan tradition or my motives," he said.

Perhaps not, but he was back to studying her. Searching her face. For what? Despite his own surprise at discovering the *Rakanasmara* between them, had he guessed her secret, hidden even from herself, when he'd looked into her green eyes?

She grasped his outstretched arm. Immediately several strands of copper hair wound themselves around both their arms, binding them together. She ignored the conspicuous symbolism. She had no intention of backing down. In spite of her years of denial, when confronted with evidence, the truth was too important to back away from now.

"Too bad, because that's what you've got. Judan, don't you realize what this means?"

He threaded his fingers through her hair, gently massaging her scalp.

"Yes," he said, quietly. "I, as you put it, collected one orphan when his parents were killed. Now I've found a second one who's discovered, perhaps not her parentage, but a piece of her heritage. Isn't that right, Myrina?

There it was, the bottom line spelled out. A piece of her heritage.

Myrina had told herself she could handle it, but the revelation came tangled with an instantaneously serious relationship. She slumped against the desk, suddenly weary.

She'd crammed so many facts about the rescue mission inside her brain she hardly had room to cope with the implications of the *Rakanasmara* to her own life. Or her feelings about the discovery.

"Myrina?" He bent and kissed her forehead.

"I'll need to run a DNA scan to confirm," she said, falling back on what she knew best. Her work.

He chuckled. "*Rakanasmara* has come and yet now you want to be the scientist. I'm surprised you never wondered before this and…"

"What? I was literally found on the steps of an orphanage when I was about two years old, Judan. Whoever left me didn't want me anymore, so early on I decided I didn't want to know about them either. Eventually it became a moot point."

"I have struggled with this truth, Myrina." Although his words were gentle his stormy features made her wonder if he didn't want to throttle her unknown ancestor. "I cannot believe a Dakokatan would abandon a child. That is not our way."

"Well, somebody did and I was raised in a Confederacy orphanage. Still, I don't see any other explanation for my having the genetic marker for *Rakanasmara*."

"Then you accept that this is what is between us?" His voice dropped to an intimate register.

Since her left arm was still pinned by his hair, she reached for the pendant hanging around her neck with her other hand. Cradling it in her palm she met his intense gaze.

"I take it that this necklace is part of one of those Dakokatan rituals you mentioned. Part of your, ah, wooing, of me."

He nodded. "I am honored that you chose to wear it today."

His lips brushed hers and he pulled her within the security of his embrace. She welcomed the steadiness of his heartbeat and the warmth of his body. She had, she realized, already accepted Judan Ringa into her life with a speed she never would have thought possible. And yet…

"Judan."

"Yes, Myrina?"

"You're right. Although I probably have Dakokatan genes, I don't know Dakokatan customs, only the Confederacy ones I grew up with."

"That's fine, Myrina," he said, soothing her back with his free hand. "We'll manage."

She sighed and her gaze flicked to the picture frame sitting on his desk.

"Is that what you do with Zane, manage? Fit him in when you have time in your busy schedule. If that's the case, I guarantee he knows he comes in second."

His hand stilled on her back. She even sensed a slight hesitation in his next breath.

"I spend as much time with him as I can when I'm home," he said. "It isn't enough. For either of us."

She lifted her head and stepped back against the desk. He released her, reluctantly, which is more than she could say about his hair, which kept a firm grip on their arms. She didn't dispute the connection, only the strength of it, because she knew if she lifted her arm, his hair would slide away.

"I grew up with not enough," she said, reaching out with her free hand to smooth the wrinkles she'd made in his shirt. "I won't settle for that again."

"What do you mean? I want you, Myrina deCarte, and I am yours for the rest of our lives together. What more is there?"

She suspected that what he wanted and what she needed were two very different things. "What about love, Judan? Or didn't you read up on that when you discovered the art of wooing in the TLC archives?"

To her surprise he nodded. "Yes, I came across the word."

"And?"

"*Rakanasmara* binds us together in a way that can never happen again. I understand what that means. It means you are my life partner, Myrina. I do not understand the word 'love'."

His words were a far cry from a declaration. But at least he'd acknowledged the concept.

*Whoa, girl. Is that what you expected? A declaration? You need to pull back real fast before you get burned. Before you lose your heart.*

She didn't want to concede it was way too late for that.

"I've been attracted to other men before, Judan," she said. Her gaze was steady though she couldn't say the same for her heart. The erratic thumps sounded like a death knell to her dreams.

"The *Rakanasmara* may be a life force to you, but without love it really is just an affair to me. A lot of hormones and pheromones kicking up a storm. The only reason this time is different for me is that in the process I've potentially found a hidden piece of my past."

# Chapter Eleven

**ဢ**

A couple of hours later Myrina was no closer to a solution for saving the Outposters. Heck, she hadn't even seen the inside of the lab since she'd left in search of a few not so simple answers. Basically she'd played hooky with the lives of seventy-seven people. She should be checking DNA. Theirs. Hers.

Way back when she'd first flirted with genetics, she'd entertained the idea of testing herself. In the end she hadn't because what could a double helix tell her that she didn't already know? She'd survived childhood, was healthy and had good job prospects. Oh yes, and she was alone in the world. Nothing new there.

Praying the coast was clear so she wouldn't encounter any other crew members, she'd retreated to the observation deck after leaving Judan's office. She'd been here ever since staring at the stars. Unlike her imaginary childhood adventures, this time she was old enough to realize there were no escape routes. For one thing, experience had taught her she couldn't trust a one of them. She really and truly was stuck on this ship. With a man who didn't understand love despite a little boy's face that proclaimed the emotion loud and clear.

She didn't dare dwell on her own wishes, maybes, or might-haves. She'd lost most of those eight years ago and the loss of one Dakokatan Warlord wasn't going to change that. She'd finish her job and then go home a lot wiser about herself and with the memory of an awesome fling.

Goose bumps marched up her arm the minute the elevator doors swished open. *Crap.* At least this time her personal alarm system had issued a warning. She didn't turn around, giving herself time to school her emotions, which had remained an uncharacteristically jumbled mess since her discussion with Judan.

* * * * *

Thanks to a suggestion from Chiara, Judan finally found Myrina sitting on the floor of the observation deck staring out into space. Since the *Ketiga Bulan* was recycling for another combined space-time jump and hyperslide, the shutters protecting the hull had retracted, exposing the dome of the ship to infinite space.

Myrina pretended to ignore his arrival, but he knew otherwise. *Rakanasmara* could not so easily be dismissed.

He had reluctantly let her go after their confrontation in his office. His selfishness had caused her pain and while he'd wanted nothing more than to comfort her, he was no longer sure he had the right. Besides, she'd needed time alone to deal with the revelations *Rakanasmara* had brought to her life. He hadn't fully understood the implications until then. Because his own Dakokatan heritage was such an integral part of himself, he couldn't imagine a life without a basic knowledge of one's ancestors. And yet, until this afternoon, that was exactly how Myrina had lived. Curious about the world around her, while denying the secrets carried within her own body.

Myrina deCarte was a strong woman. She was used to being alone. And, as she'd told him quite vehemently, looking after herself. But, while he didn't doubt the truth of her words, he refused to believe she preferred it that way. Any person with a scientific mind like Myrina's, who believed in an incomprehensible concept called "love", was searching for a way not to be alone.

Yet, he'd let her go. He hadn't argued with her. Or pointed out the irony of her rejecting the very connection she'd obviously dreamed of finding. Nor had he defended himself against her charge.

It was true. He did not understand the word "love". And he would not pretend and tell her words—even words he knew she longed to hear—without meaning them. Time and time again, he'd told her he wanted her. If she chose not to hear those words for what they meant, he would keep repeating them until she did. She may have demoted the connection between them to the level of human "lust", another word he'd discovered in the TLC archives—but that simply proved she had not done her research. She did not understand *Rakanasmara*.

*Rakanasmara*. The need to be with her. The near constant ache to touch her. And he knew Myrina was experiencing an answering need. It could be no other way once *Rakanasmara* was initiated. But these and other sensations were no mere symptoms of "lust", which reminded him of the tail of a burning comet. An uncontrollable emotion that appeared swift and fierce, burned brightly and was gone just as quickly.

Not *Rakanasmara*. From the onset of *Rakanasmara* their bodies had literally responded to each other. They would continue to adapt and change physically until the final joining created an inseparable bond between them, broken only through death. Hence the term "life partner".

Myrina scrambled to her feet and turned to face him. "Did you try to find me in the lab?" she asked.

"Yes," he said and stood waiting while she walked towards him.

He hadn't allowed his guilt to keep him away for long. Since meeting Myrina he'd come to understand there was something to this wooing business after all. He truly had spoken in arrogance all those months ago when he'd assured Zane he would find someone who wanted them both. He wouldn't be surprised if the Third Moon had heard that statement along with his prayer and deliberately challenged him by sending him to Myrina.

Challenge indeed. At the moment Myrina didn't seem to want him, though she had been drawn to the boy.

He'd experienced an odd sense of joy when he'd found her with Zane's picture. That she should be curious about the boy when she didn't know how Zane had come to be in his life astounded him. Was it arrogance to believe this proved how right the *Rakanasmara* was between them? Her empathy for a fellow orphan was transparent, which was why he'd treaded carefully.

She wouldn't meet his eyes when she reached him. Instead she stared at his shirt. Then her hand closed the short distance between them to settle over his heart. Or, more accurately, within the region of his twin scars. His most visible imperfection. A reminder that great rewards often came hand in hand with failure.

"I'm sorry," she said. "I'm not very proud of myself right now."

"Myrina."

She shook her head, silencing him. "I've never, ever neglected a job before, Judan. But then," she added with a weak smile, "I've never faced a distraction quite as powerful as my past. As you. I need to concentrate on the Outposters. I can't do this…" Her voice trailed off.

The tendrils of heat from her light touch that had warmed his body now cooled. He was not a distraction. *Rakanasmara* was not a distraction. The proof of her heritage encoded inside her was not a distraction. And, in spite of the desperate situation on Hitani, he would not let her dismiss what was happening between them so easily. *Rakanasmara* did the choosing.

"I, too, am sorry, Myrina," he whispered.

"No, Judan…" She started to pull away, but he caught her hand in his.

Regardless of her present opinions, he would not allow her to deny him the right to start fresh by making amends. "I am sorry. I didn't tell you about *Rakanasmara* because I thought it might be easier to introduce you to my customs through using yours. But, while I enjoyed wooing you, it was selfish of me to keep the knowledge of your heritage a secret."

A flash of disappointment crossed her face before disappearing behind a brief nod of acceptance. His heart thudded in satisfaction and he released the breath he'd been holding. *Enjoyed.* He'd used the past tense deliberately to gauge her reaction. She hadn't been pleased. Despite her earlier words, she did want him. And he *was* going to "win" her. On his own merit, without empty words of "love" or the help of a small boy. That is why he'd answered her questions about Zane with basic facts, truths with nothing of his own wishes behind them.

Now that *Rakanasmara* had come, he could claim Zane for his own. He also guessed that if he told Myrina this, she would probably accept the partnership between them for the sake of the boy. And while he'd once thought that was enough, he now realized it would be an empty victory. He could not do that to Zane or Myrina. Or himself. They all deserved better.

He gathered her in his embrace. She melted against him, burrowing her face against his chest with a tiny sigh. Her hair tickled his chest through the thin layer of his shirt, enticing his skin to riot. His hands itched to dip below the obstruction of her shirt and touch her skin. Instead he contented himself with rubbing her back, with the feel of her slender weight against him and her scent teasing his nostrils.

"I'll take you back to the lab so you can get back to work."

"Okay." The single word was little more than a puff of air.

Neither of them moved.

Then slowly, reluctantly, she lifted her head. But instead of stepping away from him, she stood and stared in rapt fascination at her arms, which were settled along his own.

"Your hair," she murmured. Twisting her right hand, she fingered a few strands. "It seems to like me, a lot."

Once again his locks had wrapped themselves around their arms, binding them together.

"Yes," he said.

"And it's the oddest thing. Every time I look at it, I see a different color, as if your hair was streaked."

"It's part of *Rakanasmara*."

"What?"

How did he explain without scaring her off? He shrugged. "As *Rakanasmara* grows stronger, hair color changes."

"Hum." She sounded distracted. Deep in thought. "And the liking part?"

Judan found it difficult to maintain such a casual level of conversation when all he wanted to do was kiss her, take her back to his room and… He shrugged. "Yes, it likes you a lot. Hair is a sexually attractive feature among Dakokatans, which is why I hid it under a wig the first time you saw me."

"Yet the rest of the crew don't wear wigs. Only Chiara."

"They know about the *Rakanasmara*, Myrina, and so they accept you. Amongst ourselves, Dakokatans leave our hair on display and simply tie it back. Chiara doesn't mean to be rude, she is just very conservative. Once *Rakanasmara* starts the attraction is enhanced, so I released my hair from its bindings. That's one reason Dakokatans wear long hair."

Myrina looked up at him then, a little pucker forming in the middle of her brow. "My hair is short."

"Yes," he whispered and bent to kiss away the concern. "Don't worry, I find it very, ah, attractive. It means I can do this." He slid his hands up her back and neck and into the soft curls of her hair, spreading his fingers and running them with gentle caresses along her scalp.

She arched closer to him and her eyes wide with desire. A wave of pleasurable satisfaction hit him, hard.

"You see," he whispered, intent on persuading her of what was happening between them. "In every way you respond as a Dakokatan would. The final mating will be soon."

She shuddered at the promise in his words, even though nothing was settled between them.

"No fair," she said.

Her own hands traced a path up to his broad shoulders. Her fingers spread through his hair and he bit back a groan, wondering how much longer he could last without the final mating. Then the fingers stopped moving. He refocused his gaze and saw she was frowning again.

"Myrina?"

"Shh," she commanded. Her voice had lost its dreamy quality with that single command. She sounded all scientist.

He stilled. Waited while she ran her fingers through his hair again and again.

"Damn it to hell!" she said, her voice loud enough to echo around the room.

"Myrina?"

"Damn it to hell." Her voice had softened, but he could still sense the energy bubbling up inside her.

To get her attention, he repositioned his hands on either side of her face, forcing her head round to look at him.

"Myrina. What's…"

"It's the hair." She cut him off without hearing a word he'd said.

"What?"

"Come on, we need to go to your brother. He left us a clue."

* * * * *

The puzzle pieces tumbled into place as Myrina marched through the doors of the Medical Clinic, Judan at her side. The almost lethargic confusion that had fogged her brain for the last few hours had dissipated as if a gust of wind had blown the clouds away, revealing blue sky. Even Judan's proximity created little more than a hum of excitement, enhancing the adrenaline rush pumping through her system but no longer having the power to sidetrack her thoughts.

The answer had been, literally, right at her fingertips all along. From the moment she'd walked into Fenton's office and felt that first tingle across her scalp. Staring her square in the face since her second meeting with Judan, when she'd gazed in gawky fascination at his hair. She couldn't quite believe it was that easy.

It wasn't, of course.

All she had at the moment was her finely honed instinct in search of evidence that would prove her theory. A probable answer, but no guarantee of a solution. Yet. Which is why she'd kept her mouth shut during the elevator ride down to the clinic.

Of moderate size, the Medical Clinic, situated across from the science lab she'd been using, was decorated in the standard earth tone decor. A smaller, separate area at the rear housed the morgue.

She was almost across the room when she realized that Vand was sitting at one of the data consoles. He obviously hadn't expected to be interrupted, least of all by her, because his blond hair hung loose around his shoulders. She immediately veered from her original course and headed straight for him. With a quick, questioning glance behind her, Vand hastily pulled his hair back, away from his face.

"Stop," she ordered.

Startled, he released his hold on his hair, which tumbled down his back. With a nod of thanks, she reached out and threaded her fingers through a lock of his hair. He shifted restlessly under her touch, but she ignored him. Vand was Judan's brother. Lorre's brother. Another genetic link.

"Myrina!"

She glanced over her shoulder. Sure enough Judan was right behind her. And severely unhappy she was openly admiring Vand's unbound hair. He had, quite correctly, assumed she'd been talking about Lorre when she'd told him his brother had left a clue. But she couldn't let taboos surrounding Dakokatan hair dictate a chance to decipher the Hitani problem. Or, more importantly, find a solution for the Outposters.

Releasing Vand's hair, she whirled to face him. Standing toe-to-toe with him, she said, "I'm going to touch Lorre's hair, too. Are you going to tell me off the way you did in deMorriss' office?"

"What?" he said. Behind her, Vand barked out an incredulous laugh.

"Remember?" she said. "*Tak tahu* something, something." She gestured wildly to fill in the blanks.

A wry smile touched his lips and he shook his head. "*Tak tahu adat mati,*" he said. "I suppose I do owe you an apology for that. I claimed you didn't have a proper respect for the dead."

"Oh, so you weren't swearing?" She dropped her hand. "You were defending your brother."

"Disappointed?"

She shook her head. How could she be disappointed in a man who had actual principles and lived by them?

"I'm sorry about Lorre," she said. "I meant no disrespect, then or now, but my focus is on the living. They're the ones I can help."

"Fine, Little Warrior," he said, with a slightly amused look on his face. "You do what you have to."

"With Lorre?"

He nodded.

"With you?"

His eyes blazed wide with surprise, but he didn't hesitate. "Yes," he said.

"With Vand?"

This time his features sobered and he didn't answer right away.

"Or are you afraid of a little competition?"

They both knew what she was asking and that her question really had nothing to do with Vand. Had he really meant what he'd said the other day about the pilot turned politician needing the scientist? Trusting the scientist. Trusting her. Trusting that she wasn't being capricious with Dakokatan customs or the Outposters' lives.

"If this is about the Outposters, I'll help you," Vand said. The determination in his voice was laced with a hint of his customary bravado.

Myrina turned back to Vand. He hadn't touched his hair. Despite his bold actions, though, he didn't look completely comfortable. His gaze skipped between her and Judan, suggesting he was waiting for Judan before making his final decision.

"Yes and thanks," she said.

Seconds later Judan's thumb shoved aside the edge of her shirt. His index finger traced a path along her collarbone, effectively drawing her attention back to him. *Damn the man.* Even with her systems on high alert, his touch melted her bones.

His fingers curled around her shoulder. Not painfully, but with a definite urgency. It was the only part of his body that betrayed his emotions because his face remained an impassive mask. After another moment, he nodded.

"Thank you," she whispered for his ears alone, then turned to face Vand.

"Are you willing to help me?" she asked, nodding toward the back of the room.

His features tightened, but he nodded.

"Good," she said. "I'll need three evidence packs, one for each of you."

Judan followed them both into the smaller room where they stood facing a square block of four separate compartments set into the wall. The neutral beige tones made the room seem devoid of warmth. She hadn't noticed the starkness the last time she'd visited and wondered at her sudden awareness today. Was she picking up vibes from the two men with her? She tried to shrug off the bizarre notion, yet a little voice told her she'd at least tapped into Judan's emotions.

Both men visibly stiffened when she pressed the button on the control panel. The lower right compartment door opened and the slab holding Lorre's body automatically slid out. She bent over the dead man's head. There, quite visibly, were strands of white hair interspersed with the reddish blond.

"Chiara's hair is turning white," she said, striving for a conversational tone. Neither brother so much as blinked at her insider's knowledge of what lay under the Second's wig.

"She's the oldest crew member," Judan said. He'd reverted to a monotone and his hands were fisted at his side, sure signs he was struggling to compose himself.

She wouldn't put Chiara much past forty-five. Not very old by most standards. "So it's common for Dakokatans' hair to turn white as they grow older?"

She'd already donned a pair of thin, sterile gloves and set to work separating the strands of hair, isolating a sample of a white one. Behind her she heard Vand mutter a series of words she was sure were Dakokatan expletives.

"No," Vand said. "Usually only when *Rakanasmara* ends after one life partner dies."

"Or," Judan said, his eyes on Lorre, "When *Rakanasmara* doesn't come. Is that what you think?"

So Chiara was losing, maybe already had lost, her chance for *Rakanasmara*. Myrina placed the strand of Lorre's hair in the marked evidence bag Vand handed her. She glanced up when he handed her a second bag containing one long blond strand, root intact. His hair was neatly braided behind his back.

She looked over at Judan. He'd guessed her working hypothesis, but she wasn't prepared to admit it just yet. Silently, she nodded toward the third evidence bag. He looked solemn. Grim. Her heart ached at the grief mirrored so clearly in his eyes for the loss of a beloved brother. She didn't understand her own emotions. Sympathy, yes. She'd experienced that many times during her years on the job. But empathy? She'd never had any brothers, sisters, a mother, father, cousins. Anyone she could truly mourn. Yet the hollow sensation in her stomach told her this time she wasn't imagining the connection. She felt Judan's pain.

He reached up, yanked a strand of hair from his head and dropped it into the evidence bag Vand held open for him. She collected the third bag with a nod of thanks.

Judan caught her arm, stopping her exit before she'd stepped five paces outside the tiny room.

"I want those people off Hitani, Myrina. But I also want to know why, so I can make sure something like this doesn't happen again."

"I have to go to the lab and do some tests," she said. That was all she would say or could tell either of them at the moment. Because, if her hypothesis was correct, it might well be impossible to save seventy-seven people who needed a genetic trigger to leave the hostile planet alive.

# Chapter Twelve

ఈం

Myrina ignored the fresh blast of cool air that shot out of the elevator's vents above her head. The ship's environmental control had dimmed the lights hours ago and had begun cleaning the recycled air. By rights she should be sleepy. Before she'd left the lab a few minutes ago, she'd tipped her head back and squeezed some drops into her itchy eyes. But other than a little blurry vision, she felt alert and edgy.

When she reached the observation deck, the elevator doors swished open revealing an endless expanse of black space dotted with light. The Speedlite's propulsion system was in recycle mode too, and she hadn't even noticed. Spotting a twinkling star, she automatically plotted a path to the next bright light. An old habit. Except she didn't know if she was trying to head home to TLC or onward to Hitani or to the Dakokatan homeworld. The world her grandparents had abandoned. In addition to the tests she'd run on the three brothers, she'd checked her own DNA and tracked the changes wrought by *Rakanasmara*. In the process she'd identified the relationship of her Dakokatan ancestors, but still knew nothing else about them. Least of all why they'd left Dakokata or how she in turn had come to be abandoned at a Confederacy orphanage years later.

She stepped out into the room. Off to the left three men sat together, deep in conversation. She'd found Judan in the last place she'd thought to look.

On cue Judan's head snapped up. In the dim light, his laser green eyes drew her to him like a signal flare. Her blood stirred and heated, responding without a nanosecond of resistance. She smoothed her hands against her rumpled pant legs, aware of the growing ache in her breasts and the moisture gathering in her pussy.

Her body's betrayal was a supreme irony. If the tests she'd just conducted had taught her anything, it was that *Rakanasmara* could not be easily ignored. Yet, when they'd met here this afternoon, she'd definitely shut the imaginary door in Judan's face. And tried to ignore the impact *Rakanasmara* was having on her and on her relationship with him, despite the revelation connecting it to her unknown ancestry.

The not-so-simple truth of the matter was, she'd grabbed hold of whatever excuse she could to back away. She'd survived a childhood filled with intangibles and uncontrollables and she'd vowed to never allow that kind of chaos in her life again. Once she'd earned a scholarship to university, she'd remained totally focused on her studies, on her work and on science. In her lab she controlled destiny and transformed intangibles into concrete results.

She glanced at the sky again. Someone out there was having a good laugh at her expense, because whether she liked it or not, *Rakanasmara* was changing her life. While she'd run the tests and double-checked the results, she'd had time to come to terms with that reality and make some decisions.

No more backing away or slamming doors. She'd never been much good at fooling herself. The moment she'd gone to Judan's room two nights ago and stayed, she'd accepted that something was happening between them even if she hadn't been able to put a name to it yet. It was downright impossible to fool the scientist within her. Tests had proven her Dakokatan ancestry. She straightened her shoulders and kept walking towards the men.

Judan stood up, silent except for the question blazing in his eyes. Biali regarded her with a keen, thoughtful gaze. He's waiting for an answer too, she thought, then realized how idiotic that was. Of course he was waiting, as were Chiara and Hylla, wherever they were. No one would sleep tonight until she'd announced her findings. Vand had his back to her, but as soon as he heard the door swish closed, he twirled around in his chair to face her. His own green eyes, so like Judan's, flared with barely suppressed excitement.

"Is it the *Rakanasmara*?" he asked.

"Yes," she said, relieved that in his rash enthusiasm he hadn't asked her whether or not she could save the Outposters.

"What did you find?" Judan asked, his voice deep and calm.

She admired his composure, even if it was just an act. She was no longer sure where she stood with him. Did he still want her? She hoped so, at least physically, since she was about to proposition the man for all the wrong reasons.

"More than our hair changes during *Rakanasmara*," she said.

"I know," Judan said.

In fact, since *Rakanasmara* had been triggered, their DNA had undergone a metamorphosis. Was continuing to create a uniquely compatible signature. Would continue to mutate until the final phase of *Rakanasmara* was completed. And that was the good news.

"What about the Outposters?" Vand asked.

Reluctantly, Myrina shifted her gaze to the younger man. She rubbed her hand against her pant legs again. She was used to presenting her findings to a group, but this time was different. For one thing, her objectivity was shot to hell. For another, she didn't like having her personal life exposed under a microscope. She'd much rather say what she had to say to Judan without an audience.

She'd much rather not have to say anything at all.

"Hitani doesn't just sustain its indigenous life forms," she said. "It actively nurtures them. Because the Outposters are all single, their reproductive ability is dormant, hence the planet's hostile reaction."

Vand's chair squeaked under him. "They'll remain dormant until *Rakanasmara* occurs."

She nodded.

"What do we do?" Biali asked in the silence that followed.

Myrina glanced at Judan. She knew that he, like the other two men, was struggling with the problem of finding seventy-seven as yet unknown life partners for the stranded Outposters. Impossible. Unless he accepted her alternate solution.

"I think I can simulate the genetic mutations that are activated during *Rakanasmara*. A partial test scenario I ran strongly suggests the planet will back off its attack if it believes the Outposters are experiencing *Rakanasmara* and entering a fertility cycle."

"And they'd be able to leave Hitani safely?" Judan asked.

"Yes," she confirmed. "I'm fairly certain they'd be safe, once the simulated genetic code begins to mutate."

*Tell him, you coward. Just tell him and get it over with.*

"What do mean you're fairly certain?" Vand asked. "We'll be arriving at Hitani tomorrow. Didn't you complete the test program?"

*Well crap. Now you have to tell him. Straight out. Just say what you have to say and...* "We need to complete the final *Rakanasmara* ritual before I can run the full test," she told Judan, while studiously avoiding the incredulous looks on the other two men's faces.

Without being asked, Biali dragged Vand toward the elevator, leaving her alone with Judan. He turned away from her as soon as the men disappeared behind the elevator doors.

"You call it a simulation." His voice carried no warmth. It was as cold and clinical as her explanation had been. "What happens to the Outposters once they've left Hitani. Will they be denied a true *Rakanasmara*?"

"No," she said. "The simulation will last for approximately seventy-two hours to allow their bodies to adjust to the mutations and begin self-healing. After that the effects should wear off with no aftermath."

He turned back to face her. "Over a millennium of Dakokatan tradition is nothing more than the reaction of a few pheromones and hormones that can be turned on and off. Is that what you're saying, Doctor?"

From his tone, he undoubtedly saw her as a cold-blooded alien. His facial features were stark and unyielding with none of the softness towards her she'd detected this past day. Even his hair was reluctant to seek her out. Several strands hovered between them, but didn't make contact. So, she'd lost him, now. Not that she'd ever believed she'd really had him.

She probably deserved the contempt ringing in his voice, too. She should just take it and keep her mouth shut. Except there were seventy-seven lives at stake. And, once the *Rakanasmara* was complete, she and Judan would be the only two people immune to Hitani's defenses. The only two who could safely go down to the planet's surface and administer the antidote to the Outposters.

"Look," she said. "I didn't ask for this solution." Hadn't wanted to discover just how complicated her life had become in a short forty-eight hours.

"The solution where we have to fuck each other so our DNA will finish its mutation and you can complete the test scenario. Is that the solution you mean?" he growled. "Or did I misunderstand what you said earlier?"

"No," she said, looking him right in the eye. "You didn't misunderstand."

She wasn't even shocked he'd used the word fuck. He'd undoubtedly consulted a dictionary and would claim he was using the term correctly. And he'd be right. This wasn't about wanting each other or needing love. Bottom line, they had to fuck each other to save seventy-seven other people.

"That's what I thought," he said. "Congratulations, Doctor. You've managed to reduce what's happening between us down to the level of a science experiment. Come on."

"Where are we going?"

He gripped her arm gently enough, but she didn't even try to resist when he walked them to the elevator. He was eight inches taller, quite a few kilos heavier and furious. What's more, he'd managed to make her job and what they now had to do sound sleazy. And while she could, justifiably, protest the former, she couldn't argue the latter assessment.

"To your quarters, where do you think?"

"My quarters?" She pulled out of his grasp as the elevator door opened. "Now just a damn minute."

"Get in, Doctor."

She got in. "Cut the Doctor crap, Judan. If we're going to fuck we should at least be on a first name basis, don't you think?"

No response. Which made her even madder.

"Why my quarters. Why didn't we just do it on the observation deck and get it over with?"

If he wanted sleazy, she'd give him anywhere except a bedroom. Of course, under the right circumstances and with the right person, the observation deck would be a wildly romantic place to make love. But then, since he didn't understand the word love, he obviously didn't qualify as Mr. Right. The elevator doors slid open and he marched her down the hall.

"Perhaps I don't want to get it over with," he said, stopping outside her room. "Invite me in, Myrina."

"What?" He expected an invitation into her room to, what? Fuck her in the name of science. This had gone way past the awkwardness and embarrassment she'd envisioned.

"This was your idea. Invite me into your room so we can fuck, Myrina."

*Like hell she would.* "Listen, Judan, let's get one thing straight. This was not *my* idea. This was the, yes, scientific solution I found when I ran the test scenarios. I'm sorry if it offends your sensibilities. This isn't exactly how I conduct my—"

"Affairs?"

"Your word, not mine," she said.

Talk about ironic. He was throwing everything he could back at her. Making the past couple of days together sound cheap and ugly, after she'd spent agonizing hours in the lab face-to-face with the reality of the genetic code for *Rakanasmara* embedded within her DNA. From her conception her unknown parent had gifted her with the ancestral marker.

She'd had no choice in the matter and, if she hadn't met Judan, might never have known of its existence. She'd never really had a choice whether to accept or reject *Rakanasmara*. It simply was. No, her real choice was what to do about it. What to do with Judan.

And now it seemed he was taking that choice out of her hands, too. She wanted to hate him for diminishing their time together, but she couldn't. Hadn't she done the same? How must he have felt when she'd pushed him away?

"The door's open."

She walked into her room without a backward glance, only to feel trapped moments later when the door swished closed. Judan was in the room with her.

"Pour me a glass of spring water," he said. Commanded.

She remembered they'd drunk spring water the first night they'd met in his room and he'd backed her against the door. She wasn't interested in initiating another Dakokatan ritual. Not now.

"Get your own damn water," she said, rounding on him. "Better yet, you can turn around and walk right back out again. I don't want to fuck you." *I want to make love.*

*Well crap.* Where had that idiotically impossible wish come from? From the place that remembered the teasing, the urgency, the devotion they'd each shown to the other's needs and the ultimate surrender. His. And hers. None of those feelings were in this room right now.

"Do you know what the final *Rakanasmara* ritual involves?"

*Double crap.* Instead of walking out of an embarrassing situation, she'd walked straight into the most uncomfortable topic she could think of. How was she supposed to answer? The Dakokatans might not make love, but she was sure they did a lot more than fuck. She knew firsthand they did, because she'd experienced it. Besides, since he'd asked the question the ritual had to involve more than basic biology.

"I'm sure you'll tell me." Her tone was all false bravado. She was at an uncharacteristic disadvantage and they both knew it. Everything she did know about *Rakanasmara* she'd learned from Judan, because she'd never gone back to study the information on the data-chip.

He stood facing her, all green skin and stark features. An intimidating presence that dominated the room, dwarfing her and her meager possessions. He looked every inch a *Ktua*, a leader of his people.

"The man entices his woman to his bed with the promise of his seed begetting the children they both want." His voice was rough, harsh even, and he turned away once he'd told her.

The blood drained from her face, leaving her feeling light-headed. She took a step back, but her feet had lost their coordination and she stumbled against the desk. She clung to it, steadying herself. Here she'd finally started to believe and now it turned out *Rakanasmara* really had been a sham after all.

"I...I can't." Her denial caught in her throat, strangling the words.

He whirled, a frown marring his rugged features. "You've announced your intention to fuck me for the sake of science. What do you mean you can't?"

The first time she'd ever told anyone and he'd misunderstood her. His anger didn't make what she had to say any easier.

"I'm sterile," she said. "I can't have children."

"Eight years ago." It was a statement, not a question.

She nodded, barely noticing that his voice had sounded halfway normal. So he'd wondered about the source of her anxiety attacks after all. He'd expected her to do her job despite the anxiety, but he hadn't really forgotten the issue.

"Tell me what happened."

Just like that. As if the story was so easy to tell. She'd only ever told Dr. Smith. And now Judan had made an educated guess. He wanted to know.

Why should she tell him anything?

A thin line of perspiration broke out along her forehead. To prove what she'd known all along. That he couldn't— didn't—really want her.

"A group of us were returning from a field assignment when we ran into trouble. We were able to send a distress signal before we crash landed. The planet hadn't been studied, not properly, but our initial test showed it could sustain life. Our lives."

He was listening to the bare facts of her story as if she were weaving the most fantastical tale instead of a nightmare. The elation that all twenty-two of them—students, teachers and crew—had survived the crash had been short lived.

"We soon realized we were in big trouble. The planet didn't like being invaded—that's how it interpreted our crash—and attacked with full force to drive us out. We couldn't leave without a functioning ship, of course, so we were stuck. Had to make do. The weather patterns shifted

178

rapidly. We barely found enough shelter and warmth from the storms, but they weren't our biggest problem.

"By the time a rescue ship arrived, the winds were carrying a plague. Evacuation began immediately, but three of us didn't make it off in time."

The full irony of her story hit Myrina. Just this afternoon she'd told Judan and Vand they couldn't possibly have been all-knowing and were, therefore, not responsible for Lorre's death. Yet she'd blamed herself for years for the consequences of her act of heroism. She'd chosen to stay on that planet longer than nearly everyone else. She'd chosen to give her place in line to the next person and the next and the next. Spending so much damn energy caring for everyone else she forgot about herself.

"The next thing I remember I woke up in a hospital bed. I was the only one of the three to survive." Surprisingly, the intense pain she expected materialized instead as a dull ache. As Dr. Smith had promised, time and distance had lessened the bitter memory. "Parker was the one to tell me I would regain perfect health, except... I was sterile."

A spasm of pain crossed Judan's face as she finished her story. Myrina bit back a cry of anguish, forcing herself to turn away so she wouldn't have to see his rejection so clearly.

"No. Don't think that." His own hoarse cry seemed so close she jumped at the sound of it.

In the next instant she was in his fierce embrace.

"Don't you know I experience your pain?" He pulled her closer.

*Damn the man.* His touch made her yearn for this, for the safety he instinctively offered. It wasn't fair to come so close and... If she'd learned anything by now it was that life wasn't fair.

He tipped her chin up. "Everything will be all right," he said.

She shook her head. "Until today I never had a past," she said. "Eight years ago I lost the chance to have a family of my own."

Judan had lost a brother. Tragic, yes, yet for a time he'd at least had Lorre in his life. Despite their differences, he had Vand with him to share his grief. And back home another brother and a mother and a small boy with whom he could share memories. So many people, while she had never had one. And one twist of fate had robbed her of even the option of giving and sharing life with someone who was truly a part of her. All she had was this life, right here, right now and she'd blown it.

"I can't do this," she said. "I've had casual, um, relationships with men before but not like this. I won't do it like this."

"I know," he whispered. "This isn't exactly how I expected my first time to be, either."

"What?" Startled, she pushed him away. She couldn't possibly have heard correctly. He stepped back but still kept his hands resting lightly on her arms. "You mean you've never…" She stopped, at a loss for words.

"Actually had sex with a woman before? No."

"But…" She stopped again, trying to wrap her mind around what he was saying. "So you're trying to tell me you've only…" What was she going to say? He'd obviously engaged in oral sex before, except even then he'd admitted no woman had ever touched *him*.

"Myrina," he whispered her name, refocusing her attention on him. "Like you, I've had cheap thrill affairs before." He paused, quirked a smile and shrugged. "But none of them was *Rakanasmara*, so I waited."

*Triple crap.* Now she definitely wasn't going to bed with him. He'd waited. Actually saved himself. For the woman with whom he would share *Rakanasmara*, who would be his life partner. The woman whom he could entice into his bed and give children to.

And what had she done?

Told him he had to fuck her. She'd made it sound exactly like a damn science experiment. She would not do that to him. He would just have to wait a little longer. For what or whom, she wasn't exactly sure, since he would only ever share *Rakanasmara* with her. But she ignored that complication.

"We can't complete the ritual. I can't give you children. I can't give you what you want."

The muscles in his jaw ticked. She thought about backing away, but, before she had a chance, he grabbed her and hauled her up on her toes. His green eyes flashed with frustration. "You have no idea what I want."

*I thought you wanted me.* She blinked. Had she really expected him to repeat those three words? To declare himself. To reassure her.

"I need to take a shower," she said and pulled away. Maybe if she scrubbed hard enough she could cleanse away some of her guilt. "You know your way out."

But, once the door closed behind her, she slid to the ground and hugged her knees close to her chest.

*If the job is so easy, find out what's wrong, impress the man and get sent back.* She should have followed Fenton deMorriss' advice, except the job hadn't proven so easy after all.

She was glad she'd told Judan about the accident and set the record straight. She was glad she'd walked away rather than have him think she really would fuck simply for the sake of science. She was miserable.

Weary and dejected, she stood and stripped off her clothes. Leaving them in a pile, she walked across the floor and stepped into the rounded shower stall. She rested her hand against the opposite wall and bowed her head. The warm, cleansing steam that shot out of a series of vents set into the wall massaged her sore muscles from all angles but couldn't erase the pain.

She was a damn fraud. She hadn't been out in the field in eight years and in all that time she'd arrogantly believed she had all the answers she needed in her lab. How was she going to save seventy-seven other people when she couldn't even rescue herself?

She turned at the soft squeak of the shower door sliding open and there he stood magnificently naked, his hair crackling like a living flame around him.

"Myrina."

"Oh, Judan."

His name on her lips was little more than a cry of need. Damn the hormones and pheromones and genetic triggers that worked so superbly. Damn customs and rituals. Damn her weaknesses and limitations. Her resistance to him was zilch, nil, nada. She simply couldn't say no. Didn't want to, despite the imminent danger to her heart.

He stepped inside the stall, closing the door behind him. Instantly, steam filled the small compartment again. Turning into his embrace she was caught in a firestorm. The green blaze in his eyes cut through all her doubts. If there was one thing that was perfectly true, perfectly clear about this relationship, it was that at least on this level Judan Ringa wanted her.

His mouth descended and captured hers. The *Ktua* campaigning for her surrender. His hunger was a live, devouring entity. His tongue plunged into her mouth, demonstrating the one act they had yet to share together. Her resistance all but shattered and she gave him what he asked for.

After two nights at the mercy of his exquisitely talented hands and mouth and hair, her body was primed to respond. She arched against him, melting under their mutual body heat. Her nipples, taut and aching, were crushed against his chest.

And, when his hand ran the length of her spine, pulling her hard against his fierce erection, her pussy wept.

Yet, even as she gave herself to him, she demanded a piece of him. Just as insistent, she dueled for a taste, a touch, anything she could get her hands on. Hands. Hers slid up his arms. Got no further than his shoulders and hung on for dear life when he began trailing kisses along the edge of her jaw.

*Sweet heavens.*

Each brush of his mouth sent a trail of fire straight to her womb. Ravenous, she bent to kiss his shoulder, gorging on the taste of him. That unique, desalinated flavor of Dakokatan skin. Intoxicated. That's what she was. Inebriated by the large sample of male Dakokatan flesh. She traced the twin lines of scar tissue.

Still, much as she wanted to, she couldn't totally surrender to him. "Judan," she whispered against his skin.

He pulled his head back to look at her, his features suddenly sober. And yet, there was no mistaking the banked lust or the deep desire etched in the rugged lines of his face. The wanting was still there, still as powerful, still as compelling. He made a fiercely intense lover, this Dakokatan man with the mane of wild hair.

"I want you, Myrina. For tonight let that be enough."

# Chapter Thirteen

ജ

By the Third Moon, if Myrina said no, he'd go mad.

If he didn't bury his cock deep inside her this eve, he'd go mad.

Undoubtedly he already was mad because he'd done his best to drive her away, even while his body had screamed at him to accept her cheap thrill offer.

Would it have been so bad to take what he could get? It would be easy enough to do so even now. She was in his arms, her naked body pressed against his. Her eyes wide with indecision.

A groan caught in his throat. No, he couldn't do that to her. She had to tell him yes or no.

He hardly dared to breathe as he waited. Wanted. More than he'd ever wanted anything in his life. Because those pale green orbs confirmed that, despite her initial offer, his Little Warrior had a conscience. Whatever happened between them tonight would not be a fuck for the sake of science.

She sighed and pressed a little closer. His hands roamed across her back, pulling her a little tighter within his embrace. Offering her the safety he'd neglected to give her earlier in his arms. In spite of her strength of purpose, she was delicately made. The top of her head barely reached his collarbone and his hands easily encircled her waist. He barely felt the weight of her head resting against his chest.

She was his. His to protect and he'd failed miserably.

Sweat trickled down his back and the front of his chest. He wanted to blame it on the shower's steam, but knew it would be a lie. Her hand reached up between them and flicked his hardened nipple. A growl rumbled in his throat and he fought for control.

When she flicked his nipple for a second time, her stomach rubbed against his engorged shaft. He closed his eyes, but it was no use. The smell of her skin, her touch, she herself unleashed his sexual energy. From deep inside him the energy core raged to life, shooting its heat straight through his cock. The bulbous head pressed hard against her as it grew. The tiny hairs covering her stomach tickled and teased the sensitive hole as it expanded to double its size. His balls pulled tight and he shuddered.

Her tongue, slightly rough and warm, licked his chest. "Show me, Judan Ringa," she whispered. "And for tonight I'm yours."

His body instantly obeyed her command and he shot pre-cum onto her stomach with a hoarse cry. She trembled against him and his nostrils flared as he caught her answering scent.

He bowed his head and hugged her tightly against him, not caring that his essence coated both their bodies. With a tiny moan of pleasure, she rested her head against his chest, her hand covering his heart. He kissed the top of her head.

She'd come to him as the scientist with a solution and he'd reacted in anger. Hurt that she'd once again found a way to shut him out. And scared that maybe, after all, she was right. What if the bond between them was as fake as the *Rakanasmara* simulation the Outposters were going to experience tomorrow?

He couldn't accept that. Any more than he was willing to accept that his anger had cost him. That instead of winning, he'd lost Myrina.

Uncertainty rode him, but, for tonight he would take what he could get.

Steam pounded against their bodies, washing away the last of the tension between them. Mist rose from the floor, fogging the glass door and enclosing them in their own world. This moment.

He needed to appreciate it. Enjoy her. He needed to…

Push her away from him. "Turn around, Myrina."

"What?" She lifted her head, looking a little dazed, and frowned up at him.

"Turn around."

"But…"

She sputtered a protest, only he wasn't listening. His mini-ejaculation had only primed his cock. Still as hard as a meteor it jutted proudly toward its destination. After days and nights of wanting her, he wouldn't last much longer. Especially when each of her sighs and moans of pleasure fanned his skin and heated his blood. And her soft caresses sent tiny shock waves through his system. For the sake of his sanity, he had to prevent her from touching him until he'd buried himself deep inside her.

But therein lay the challenge. Unlike a Dakokatan woman who knew better than to inflame a man's passion in the heat of *Rakanasmara*, his Little Warrior seemed determined to instigate a riot. She craved his skin, touching and tasting him at every opportunity. And challenging him for her right to do so.

She licked her lips and he remembered the hot, wet feel of her mouth on his cock, sucking him dry.

Enough.

Threading his fingers through her hair, he hauled her up onto her toes. Caught off balance, she gasped and her hands came to rest on his shoulders. He shook his head, bemused.

"Tonight you are mine. Remember?" he asked.

Silently she nodded.

"And you trust me to bring us both pleasure."

Another nod.

"Then turn around."

She swallowed, hard, and her mouth opened. An invitation to kiss her again, perhaps, but one he'd have to forgo for the time being. His cock nudged the silky hair hiding her yoni and wept for more. He brushed his lips across her forehead and set her down.

His anger had hidden his fear. It had also blinded him to the truth. Too late he'd seen the uncertainty in her eyes when she'd told him what they had to do. The embarrassment and hesitancy that lay behind her own fighting words. Neither of them had asked for the solution she'd found. He understood that now. But he wouldn't risk more words to tell her that. He would show her instead.

"Turn around, please."

The soft, round globes of her backside deliberately brushed against his cock when she complied. He didn't care. The crack of her buttocks beckoned. Wrapping his hands around her waist, he pulled her tight against him and snuggled his cock in place.

"Judan." His name was a hoarse cry from her lips and her arms flailed as she sought to stay balanced.

"Brace your hands on the wall," he told her.

To comply she had to bend her body at an almost ninety-degree angle to reach the rear wall. His cock nestled deeper in the tight warmth of her cheeks.

"A little lower," he urged, skimming his hands up her sides to the sweet curve of her breasts.

"Judan," she gasped, but did as he asked.

Her skin was damp and his hands slid easily over the twin mounds of flesh. Each breast filled one of his hands. The fine texture of her skin teased the sensitive nerve endings in his fingers. And her nipples, already hard nubs, stabbed into his palms. His hands took much delight in bringing her to the peak of climax simply by playing with her breasts.

When he sensed she was hovering on the edge of the intense excitement he'd built, he cupped her breasts, tipping them up just a little. She tossed her head back with a wild cry and bucked as a jet of steam hit her nipples full force.

Sweat poured off his skin and his heart hammered in his chest. His control was tenuous at best. Yet he took the time to savor the delicate ripples of energy coursing through her body as the steam did its work.

Nudging her feet wider, he adjusted his hold so one of his large hands could cup both her breasts. His free hand slid down her flat belly until his fingers delved beneath her folds and found her clit. The faint effects of another spray of steam hit the exposed nub. A few hard flicks of his thumb and her body surrendered to his touch, writhing beneath him. He held her tightly so she wouldn't fall. So she'd know he was there and wouldn't let her go. Ever.

Both of them were breathing hard by the time her orgasm subsided. The scent of a woman in heat rose through the steam, urging him to mate. Swiftly, he shifted his stance until the head of his shaft nudged the opening of her yoni.

"Yes," she sobbed. "Please, Judan, now."

Her plea was all it took. With one swift thrust, he rammed himself home. She screamed and arched her back pulling him deeper inside her. Her pussy gripped his cock like a Situsian watersuit, tight and wet, and her juices soaked his balls. He pulled back slowly, reluctant to leave the warmth of her snug embrace.

She glanced back at him over her shoulder. "Please, Judan," she said. Her voice was raspy and pitched so low he had to strain to hear her.

He obliged. Setting a fierce pace, he thrust deep inside her again and again. Burying the full length of his shaft up to his balls in her welcoming warmth. Feeling the tiny pulses that gripped his cock each and every time. Frantically, he pulled her hard against him and shoved his cock deeper still. Then, for a brief moment, time seemed to stop.

All he could hear was his own harsh breath. And hers. His body was on fire. Hers too hot to the touch, yet he willingly scorched himself. The tension built inside him and she tried to jerk away.

"Hold still," he rasped.

"Please," she whispered.

He nudged her. Once, twice, but filled her so completely he could barely move. He labored for each breath, waiting. And then he felt the tip of his cock expand, preparing itself. His balls, already high and tight, ached for release. He rocked against her, desperate to push himself over the edge. Then, with one tug of her nipples, one stroke across her clit, her orgasm broke. In a quick, spasmodic rhythm, her yoni squeezed his cock tight, then released it, again and again and again. Already primed, his core of sexual energy burst forth and he shot load after load of cum deep inside her.

Dazed, they both stumbled forward to rest against the wall. His big body covered hers. His cock, still semihard, stayed lodged inside her. Warm steam prickled his sensitive skin and he shuddered.

Her hands were braced against the wall beside her head. Her forehead rested against the heated surface. She was panting. Fast, labored breaths. And every so often a whimper escaped from her lips. And with each whimper, her yoni squeezed his cock. Encouraged it to grow and fill her more fully.

"Gee," she whispered with a hoarse laugh. "You got it perfect the first time. We didn't even get to practice."

Laughter bubbled up inside him. But, not that he disputed her claim, he decided he could well do with a little more practice. Bending his head, he nuzzled her ear, his tongue tracing the delicate whorls until she sobbed.

"Is that so?" he asked.

She sucked in a tiny breath that sounded more like a moan of need. He set his hands on her waist and widened his stance, nudging himself more firmly inside her. She groaned and her delectable bottom arched against his groin in answer. The fine hairs covering her mound tickled his balls. Teasing them. Enticing them closer.

He rocked against her again, barely pulling out before shoving himself as deep as he could.

"Take me," he said. "Take me, again. Show me how much you need me inside you."

*Let me prove to you that the* Rakanasmara *we share is real.*

Her sobbing turned to a low keening wail and her pussy clenched his cock in a fierce grip. He slid his hand up her sides and along her arms. Her skin was soft and slippery from steam and sweat. Their hands met and their fingers intertwined, locking them together in an erotic embrace.

His thrusts turned almost savage in their intensity, matching his mood. He was almost desperate now to imprint himself on her body, on her memory, so she could never deny that she was his. Lost, he gave himself up to the sensual reaction of her body. She welcomed his wild taking of her with a fierce urgency of her own. He'd already blasted two loads of pre-cum into her when her orgasm hit. His own body trembled and then exploded as the waves of energy zoomed between them.

Ever so gently he pulled out. Keeping one arm around her, he gratefully used the wall to prop himself up. She squirmed in his embrace, turning to face him. Her arms slid up his chest and around his neck and she kissed his jaw.

"It's a good thing you're holding me up or I'd slide right to the floor."

He chuckled softly, unwilling to admit he was barely able to stand himself. Not when he was trying to decipher how he'd lived for so long without her in his life. They stood together for a while, allowing the steam to cleanse their sweat-soaked bodies while they nuzzled and kissed and touched. She hooked one of her legs around his hip, opening herself to him again. And his cock responded eagerly. He'd already had her twice and yet it barely felt as if he'd had a taste of her. She took the hint and wrapped her other leg around his waist.

"Take me again, Judan Ringa," she whispered.

A sense of relief filled him. She wanted him just as badly as he wanted her. The *Rakanasmara* between them was not a product of science or human lust. It was real.

His hands slid down to cup her bottom and hold her steady. Then inch by inch he pushed into her slick channel. Her yoni clenched his cock tightly and her whole body trembled. He pulled out just as slowly, until only his tip lay embedded in her sweet yoni's embrace. She gasped and sobbed for breath as he teased her with shallow strokes, building their sexual energy at a slow, deliberate pace.

This time it didn't matter that her hands roamed across his skin. This time he kissed her. Dipping his tongue inside her mouth to taste her. She answered his call, threading her fingers through his hair to hold him fast so her tongue could duel with his.

This time they took their time. He slowed almost to a stop whenever either one of them got too close to the edge. She urged him on until they came so close her yoni drained him of pre-cum. And still he rode her. When they came, their orgasms—his first, hers following moments later—rippled through their bodies leaving them deliciously sated with pleasure. Reaching out he shut the steam off and turned on the drying mode. It didn't take long before they were dry. By rights he could leave. They'd more than fulfilled the requirement to complete the changes to their genetic code. By morning, Myrina would have her sample to test.

But there were still many hours until the ship's environmental controls declared a new day. Picking her up, he carried her to the bedroom and set her on the bed before joining her. If he could, he'd stay buried inside her the entire night.

He didn't think he would ever get enough of her. But it was, perhaps, best not to tell her that just yet.

\* \* \* \* \*

Late the next morning, Myrina arrived at one of the two docking bays located at the rear lower level of the Speedlite. They'd arrived above Hitani an hour ago. Vand and Chiara were already there, double-checking the two cases packed with hypodermic injections that she and Judan would be administering to the Outposters. She noted, with some surprise, that the Second's hair was neatly tied back in a braid. There was no sign of her wig. There was no sign of Judan yet, either.

The shuttle craft took up most of the room in the long, narrow space. Stepping inside the docking bay she felt neither claustrophobic nor alarmed. If she'd wanted to, she could have pretended this was just another shuttle trip to one of the satellite meeting stations above TLC. But she wasn't in the mood to fool herself. She glanced at the shuttle's open hatchway without so much as a twinge of anxiety. After a morning spent completing the testing on the DNA sequence and then manufacturing the simulated immunization, she was hyped. The adrenaline rush felt like old times.

She sat on a crate and set the pack she'd been carrying beside her. While she was down on the planet's surface, she planned to take various samples to analyze later. She took the extra time, while she waited, to double-check her personal equipment, but her thoughts wandered, as they had all morning, to Judan.

She'd woken early this morning from a deep sleep. Her second in as many nights while aboard a ship imminently due to arrive above a hostile planet. Her ability to sleep at all was obviously due to Judan. At some subconscious level she trusted him to keep her safe. To guard her from her nightmares.

Then there was the sexual chemistry between them. Hot and so intense it made her breathless just remembering the feel of his hands caressing her body, his lips touching her skin. She'd experienced lust before but it had been light years away from the powerful connection she shared with Judan.

Last night, despite the harsh words that had come before it, they had made love. There was no other term for the fierce tenderness they'd found in each other's arms. A genetic trigger might have brought them together, but instinct told her there had to be…much more.

Funny how she'd claimed she wouldn't settle for anything less than love from him while neatly sidestepping the issue herself. Instead of asking whether or not he loved her or even understood the concept, she should be asking herself what she felt for him.

And this morning she'd come face-to-face with a reality check. She'd crouched by the bed and watched him sleep before slipping quietly from the room. As long as Judan slept she could pretend for a little while longer. That they hadn't hurt each other. That they had a future together despite the complications. That he was hers.

Because she wanted Judan Ringa.

The knowledge that he had such a profound affect on her psyche disconcerted her.

She'd never wanted any one person before. Security, absolutely. A good job and a home she could call her own, definitely. But she didn't like the idea that after such a short time she was getting used to being with this man. Wanting him. Where was her sense of independence? How could she suddenly hunger for Judan to be part of her life?

She knew he'd arrived even before she heard the soft snick as the docking bay door slid open. He nodded toward Vand and Chiara before turning his attention on her. She hadn't seen him all morning, which was probably a good thing for her sanity. Lucky for her there were barely any traces of the naked lover she'd left sleeping in her bed. Except for the absence of the quilled cape, he looked every inch the *Ktua*.

When he reached her he pulled her off the crate. His large hand radiated heat along her arm and knocked up her pulse a few notches. He bent his head, his body blocking Vand's and Chiara's view, but if they were watching, they had to guess he meant to kiss her. He didn't.

"Do I have your permission to tie my hair back for this mission?" he said instead.

*Is he serious?*

Startled, she drew back a little and studied his face. Maybe he was, because while his eyes twinkled bright green, the rest of his features didn't come close to cracking a smile. Okay, she had told him she preferred him to keep his hair down and he had. So did this request mean he wanted to please her, after arguing with her last night and then touching her, making love to her until she screamed? She desperately wanted to ask him what was going on between them, but right now didn't seem the best time.

She nodded. "Of course. Are we ready to go?"

He released her. "I have the coordinates of a landing site near the camp and the reconnaissance vessel is standing by."

"Good," she said.

A pilot and a couple of medical staff aboard the reconnaissance vessel had volunteered to use a low dosage transdermal patch to resist the planet's defenses so they could assist with the evacuation. Because of the high risk of exposure they were on standby until she and Judan had done their job and the Outposters were ready to leave.

"What about you? How are you doing?" he asked.

"I'm fine." Nice, short and basically truthful. She was fine, at the moment. With not a whisper of anxiety in sight, she was primed to go into battle. Literally.

Between the space-time jumps, the hyperslides and their arrival only a short time ago above the planet's surface, she'd been forced to rely on outdated data because the planet was constantly reacting to the Outposter invasion. Using the GCS she'd predicted a few possible simulations for what conditions on Hitani would now be like, but she couldn't be absolutely sure what they would encounter once they landed.

"Myrina."

"I'm serious," she said looking him straight in the eye for good measure. "Everything will be all right."

At least she damn well hoped so. Although she wasn't about to tell Judan that. She'd run the final simulation five times, but unlike Biali and his beloved hyperslides, her results had been much bleaker.

Judan would be all right. No matter what simulation she'd tested, he'd suffer only minor reactions, if any, to Hitani's hostility, depending on how quickly the planet adapted to the latest "invasion". And, once the *Rakanasmara*-enhanced DNA sequence was initiated, the Outposters would recover sufficiently to leave. But no matter how she'd played it, her own prognosis was grim at best. Her newly enhanced DNA offered virtually no protection from the planet's malevolence because of her sterility.

"Okay," he said with one final, steady look at her. "I have to perform a preflight check. I'll see you onboard."

"Okay," she said. "I'll be right there."

He walked away and she turned back to her equipment, relieved she'd passed muster. Not so much as a shaky hand in evidence.

If he'd asked about the test results and the conditions on the planet's surface, she'd have told him. Since he hadn't, she hadn't had any qualms about omitting a few facts from her answer.

There was no way he could save the Outposters himself. They were pushing their window of opportunity as it was with only the two of them.

This was her job. The reason Judan had come to TLC and the reason she'd boarded the damn Speedlite and gone into outer space. This time she knew the consequences and was ready for the coming battle. So the decision to take her chances was hers alone to make. Not Judan's. Especially not after his angry reaction to her scientific solution last night. They'd ended up making love, but they had yet to clear the air between them. Besides she hadn't come all this way to back out of a fight just because her lover had a macho protective streak the size of an asteroid belt.

"Doctor."

At the sound of Chiara's voice right in front of her, Myrina glanced up.

"Please, call me Myrina," she offered, remembering Judan's comment that the Second took a highly professional approach to her work.

The woman nodded. "I'm concerned about the Outposters who are critically ill," she said.

Myrina tried to decipher the hidden message in the Second's observation but drew a blank. Everyone was concerned about the critically ill Outposters. By now they were also being weaned off their meds. Still, they faced the toughest battle yet, because she hadn't been able to accurately predict the reaction of the simulated DNA sequence with the various drugs in the Outposters' systems.

"I am, too," she said for something to say.

Chiara smoothed back her already neat hair. A self-conscious gesture that reminded Myrina of Hylla's discomfort when Myrina had first met the navigator in the mess room. She now realized that Hylla had definitely felt awkward about revealing her hair to a relative stranger, even if that stranger was experiencing *Rakanasmara* with the Captain. The Second obviously didn't feel completely at ease either showing her hair to Myrina so why had she exposed herself?

*She wants something.* That thought was quickly followed by another. "You're worried about someone."

Myrina wasn't quite sure if she was asking a question or making an observation.

Regardless, Chiara nodded. "He's older than the others," she admitted. "I'm concerned he won't..."

*...make it.* Myrina filled in the blank and wondered if she'd stumbled across another case of a Dakokatan cheap thrill affair. It must be difficult for Chiara to look in a mirror each morning, see the grey hair and know her chances of finding her life partner were rapidly diminishing.

Normally, Myrina wouldn't hesitate to offer the woman a hug, but she held back. For one thing, she hadn't noticed any casual physical contact among the crew, which made her wary of transgressing another Dakokatan custom. For another, the Second appeared highly embarrassed by her emotional display. Her relationship with this man was obviously important, probably all she had.

So she kept the conversation strictly professional. Besides, she knew exactly who Chiara was worried about. At this point, Myrina could probably list the personal data and symptoms of each of the seventy-seven Outposters from memory.

With one last look at her pack, she closed the lid. She wasn't about to make any rash promises, but that didn't stop her from offering some positive hope. Especially since there were two or three other critically ill Outposters who might not make it.

"I know how it looks," she said. "But he has a pretty good chance."

She glanced at the shuttle's hatchway. If only those kind of odds were in her favor, too.

# Chapter Fourteen

ဆာ

He couldn't smell it, but every breath Judan took tasted metallic. He'd avoided food after one bite of a protein bar two and a half hours ago. After five hours of breathing in the deadly air he understood why the handful of Outposters who'd met them at the landing site looked haggard. On top of their illnesses, malnutrition had set in.

He'd since wondered a time or two what Myrina had meant when she'd told him before their flight down to the planet that everything would be all right. She certainly hadn't warned him that he'd come to regret the necessity of breathing, shun food and have less energy than a giant sand lizard basking under the rays of the Dakokatan sun. It seemed his immunity offered only limited protection against Hitani's wrath.

He kept walking toward the other side of the Outposters' camp anyway and ignored the deceptively benign-looking landscape. Blue, cloudless sky, an abundant variety of foliage of mostly unknown species and, a short distance away, the silvery sparkle of the sun reflecting off the clear waters of a lake. Myrina's base of operations was situated on a flat rise above the lake, which afforded an excellent view of the deceptively deadly countryside.

They'd each overseen the recovery of half the complement of Outposters. The simulated DNA injection had only been the first step, hence the five hour wait until the Outposters' bodies had adjusted to the changes and it was safe enough for them to leave the planet's surface.

A few minutes ago the second shuttle had landed. It was time to begin the evacuation. He planned to take a handful of

Outposters back to the *Ketiga Bulan*, the rest, including the most critical cases, would be taken aboard the reconnaissance vessel to receive more extensive care.

He passed several Outposters sorting through their personal belongings. Though he didn't expect it, a few of them managed to stand and nod as he walked by. He found the rest of the group Myrina had treated huddled stoically in a tent. The high velocity winds that had plagued the camp a few weeks ago had torn gaping holes in the tent's supposedly durable fabric. Three hover transports stood nearby ready to load passengers for the short trip to the shuttles. Much as he regretted leaving the ravaged remnants of the camp, no one had the time or energy to dismantle the tents and prefabricated buildings or to pack supplies.

He glanced around the group, conducting a quick assessment of how much assistance these people would need to reach the shuttles. He expected to see Myrina tending one of the more critically ill patients, but she wasn't in the tent. A young man with light blond hair who looked to be in slightly better health than many of the others stepped forward.

"Can I help you, *Ktua*?" he asked.

"I'm looking for Dr. deCarte," Judan said.

"Myrina, the doctor, left over an hour ago to collect samples," the man said. "She went that way." He pointed east toward a stand of stubby, thick-trunked trees.

"Start loading the hover transports," Judan instructed. "As soon as I've found the doctor, we'll leave for the shuttles."

The young man nodded.

With one last look around, Judan left the tent. They hadn't had much of a chance to talk this morning. Myrina had been gone by the time he woke, uncharacteristically late, his cock hard and aching for her again.

One night hadn't been nearly long enough to sate him. The problem now was, how was he going to coax her into his bed? Out of necessity, he'd deferred the final ritual, but he'd made a deliberate choice. Instead of coaxing her into *his* bed, he'd taken her in the shower and in her bed. So, even though the final stage of *Rakanasmara* had occurred last night, the ritual itself could still be completed.

Meanwhile he had to find out what Myrina was doing. He'd noticed her sample pack this morning in the docking bay. He understood she was a scientist with the need to analyze what precisely Hitani had done to these people. And yet, he never would have taken her for someone who would leave her post. Who would place sample collecting above people's lives.

He entered the stand of trees, surprised to realize the air here smelled and tasted somewhat better. A little later he spotted Myrina's backside. She was bent over, one arm holding the trunk for support, and appeared to be studying the ground underneath a huge tree. There was no sign of her specimen pack.

"Myrina," he called out.

She straightened instantly and turned, the back of her free hand wiping her mouth. Using the tree as leverage, she pushed herself forward, swayed and then lurched across the ground to the next tree. When she looked up at him, her smile barely reached her lips.

"I sure hope you're here to tell me we're ready to start the evacuation," she said.

Something was terribly wrong. She had, he realized, been vomiting.

She stayed at the tree waiting for him. In fact she sagged against it. Pale didn't come close to describing the lack of color in her face. Her features were pinched tight and she'd curved a protective arm across her middle.

"What's going on?" he asked.

"I'm getting a breath of, well, fresher air," she said with a slight shrug. "There's a higher level of oxygen here and less contaminants because of the trees."

Her voice sounded much stronger than she looked, so he concluded she was trying to put on what in English was called "a brave front". He knew anxiety attacks sometimes included extreme reactions but his instincts told him that's not what was happening here.

He gestured towards her and kept walking closer. "I understood you were collecting samples," he said.

She grimaced. "I had to give some story so they wouldn't worry, or worse, panic. Besides, it wasn't exactly a lie, I did want to collect specimens. I just didn't get the chance."

"Is that what you were doing in the docking bay this morning?" he said coming to stand in front of her. "Not exactly lying when you told me everything was going to be all right."

He picked up her wrist.

"What are you, the doctor all of a sudden?" She tried to snatch her hand away, but she didn't have the strength to pull free. Her pulse raced underneath his slight touch and her skin was burning up.

"It's Hitani, isn't it?" he said. All the time they'd been talking, his brain had been scrambling for an answer. He'd found it in the story she'd told him last night.

"The *Rakanasmara* didn't make any difference to you. You don't have much immunity because you're sterile. Isn't that right, Myrina?"

"More or less," she said with another wan imitation of a smile. "I managed to last three quarters of an hour before the nausea and stomach cramps came on."

And yet she'd ignored the symptoms for over another three hours before giving in to the pain. He scooped her up in his arms, ignoring her protests and nearly staggered under her weight. A reminder that he'd better get them off this planet before his immunity gave out on him.

"Why didn't you tell me?"

Under normal circumstances he'd welcome the feel of her in his arms, her head nestled against his shoulder, her soft green eyes gazing up at him with longing. Except it wasn't exactly longing he saw reflected in her eyes, but relief. She'd obviously been lurching from tree to tree on her way back to the camp. If he hadn't come along, she never would have made it.

"Tell you what?" she finally whispered. "That you had to come down to Hitani alone? Don't be ridiculous."

"What's ridiculous is you didn't tell me that neither one of us would be fully protected by the immunity."

"Didn't know for sure," she wheezed. Now that they'd cleared the trees she was having a hard time catching her breath. "Hitani adapted. Hoped we had time…had to fight…to face it and win this time. Knew you wouldn't like my decision, get mad."

It took her a while to get the full explanation out. When she had, he didn't answer, deciding it was more prudent to save his own breath for the walk to the camp rather than risk it arguing with her.

Was he mad? How could he be mad at Myrina for facing her greatest fear and sticking to her principles to save the Outposters? Furious, maybe, at the irrational wrath of this planet against his woman. And definitely terrified. He'd just spent five nerve-racking hours working with nearly forty Outposters, willing the injection he'd given them to make them well enough to leave the planet. He wasn't about to accept that he'd worked so hard to lose the one person he most wanted to keep.

By the time he made it back to the camp, Myrina was unconscious. Most of the Outposters were now on the hover transports, making his job easier. He staggered to the tent and leaned against one of the posts for support. Several of the people sitting in the nearby hover transport gasped when they saw Myrina's condition. He paid no attention, too busy searching for a face. Once he made eye contact with the blond man, he issued his order.

"Follow me, we're evacuating the planet. Now!"

He didn't wait to see if everyone came. The man known as the last to leave anyone in need was the first on board the shuttle. Gently, he lowered Myrina's limp form onto one of the few available beds. Reaching behind him, he swiftly undid his braid, letting his hair fall in a curtain around them. He breathed a little easier when his hair reached out and wrapped itself around her arm. The connection was still strong between them. Nevertheless, he rechecked her pulse. It fluttered irregularly.

"*Ktua. Ktua.*"

He looked up into the earnest face of the young blond man.

"The others need help, *Ktua*," he said, pointing back to the shuttle's hatch.

Judan nodded. He stood, reluctant to leave Myrina, but having no choice.

"Watch her," he told the man and left.

For once in his life Judan worked on automatic pilot. He didn't allow himself to think, he simply did what he had to do. Once his passengers were aboard, he completed the preflight check. They were so close to getting off the planet, he didn't want anything to go wrong. Both shuttles left the planet's surface and blasted through Hitani's atmosphere without encountering any further hostile reaction. The other ship veered off toward the reconnaissance vessel while he headed back to the *Ketiga Bulan*.

Only when the shuttle was parked back in the bay and he was by Myrina's side again did he relax. While Vand and Biali assisted the Outposters to the makeshift medical facility in one of the lounges near the clinic, Judan sat at Myrina's side and talked.

Robie Madison

He apologized for his anger the previous day. He hadn't last night, an oversight he now regretted. They'd shared something far more intense and connected than a simple fuck. At the time, he'd thought it was *Rakanasmara*. But at some point during the night he'd begun to wonder if there wasn't something to this "love" business after all.

He still didn't understand it, but he felt...an intangible force that drove him. He shook his head. He wasn't at all sure he liked "love". The whole relationship had seemed easier when he'd simply wanted Myrina.

But now.

What if he did "love" her?

He wasn't sure. The idea was too startling, too new. But he wanted the chance to find out.

"I want you, Myrina deCarte. Don't you dare die on me."

No answer. Not that he'd expected one. He just couldn't face the alternative if she didn't wake up.

\* \* \* \* \*

The next time Myrina woke, the grogginess had receded and her memory had returned. Or at least part of it. She'd been leaning against a tree, reluctant to lose its support and wondering how she was ever going to make it back to the camp when her legs and her stomach refused to cooperate. The onset of dehydration hadn't helped.

Bottom line, she'd been in big trouble. She'd rushed too far into the woods. Lost her lunch, her breakfast and any other meal she'd ever eaten. And hadn't had the strength to walk, crawl or, heck, drag herself to safety. For the second time in her life, she'd needed rescuing from the demonic clutches of a hostile planet. Some great savior she'd turned out to be, when she was the one who'd ended up needing to be saved. And then Judan had come along to do the job, even though she hadn't stayed out of another fight. She clearly remembered him picking her up in his arms and carrying her out of the

204

trees. After that, her memory was a complete blank, except for the occasional foggy images of faces and noises.

It was quiet now and she was lying in a bed. Naked. Well, okay, she had her panties on, so technically she was almost naked. She blinked, adjusting her eyes to the dimness. They'd put her in the bedroom Judan had given her. A moment later she was forced to close her eyes against a sudden light.

"Sorry, is that too bright?"

Judan's voice. Judan was here in the room with her.

She started to shake her head, then thought better of it. "Give me a minute," she said.

A hand brushed against her own and fingers curled around hers, holding tight. A thumb drew lazy circles across the back of her hand, sending tingles along her arm. She sighed with relief at the familiar sensation and squeezed back. The strokes were soft and gentle and hypnotic, lulling her back to sleep. She blinked again, determined to stay awake, and looked up into Judan's grim face. He was kneeling beside the bed, but still looked imposing from her prone position.

"Better?" he asked. His voice, unbelievably tender, sounded the exact opposite of how he looked.

"Yes," she said. "How long?"

He eased back to sit on the floor, but didn't let go of her hand. "You've been asleep on and off for a day."

She closed her eyes briefly. "Faster than I thought," she said. Given how badly the conditions on the planet had deteriorated, she'd expected far worse.

"Vand found your test program. He had a combined sedative antidote to counteract the toxins attacking your system ready when we arrived back."

"What?" Carefully she turned her head and looked at him. "He doesn't know how to use the GCS."

He shrugged, looking totally unrepentant on his brother's behalf. "Vand's always been good with technology. He apologizes for using your equipment but since our discussion in the lab he's become, how do you say in English…"

"Driven," she said, because the word exactly described the man's intense nature.

Judan nodded. "He's determined not to repeat his mistakes, but to learn from experience." There was a definite measure of pride in Judan's voice as he spoke of his brother.

"I take it things are better between the two of you."

"We're working together," he said. "But once this is over, he wants to go to TLC and study colonization dissonance under the esteemed Dr. deCarte." He grinned at her. Obviously he thought this was a great idea.

*Once this is over. Once this is over. I'll be back at TLC, but where will you be?*

"Hardly esteemed," she said and stared up at the ceiling. "I couldn't even fight my way out of a paper bag."

"You took a calculated risk and did all right," he said softly. "We both did and we got everyone off the planet safely."

She'd become a "we". When had that happened? When the *Rakanasmara* between them had been triggered in Fenton deMorriss' office? When they'd had wild oral sex? When they'd made love in the shower? And what did any of those events prove anyway?

Not a damn thing except that they enjoyed mind-bogglingly hot sex. Not a damn thing except that she was a total wimp. Sure, a couple of days ago she'd admitted to herself she wanted him, but now… She'd taken a calculated risk, pitting herself against Hitani to save the Outposters, and she'd barely survived. She still wanted Judan, but was she willing to take another calculated risk to keep him? Commitment scared the heck out of her. What if she said yes and it didn't last? Worse, what if this was her only chance at happiness? What if she said no and regretted the decision for the rest of her life?

She reached up and tugged aside the collar of his shirt. Her fingers found the now familiar path of scar tissue. She'd touched, kissed and been fascinated by those lines. The twin scars made him seem more...human, the way they marred his otherwise perfect body. Judan was a *Ktua*, the captain of his own ship and a man who made mistakes. And survived them.

"You're being awfully calm about what happened down there," she said. "What I did."

Except he wasn't calm at all. The moment she'd touched him, she'd picked up on the tension radiating from him like the aftermath of an ion bomb explosion. He'd obviously spent the last day and a half watching over her rather than looking after himself. It was rather sweet. Not too many people had ever gone out of their way to be sweet to her. It felt good. A warm and fuzzy kind of good.

"I promised to protect you. That's what I did," he said.

"As I recall, when you told me that you also ordered me to stay out of a fight. I didn't."

He rose to his knees and bent over her. "No, you didn't. By keeping quiet and not telling me what we might face down there, you jeopardized the mission."

"Judan."

"No, listen. I regret you didn't trust me, Myrina, but I understand why. You are not the type of person to, how do you say in English, 'back down from a fight'."

"A Little Warrior."

"My Little Warrior," he said.

"Glad you figured that out."

"What I, as you put it, figured out, is that I should have apologized the other night. We are now even, because for a little while, I didn't trust you, either. I sensed the warrior spirit inside you the first time we met. I just didn't realize until yesterday that you've spent your whole life fighting. It was foolhardy of me to forbid you to fight. To change who you are."

She pulled on his shirt, tugging him a little closer. "Are you sure I'm not still asleep? I could have sworn you just said you were wrong."

His eyes crinkled with laugh lines. "Not wrong, Little Warrior. I just, how do you say, revised my game plan."

"Oh?"

"I respect your need to do what you have to do to keep people and environments safe, but from now on I stand with you."

*I will keep you safe.* She heard the words as clearly as if he'd spoken them aloud. He seemed willing to endanger himself to safeguard her. He was saying they were now definitely a "we", a partnership. Yet she'd sent him down to the planet without warning him of the dangers. She hadn't been operating as a "we", and yet he'd still protected her.

Her fingers came to rest on his left pectoral. He wasn't invincible. So, who protected him?

"Tell me," she whispered, tracing the length of each line. "Tell me how you got the scars."

# Chapter Fifteen

### ✀

The muscles under Judan's skin jumped reflexively at Myrina's request. For a second his eyes were shuttered, cutting her off from his emotions. From him. She waited and finally he glanced down at her hand where it rested against him. Because of her illness, her hand looked unnaturally pale, a sharp contrast to the healthy green of his skin.

"I told you I was a pilot," he said.

She nodded.

"Nearly four years ago I was returning home after making a delivery to an outpost. My cousin and her husband were stationed on a satellite trading post not far off my route so I decided to make a surprise visit."

The moment he mentioned his cousin, Myrina knew the story was about Zane, the little boy whose picture she'd seen in Judan's office. Since the boy hadn't looked much older than four, she guessed he'd been a baby when Judan had made his visit.

"First no one answered my hail or request for docking privileges and then I discovered one of the satellite's docking bays was wide open." Judan was saying. "I sent out a subspace distress signal, but decided I couldn't wait, so I docked my ship."

Myrina nodded again. That sounded like him. He would follow standard protocol procedures and then rewrite the rules to suit himself and go in alone. "What did you find?" she asked.

"Near total destruction. It looked like a laser gun had been let loose on the place. Holes had been punched through walls, equipment smashed, goods scattered. There'd obviously been a few fires. I was amazed the environmental controls remained intact given the amount of damage. I couldn't find anyone."

Myrina grazed her fingers over the scars again. "Let me guess. You didn't retreat."

Judan shook his head although he didn't look as if he was happy with the decision he'd made. "I headed up toward the control room to see if I could find any clues about the attack on the station and why it had happened."

He covered her hand where it rested on the damaged skin with his own. "This happened when I tried to bypass a blocked passageway. A beam in the ceiling broke apart and crashed down, nearly crushing me. I don't know how long I was knocked out. When I came to I'd lost a lot of blood. I could barely walk, but I needed to find help."

"You found someone?"

"They found me. My cousin's husband and a couple of other members of the trading post plus two children. Space pirates had attacked without warning. Somehow they'd managed to sneak past the satellite's warning sensors. The trading post had been outmanned and outgunned."

"What about your cousin?" She really wanted to ask about Zane. He had to have been one of the two children he mentioned. How had the boy and Judan survived while the parents hadn't?

"She and the other members of the trading post had been taken hostage. They were being held in a docking bay on the other side of the trading post while the pirates loaded their ships. The three adults I met had been launching a rescue attempt when they found me. I was too weak to go with them."

He caressed her arm and then let his hand and his gaze slip away.

"I took the children and retreated to the docking bay and my ship. A while later a couple of blasts rocked the station. No one else appeared. I had no choice. I had to leave with the children before the place blew apart."

She heard the gut-wrenching anguish in his voice as if he again had to make the same decision now instead of four years ago. Rubbing the back of her hand along his skin, she offered him a little comfort. And looked into those gorgeous green eyes of his.

The crazy thing was, she'd always thought she would know for sure what love felt like when she encountered it. And now, one look into his eyes—the eyes she'd stared into countless of times, the eyes that had watched her every chance they got—and she smacked face first into the certain knowledge that she loved him.

*Well crap.* She loved him. Pure and simple. Though there was absolutely nothing pure or simple about it. How had this happened? And, more to the point, what was she supposed to do with it?

She reached over and grabbed the edge of his shirt, pulling him close. "You took a calculated risk and did all right," she said. "You saved the kids."

A grin tugged at, but didn't quite reach, his mouth. "And the moral of the story is?" he asked.

"Whatever you want it to be," she whispered back.

She tugged him closer. Close enough that his hair, which had been uncharacteristically tame up to that point, spilled around them. Close enough to kiss. She kept it light and a little teasing.

"Myrina," he growled low in his throat and licked the seam of her mouth.

One little kiss and she was out of breath. One little kiss and her breasts ached for his touch. One little kiss and…

"Why don't you come in here so I can thank you properly?" she asked him.

He chuckled and his shirt came off. His boots followed in record time. He dimmed the lights. And then he crawled into bed with his leggings still on. She sighed and snuggled close. Probably just as well. Her brain might be willing, but her body was still in recovery.

He turned on his side to face her, sliding one arm beneath her to cradle her head against his broad shoulder. He wrapped his other arm around her. Then her arms slid up and around his neck, aligning their bodies from head to toe. He pulled her into a snug embrace. She sniffed, filling her senses with the familiar scent of alam and her man.

They held each other for a long time. She threaded her fingers through his hair, luxuriating in the vibrancy of the strands as they tangled around her fingers. Starting at the base of her spine, his hands kneaded the tension from her back. Slowly she began to relax. Her skin warmed beneath his caresses, creating a delicious sense of lassitude. In the silence she became aware of the steady beat of his heart. Her own echoed the rhythm. Reassuring her. Affirming life. She'd made it.

*What's the moral of the story?*

*Whatever you want it to be.*

He'd told her one heck of a bedtime tale. She hadn't intended to open old wounds, figuratively speaking, just learn about the scars. They made quite a pair, though, given their recent escapades. Both of them were stubborn to a fault when it came to this rescue business. The thing of it was, this time they'd both come through with less damage. They'd been, perhaps not invincible, but definitely stronger together, which was one heck of a moral.

His finger skimmed along her jawline, lifting her chin. The kiss, when it came, was unbelievably tender. No more than a brushstroke across her lips. His tongue traced a highly inflammable path along her mouth. She bit her lower lip, not sure how long she could hang on.

"Jud—"

"Shh," he said with a brief shake of his head. Two fingers reached up to silence her then stayed to trace the edge of her mouth. She couldn't resist and her tongue darted out to taste him. He took her action as an invitation and gently inserted his fingers, both of them, inside her mouth.

"Show me," he whispered.

She closed her eyes, savoring the taste of his skin. She suckled his fingers, drawing them deeper inside her mouth. Her tongue glided along each smooth length, teasing him and herself with memories.

He groaned and pulled his fingers out before dipping his head to taste her again. Lips on lips, the faintest touch of his tongue skimming across her teeth. She gasped when one wet finger brushed across her already swollen nipple. Involuntarily, her body arched, thrusting her breasts into his waiting hand. He smiled against her mouth and stroked the other nipple. Her body jerked and this time she felt it. His erection straining within the confines of his leggings. She tried to wiggle closer and he got her meaning. His hand clamped around her butt and he notched his shaft in the V of her legs.

A moan, her moan, echoed in the barely there space between them. Her pelvis tilted and she bucked against his erection.

One, two, three strokes and a low groan rumbled deep in his throat. Though she would have preferred his bare shaft, her clit welcomed the friction from rubbing against the cloth of his leggings. Four, five caresses along his cock and his breathing turned harsh. Tiny beads of sweat glistened on his chest and she set to work licking him clean.

His hand slid south to her thigh, pulling it high over his leg. Opening her to him. His fingers dipped beneath the edge of her panties and stopped.

She'd stopped licking, her face buried against his chest while she tried to control her breathing as she waited. It was an exercise in futility. She arched her ass, hoping to bring his fingers closer to her hole, but they remained the same tantalizing distance away. Close enough to make her wet with wanting, just not close enough to satisfy her. Her heart pounded erratically against her chest. She lifted her leg higher, grinding his erection in a desperate attempt to bring herself nearer to climax. He caressed her back, his hand gliding across skin slick with sweat. Finally, his fingers moved closer, grazing her folds and coming to rest at the entrance to her hole. Her pussy clenched, coating his fingers with cum.

"Are you sure," he said, his voice harsh with passion.

"Yes, please," she whispered back.

Without another word, he pushed two fingers inside. Her entrance was slick, allowing him to push deep. She cried out and tightened her hold on him when he began to pump. Slow, gentle strokes that stoked the flame higher, stirred her body to a greater sense of urgency. Each time she caught the rhythm he changed it, driving her to distraction because she still couldn't quite reach that next level.

His thumb roamed northward, inserting itself between her butt cheeks. She bucked, moaning in anticipation. He waited until he'd nearly pulled his fingers out of her pussy. Then he caught his downstroke and pushed his thumb up her ass, stuffing her holes.

On a half moan, half scream she climaxed. Ripples of light and energy coursed through her system at faster-than-light speeds and her body shuddered violently.

A while later she became aware that Judan had rolled onto his back and she was draped across him. She blinked and lifted her head to study him. He was watching her.

"Are you all right?" he asked. One of his hands traced lazy patterns across her back.

"I'm fine," she said and contrived to look serious. "Just concerned."

He frowned so she gently nudged his erection with her knee.

"You seem to be in a predicament."

He grinned and rolled over, tucking her beneath him. His hair cascaded like a fiery waterfall around them. "That seems to be a regular state around you, Little Warrior."

"Judan." She might have started this conversation by teasing him, but she wasn't a tease. Her only problem was, she wasn't sure she had the energy to do more than talk.

"It's all right," he said. "This time was for you."

*I love you.*

The words burst into her brain, barely giving her time to catch them before she spoke out loud.

*Tell him.*

*No. I can't tell him, yet.*

The feeling was too new to her. A secret she wanted to keep and take out to look at when she was alone before sharing it with anyone else. With him.

Besides, she'd discovered something else in Judan's arms.

She really hadn't had a clue what love looked like. Because if she had she might have seen it a lot sooner.

Judan might claim he didn't understand the word, but he loved. Her. Zane. His family. He was a man who demonstrated his love with actions, not words. Maybe all he would ever be able to say was "I want you", but she knew what he really meant.

So she'd keep her words tucked away and give him the ones he understood. She met his steady gaze, reached up and caressed his cheek.

"I want you, Judan Ringa," she said.

His body trembled slightly. He rested his forehead against hers and closed his eyes. "Thank the Third Moon," he said.

She tilted her head and brushed a kiss across his lips. "You have a real thing for this Third Moon. Is she a goddess or something? You keep invoking her name."

"What?" He opened his eyes and lifted his head. "The *Ketiga Bulan*?"

"Your ship?" she asked, confused.

He shook his head. "*Ketiga Bulan*, the Third Moon. My favorite of the Three Sisters, the moons of Dakokata. I named my ship for her."

"And you believe she helps you?"

He nodded. "She led me to you, didn't she?"

* * * * *

Two hours after landing in the Dakokatan capital of Bandar Besar the following morning, Myrina knew exactly how the live specimens she often studied must feel like.

Moments earlier Judan had arrived at his apartment, where she'd been waiting for him, with two other *Ktua*, a man and a woman, all of them looking very official in their quilled capes. She was very glad she'd worn her TLC uniform this morning and then, as a courtesy, had asked Judan's permission to wear it. She might not be as ornately dressed, but at least she looked like a scientist.

A scientist under microscopic scrutiny.

From the moment they'd walked through the door, both *Ktua* had been openly assessing her. As politely as possible, she'd studied them back. Aside from their capes, their most notable feature was that neither of them wore wigs.

Judan immediately removed his cape and came to stand beside her, placing a hand on the small of her back. A proprietary gesture that didn't go unnoticed, especially by the man.

"Myrina, these are *Ktua* Barrin and Longi," he said. "They're here to verify the *Rakanasmara* between us."

"Verify?" *Well crap.*

She shot Judan a startled glance. Once they'd touched down, he'd stood out in the middle of the landing field,

216

directing the transportation of the Outposters to a nearby medical facility. Fortunately all of them, even the more critically ill patients, were responding well to treatment once they were away from the poisonous environment on Hitani. In the midst of loading a fourth hover transport, a young man in uniform had approached him. Judan had accepted the tightly rolled sheet of paper, broken the seal, read the contents and left. Vand had been the one to bring her to Judan's apartment.

Until now she hadn't thought about the nature of the urgent business Judan had been called away on. It was a little disconcerting to realize that she—they—had been the subject under discussion.

"Didn't you show them the results of the genetic testing I did? I don't think there's much dispute I have the Dakokatan trigger for *Rakanasmara*."

"The genetic connection is only the first step in *Rakanasmara*," *Ktua* Barrin said. She was a tall, dignified-looking woman who, Myrina guessed, was in her late sixties. Given the faint traces of white in her hair, Myrina also surmised she'd recently lost her life partner.

"A series of rituals confirms compatibility between a couple," *Ktua* Barrin continued, "And ensures that each person understands what it means to be a life partner."

"So, what does that mean?" Myrina asked, totally confused. Granted Judan hadn't explained *Rakanasmara* when they'd first met, but from the beginning he'd told her repeatedly he wanted her and later that he'd observed the rituals as part of his wooing of her.

*Ktua* Longi stepped forward. He was slightly younger than the woman, no more than sixty. And in his case, his brown hair was liberally streaked with blond highlights. A man in his prime. But, unlike Judan or *Ktua* Barrin his eyes were a pale green, a shade or two lighter than her own.

"It means," *Ktua* Longi said with a gesture towards her, "that during the ritual phase it is rare but possible for either party not to accept the other as their life partner. As long as any of the rituals are not completed in the order prescribed, the *Rakanasmara* cannot be verified and the partnership is dissolved."

"You mean I had a choice to accept the *Rakanasmara* or not?" she asked. *But that makes no sense. If* Rakanasmara *only happens once in a person's life, my life, by saying no I condemn myself to never finding another life partner.*

"Yes," *Ktua* Barrin said. "Did *Ktua* Ringa not explain this to you?"

At the *Ktua's* question Judan's fingers dug into her back. Not painfully, but enough to indicate his agitation with her line of questioning. Or the outcome. He'd been gone for two hours and returned with two *Ktua* in tow to verify the *Rakanasmara* between them. Had he presented his case for *Rakanasmara* to the *Ktua* and what? Been denied immediate approval until they got a look at this upstart foreigner who claimed to have the genetic compatibility to mate a Dakokatan. She bristled at the notion.

"There wasn't any need," she said at the same time Judan said, "It wasn't an issue."

She quirked a smile at him and stepped closer into his embrace. He didn't smile back, but his fingers unclenched and his hand slid around her waist, securing her next to him. *Ktua* Longi watched their interaction with rapt interest.

What was it with these people that they kept watching her? Looking for…what? An outbreak of green skin? It wasn't going to happen. Did she need to paint a sign on her forehead saying "Dakokatan genetic code found inside, honest"? Except, of course, it now appeared carrying Dakokatan DNA wasn't proof enough.

"Are you doing this because I don't look Dakokatan?"

"Myrina," Judan said, rather sharply. "The verification is necessary. It's standard procedure for everyone."

*Okay, I get it, big guy. Standard procedure, but I'll bet this house call isn't very usual because something about the verification has you worried.*

"The doctor is correct, though. It has never been heard of," *Ktua* Barrin said. "*Rakanasmara* occurring with an outsider."

"Not quite," *Ktua* Longi said in a quiet voice.

"What?" Myrina asked, glancing around the small group.

"Why don't we sit down?" Judan gestured towards a group of oversized chairs at one end of the room.

Judan's spacious apartment, much like his office aboard the Speedlite, was filled with wood and a minimum of metal. He had many water-themed decorations, including a fish tank filling one corner of his living room. Not surprising, once she'd discovered that Bandar Besar was situated at the edge of the Tekur desert. The same Tekur desert that was home to the giant sand lizard and tekurilite.

Judan steered her toward a soft, sky blue chair. She caught him glancing at a picture of Zane which sat on a nearby table before he pulled her down to share the seat with him. The picture was one of several she'd found of the young boy in the apartment along with a bedroom that seemed to belong to Zane. At least part-time.

*Is he somehow mixed up in this, too?*

*Ktua* Barrin kept her cape on, but Longi removed his before choosing a seat opposite Myrina.

"Tell Myrina what you told the *Ktua*," Judan said to *Ktua* Longi once everyone was sitting down.

It seemed as if a pair of moths chose that moment to set up residence inside Myrina's stomach. "Tell me what?" she asked.

"I am Spar Longi." He paused as though waiting for some sort of reaction. After a moment, he added, "I see that my name means nothing to you."

"I'm afraid not," she said. Judan's fingers threaded their way through her hair.

Spar Longi sighed and shook his head. "I was expecting too much. I suppose it is not surprising, though, given what Judan told us of your personal history."

"My personal history?" She couldn't seem to string a coherent sentence together. She felt as though she was balancing on the fine edge of anticipation. "You mean the fact that I'm an orphan."

Longi winced, then nodded. "I have every reason to believe," he said, "That my eldest uncle was your grandfather."

# Chapter Sixteen

### ✀

"We have not yet verified the familial connection," *Ktua* Barrin said. She did not sound pleased by Spar Longi's revelation. She seemed to be a real stickler for regulations. And, for the first time, Myrina understood Judan's concern. This woman wasn't going to give them any latitude.

"A DNA test is simple enough," she said then turned back to Spar Longi. "Please," she said. "Tell me what you know."

"Have you heard of the hill dwellers?" he asked.

Myrina shook her head.

"They are the indigenous peoples of Dakokata. Our race settled here much later, but we enjoyed a peaceful coexistence for many centuries. The hill dwellers tended to keep to themselves, living in caves and valleys deep in the Gunun Mountains that border Bandar Besar to the north.

"Many years before I was born, my uncle declared that he'd experienced *Rakanasmara* with a woman of the hill dwellers. At that point in our recorded history," he said with a stern look at Barrin, "there were no instances of this happening. Unfortunately, despite some support from his family, their *Rakanasmara* was not validated.

"I think he would have gone to live with her anyway, but her family didn't support the partnership at all. My uncle owned his own ship, a prototype of the Speedlite model. One night they disappeared and nothing more was known of them until now."

Myrina hadn't realized how hard she was gripping Judan's hand until he caressed her arm. Moved by Spar Longi's story, she blinked back the suspicious wetness that filled her eyes. She didn't dare ask how many Longi relatives there were. After twenty-nine years alone, having one living, breathing cousin of sorts sitting across from her, talking about her grandfather, was about all she could handle at the moment. Still a feeling of elation stole over her. Threatened to overwhelm her.

"Did you know?" she asked Judan.

"I just found out the story this morning," he said, giving her head another caress.

"I'm afraid I can't tell you anything about him or my grandmother," she told Spar Longi with regret.

"But you already have," he said. "You are here. Proof that my uncle and his wife had a child who also found a life partner." Here he paused to pull a piece of cloth from his pocket to wipe the corner of his eyes. "I profoundly regret, Dr. deCarte, that none of them felt able to return here. To see that you had a proper home."

"Please," she said. "Call me Myrina. The other name isn't really my own. It is the family name of the patroness who sponsored me and was given to me at the orphanage."

"And I," Spar Longi said, "would be honored if you called me cousin."

"This is all very well," the woman said. "But it does not help us validate the *Rakanasmara* between the *Ktua* and the doctor."

At least she hadn't called Myrina an outsider, again.

"Did you explain the rituals to Dr. deCarte when *Rakanasmara* occurred between you?" Spar asked.

"No," Judan said. "I wooed her instead."

"Wooo-ed?" the woman said, a puzzled frown on her face. "What is that?"

"An old custom that involves chocolates and flowers and dinner dates," Myrina answered. "I don't suppose any of those things are on your list of rituals."

The woman shook her head, obviously confused by the answer.

"Careful, Little Warrior," Judan growled. "This *is* serious."

Then he reached over and unsnapped her jumpsuit straight down to her cleavage.

"Don't you dare do that again," she shouted and tried to bat his hand away. "You said I could wear this."

"Yes," Judan said, delving past her hand to reach inside her jumpsuit. "I'm also honored you choose to wear the pendant I gifted you with."

Myrina felt the heat of a blush creep up her neck when he pulled the pendant out to show the two *Ktua*. Okay, so she already knew the pendant was a ritualistic symbol, but she preferred to keep her exhibitionist tendencies strictly private.

"You could have asked," she grumbled as she re-snapped the suit.

"Judan has obviously fulfilled the requirement for the *Token of Wealth*, if Myrina has been wearing the pendant for a few days. I believe we can assume the gifting occurred after the other two tokens were shared." Here Spar Longi glanced rather pointedly at Judan, who nodded.

"Fine," *Ktua* Barrin said. "What of the first token, the *Water of Life*?"

"Hey," Myrina said, sitting up straight. "I can answer that one. That's that glass of water thing we did the first night we met, right?"

"Right," Judan said.

He was leaning back in their chair, one arm behind her while he fingered her hair. His casual gesture was a little odd considering he'd told her twice how serious this was. But his relaxed manner helped Myrina ease up a little, too, which was probably his intention. She grinned at him. Judan really had covered the bases. And he'd been creative and sexy and...*loving* while teaching her Dakokatan customs.

*Ktua* Barrin nodded as if she had a damn checklist hidden under her cape. "What about the second ritual, the *Token of Welcome*?" she asked. "The *Ktua* had to pay a visit to your relatives, doctor, who would gift him with a token, welcoming him to the family."

"Myrina," Judan said, pulling her back into his arms.

She waved him off.

"But I'm an orphan. I have—had no family."

It was on the tip of her tongue to ask if there were any exceptions. Then she remembered that no one on Dakokata went without a family. Which meant…

She looked at Spar Longi. The concept was still too new, too weird to think of him as a long lost cousin who could help her out of this mess. Besides, according to his story, she was the one who'd been lost.

"I'm sorry, Myrina," Spar said with a helpless shrug. "If we had met sooner, my family would have been proud to gift Judan on behalf of your grandfather. But, I'm afraid the order of the rituals is quite precise, as is the requirement of a gift."

And that was what was wrong here with this whole validation process. Everyone was so concerned about the rituals being done in the correct order. Being done properly, that the meaning behind them was lost in translation. No wonder Judan didn't understand love. Where was the time to stop and experience it when you were suffering from performance anxiety…of the ritualistic kind?

"Myrina," Judan said, again.

She shook her head. "No, wait," she said. "I just want to understand this."

If she'd wanted to take it this was her perfect way out. Heck, she hadn't been too enamored of the complications *Rakanasmara* had brought to her life when she'd first come face-to-face with it. So, who needed it?

*Judan does.*

The thought shot through her brain like a falling star. The kind you made a wish on and then believed that wish comes true. Was Judan that kind of man? A man to make a wish on. A man to take a risk on. He'd certainly been stubbornly dogged in his pursuit of her.

*Who needed Rakanasmara?*

*I do.* Because she did. She wanted him.

She shook her head. Judan was right. This was serious. Too serious to wimp out on.

She turned to Spar and *Ktua* Barrin. "So what you're both saying is that even though I have the genetic code, even though the *Rakanasmara* kicked in when Judan and I met, even though we performed the *Water of Life* and he gifted me with a pendant and even though neither one of us wants to deny our partnership, the validation is bust because he couldn't get a gift from my nonexistent family. Is this what you're saying?"

The *Ktua* glanced at each other in pained silence, which was answer enough. No wonder her grandfather had decided to leave Dakokata where customs meant everything and there were no exceptions for the surprise of love. Until now.

"Then," she said. "It's fortunate that Judan followed my traditions."

She shuffled forward in her seat and then lowered herself onto one knee on the floor and faced Judan. She ignored *Ktua* Barrin, though she didn't mind Spar Longi watching. She picked up Judan's hand and he sat a little straighter, a quizzical look on his face.

"I didn't exactly tell the truth yesterday when I told you I want you," she said.

The brilliant sparkle in his eyes dimmed a little with her words. Still he nodded in understanding. "What is the truth, Myrina?"

"I love you, Judan Ringa," she said. "Will you follow my customs and marry me?"

A grin quirked the side of his mouth and then he laughed. "A, what do you call this, a proposal. Yes, Little Warrior," he said. "I'll marry you. I love you, too."

With that he hauled her up into his lap. She had just enough time to wrap her arms securely around his neck before his mouth descended onto hers. The kiss warmed her straight to her toes.

"This is most curious," Spar Longi said when they came up for air.

Myrina tried to shuffle over so she could sit beside, rather than on top of, Judan. He was having none of it and simply shifted his own position on the chair to hold her more securely on his lap.

"It does not change the problem before us," *Ktua* Barrin said.

"No, no, that is not what I meant," Spar said. "Judan, you said you loved this woman. I have heard of the concept, but don't understand it. Can you explain?"

*Well, hot damn.* Myrina turned to look at Judan. He had told her he loved her, hadn't he?

Judan shook his head. "I don't understand it. Can't explain it. And don't care to. I just know how I feel."

"But this is truly extraordinary," Spar said. "I have spent most of my life studying *Rakanasmara*. It has been my dream to somehow validate my eldest uncle's claim, but there is one point that has always baffled me."

"Love?" Judan asked, a look of stunned surprise on his face.

"Do any of you know what *Rakanasmara* really means?" Spar asked. The question appeared rhetorical because he proceeded to give them an answer. "Although we have come to understand the term as meaning a life partnership, the ancient texts in fact give an entirely different explanation. *Rakanasmara* refers to finding one's love partner, although until now I had no idea what that meant."

"A love partnership, huh," Myrina said with a grin. "I like that. It means I haven't so much started a new tradition as resurrected an old one."

"That may be so," *Ktua* Barrin said. "But without the *Token of Welcome* the *Rakanasmara* as it is currently understood cannot be validated."

*Well crap.* Hadn't she been listening?

"The validation doesn't matter anymore," she said.

"Yes, it does," Judan said.

*Double crap. What is he doing messing with my plan?*

"It does? Since when?"

"Since always, Little Warrior. You do not think I would, how do you say, come this far without making sure the *Rakanasmara* between us would be accepted. That you would be accepted."

Just like that she melted at Judan's words. Then she remembered that he'd agreed with Spar Longi that he'd given her the pendant after completing the first two rituals. Then she remembered the coffee, her adoptive brother Parker's, coffee, that he'd served at the midday meal the first day she'd come aboard the Speedlite. And those tears she'd held back before pricked the corners of her eyes.

"Made sure you covered all the bases, huh," she said. "Protecting me as best you can."

Judan nodded. "That's what you do when you love someone."

\* \* \* \* \*

*Well crap.* So much for romance and a cool, breezy apartment. Myrina was hot and sweaty and her limbs were definitely starting to ache.

About two seconds after resolving the *Token of Welcome* issue, she and Judan had faced one more hurdle. While the requirements for the three ritual tokens had now been validated, thank you very much, there was still the matter of final acceptance. And wouldn't you know it, her marriage proposal and his acceptance of it didn't count. Because she was the one who had to do the accepting.

The moment the woman had started in on her explanation, Myrina had cringed. Judan had been stoic and blunt. Yes they had mated, but no he hadn't enticed her to his bed — they'd used hers. More or less. Her newfound cousin had immediately declared this lapse in protocol understandable, given the circumstances, and stated he was sure the situation would be rectified, soon. He'd then hustled both himself and *Ktua* Barrin out of the apartment. Myrina swore she'd seen him wink at Judan.

Who hadn't waited two seconds longer to invite her out.

So here she was tramping up some damn mountainside rather than warming his bed. The least the man could have done was to show a little appreciation. Thank the second moon or the first moon or heck, maybe all three moons. She'd taken a big risk back there, they both had.

She paused on the trail, hoping to catch her breath. Below her Bandar Besar snaked like a green ribbon on either side of the meandering river that ran between the desert and the mountains. She still had only fleeting impressions of the Dakokatan capital. The town her grandparents had fled so many years ago. Heat, humidity and bright, rich colors all vied for her attention. And she'd been curious and eager to explore, but Judan hadn't given her time. He'd headed straight for the suburbs, past the small farms and into the foothills.

In the distance she glimpsed the flat sea-green delta that led to a sea. And on the edge of the green, stretching as far as the eye could see was the desert. Surprisingly not flat, but undulating rolls of sand. She looked back up the trail and beyond to the sharp peaks.

"I've got to tell you. If this is my grandmother's definition of a hill, I'd hate to see what she called a mountain." She grinned in spite of herself. She'd just mentioned a relative in casual conversation.

"To the hill dwellers, these lower elevations are hills. Myrina."

"Umm." Geesh, the green guy wasn't even breathing hard.

"I too have a confession to make."

*Double crap.* It couldn't be anything serious, could it? She'd declared her love for him and he'd declared his love for her. So what did he have to confess? That she was going to be shipped back to TLC and he was duty-bound to stay here and be a leader of his people. True, they hadn't exactly ironed out all the issues of this life—love—partnership but, weren't those mere details?

"What?" she asked. She did, after all, have a policy of finding out where she stood with people.

"I hate chocolate."

"You've got to be kidding?" She collapsed on a nearby boulder in a fit of laughter.

"No, I'm serious. I've tried it, but I just don't like the taste."

"No, no," she said, waving her hand madly in the air as she tried to get her breath back. "I don't mean are you serious, as in are you serious. I mean, you had me worried."

"Then you don't mind?"

"No. Why should I mind? It's not as if I can't eat it, just because you don't like it. Right?"

"Alone," he said.

"Huh?"

"I don't like the smell, either, Myrina."

"Oh. Okay, alone then. As long as you understand I'm not giving it up."

She stretched out her arm to him and he helped haul her back onto her feet. They set off along the trail again. Eventually they veered to the left, following a secondary path that seemed steeper than the main road they'd been on.

"During the meeting with the *Ktua* this morning," he said a while later, "I was elected Council Commander."

"Congratulations."

As Dakokata's representative to the Confederacy, he'd be expected to attend Council meetings regularly. Which meant when she went back to TLC, he'd be along for the ride, too. His appointment effectively solved one of their biggest problems — the long-distance relationship. So why didn't he just say so?

Because he was involved in one of his convoluted jumps in logic, which only made sense to him and confused the heck out of her.

"I thought that if your mother doesn't object, we could adopt Zane."

She was three paces past him before she realized Judan had stopped cold in his tracks. She swung around to face him.

"What did you say?"

He seemed a bit dazed and she wondered if he had a touch of altitude sickness.

"That we should adopt Zane. Give him a home, with us."

He swayed a little and she rushed forward to catch him in case he fell. He gripped her arms and hauled her to within a few centimeters of his face.

"Why?" he asked.

"Why not?" she asked back.

They marched double time after that, his hand clasping hers so she wouldn't fall behind. There were no more convoluted conversational gambits. She watched the road to keep from tripping on the pebbles, so she didn't see when they reached the top of the next rise. And the path fell away down a short but steep incline to a valley bounded by rock on all sides, except for the narrow path they'd walked in on.

"By the Three Sisters, it's beautiful," she said.

"The valley is owned by my family. I gift it to you, Myrina, so that you can have your wildflowers."

Everywhere she looked that was all she saw. An entire meadow filled with wildflowers.

"What? You mean all of this is mine? I own it?" Other than her small apartment, she'd never owned a piece of property in her life. She'd never aspired to be a landowner either, because unless you were born into property or went off and colonized a hunk of rock, forget it.

"Yes. You own it," he said. "You can come here anytime."

"Do anything I want?"

He quirked an eyebrow. "Yes."

"Good." She slapped his arm to tag him "it". "Race you," she said and set off at breakneck speed down the slope and into the flowers.

By the time he reached her, she'd collapsed in a heap somewhere near the center. He must have walked, because she'd had plenty of time to strip off her jumpsuit. The sky above them was a cloudless blue until he arrived. He loomed over her like a great shadow, his hands on his hips.

"I've always wanted to do this," she told him.

"You're crushing the flowers."

"Fantastic, isn't it?" She patted the ground next to her.

He flung his shirt and boots to one side, but his leggings caused a large problem. He had to ease them past his engorged cock. His shaft and balls glistened with pre-cum. When he lay down beside her, the air around them filled with the sweet scent of crushed blossoms.

"There's something you should know," he said after the third butterfly flitted past.

*Triple crap.* She really wished he'd get to the point rather than ruin her perfectly good erotic fantasy. She rolled over and straddled him. Her pendant swung low between them, a reminder of what they'd already promised and shared. She sat just far enough down that the tip of his cock grazed the entrance to her pussy. He hissed and grabbed her thighs. She wasn't sure whether he meant to push her down on top of his shaft or pull her away. She didn't think he was too sure himself. Either way, she stayed right where she was.

With his copper hair spread around him, his body gleaming with sweat, he looked like a wild creature. Her wild man, one who wouldn't easily be tamed. But then, who wanted tame when she could have Judan?

"Later," she said. "There's something much more important I need to do first." She bent down and kissed him on the mouth. His hands didn't waste much time. They brushed up her sides to settle around the curves of her breasts. He pinched and stroked her nipples until she squirmed with need.

"Enjoy," she whispered. "This one's for you."

She sat up, impaling herself on his cock. He cried out and arched beneath her, shoving his shaft as deep as possible. She rode him hard and talked dirty. Describing in exquisite detail all the things she planned to do to his body.

He came with a mighty roar that echoed off the rocks around them. She bowed her head, panting as she always did when his cock filled her almost too full to breathe. She shuddered and her pussy clenched, tightening its hold and then, slowly, releasing him.

She collapsed on top of him and his arms encircled her in his fierce embrace. One of his hands scooted up her back and his fingers threaded their way through her hair. His other hand drew lazy circles across her back. Contented, she caressed his chest.

"I should tell you about Zane," he said.

She lifted her head to look at him. He was staring at the sky.

"I know all I need to know," she said.

He looked at her then, a quizzical expression on his face.

"He loves you," she said. "And you love him."

Judan nodded. "I've wanted him as my son since the beginning, but, until today, he could never truly be mine."

"What?" The green guy looked dead serious. Which, in her estimation, should be pretty darn impossible when lying naked in a field of wildflowers.

"This doesn't have anything to do with some complicated Dakokatan custom, does it?"

"I thought it did, because I wasn't listening."

*Okay.* He was getting deep, sinking into more convoluted thoughts.

"To Zane?" she asked.

He shook his head and shifted her hand until it rested over his heart. "I wasn't listening here," he said. "Otherwise it wouldn't have taken me nearly four years to realize I love Zane. And it wouldn't have taken nearly losing you to realize I didn't just want you, I love you."

She sniffed and blinked and shook her head. "That's okay," she said. "It took me a while to figure out I love you, too."

They lay together, mostly side by side, in her field of wildflowers for the rest of the afternoon. Talking, laughing, not talking. Every so often a soft breeze blew through the tall grasses and flowers, cooling their bodies. At last, the sun touched the edge of the jagged rocks around them. Judan caressed her hand.

"I intended to bring you out here, show you the valley and then take you home," he said. "I still haven't coaxed you into my bed."

Myrina laughed and rolled over, propping herself up on one elbow. Her fingers traced the twin scars and settled over his heart.

"Don't worry," she said. "You have fifty or sixty years to keep trying."

# Why an electronic book?

We live in the Information Age—an exciting time in the history of human civilization, in which technology rules supreme and continues to progress in leaps and bounds every minute of every day. For a multitude of reasons, more and more avid literary fans are opting to purchase e-books instead of paper books. The question from those not yet initiated into the world of electronic reading is simply: *Why?*

1. ***Price.*** An electronic title at Ellora's Cave Publishing and Cerridwen Press runs anywhere from 40% to 75% less than the cover price of the exact same title in paperback format. Why? Basic mathematics and cost. It is less expensive to publish an e-book (no paper and printing, no warehousing and shipping) than it is to publish a paperback, so the savings are passed along to the consumer.

2. ***Space.*** Running out of room in your house for your books? That is one worry you will never have with electronic books. For a low one-time cost, you can purchase a handheld device specifically designed for e-reading. Many e-readers have large, convenient screens for viewing. Better yet, hundreds of titles can be stored within your new library—on a single microchip. There are a variety of e-readers from different manufacturers. You can also read e-books on your PC or laptop computer. (Please note that Ellora's Cave does not endorse any specific brands.

You can check our websites at www.elloraescave.com or www.cerridwenpress.com for information we make available to new consumers.)

3. *Mobility.* Because your new e-library consists of only a microchip within a small, easily transportable e-reader, your entire cache of books can be taken with you wherever you go.

4. *Personal Viewing Preferences.* Are the words you are currently reading too small? Too large? Too... ANNOYING? Paperback books cannot be modified according to personal preferences, but e-books can.

5. *Instant Gratification.* Is it the middle of the night and all the bookstores near you are closed? Are you tired of waiting days, sometimes weeks, for bookstores to ship the novels you bought? Ellora's Cave Publishing sells instantaneous downloads twenty-four hours a day, seven days a week, every day of the year. Our webstore is never closed. Our e-book delivery system is 100% automated, meaning your order is filled as soon as you pay for it.

Those are a few of the top reasons why electronic books are replacing paperbacks for many avid readers.

As always, Ellora's Cave and Cerridwen Press welcome your questions and comments. We invite you to email us at Comments@ellorascave.com or write to us directly at Ellora's Cave Publishing Inc., 1056 Home Avenue, Akron, OH 44310-3502.

# COMING TO A BOOKSTORE NEAR YOU!

# ELLORA'S CAVE

*Bestselling Authors Tour*

UPDATES AVAILABLE AT

www.EllorasCave.com

MAKE EACH DAY MORE EXCITING WITH OUR

# ELLORA'S CAVEMEN
## CALENDAR

WWW.ELLORASCAVE.COM

erridwen, the Celtic Goddess of wisdom, was the muse who brought inspiration to storytellers and those in the creative arts. Cerridwen Press encompasses the best and most innovative stories in all genres of today's fiction. Visit our site and discover the newest titles by talented authors who still get inspired - much like the ancient storytellers did, once upon a time.

780899

Printed in Great Britain by
Amazon.co.uk, Ltd.,
Marston Gate.